I'd been hit quite a lot by then, and I was running out of steam. The stranger was big; I'm six foot two, and he was two or three inches taller than me. But he wasn't seeing too well, so I had a chance. All or nothing. I took a run at him with my right fist brought back as if I was trying to king-hit him, and he leaned back ready to take me, but at the last moment I dropped my shoulder and shoulder-charged him in the midriff. I caught him off balance and he went backwards out through the panorama window, falling God knows how far – four feet, ten, twenty? I'd never looked in all the time I'd been going there. I watched the glass fall in slow motion out of the window after him, lights catching and twinkling in the shards. Then I realised that the wailing in my ears was more than just concussion: the police car must have been just around the corner.

Evelyn was screaming something, and I was going towards her when the first policeman caught me, and then another got me from behind. There was a terrible bang, and the lights came back on again, then another bang, and everything went black.

Bill Hallas was born in India, and has lived in England, Guernsey and Australia. He was educated at the Universities of Cambridge and Sydney. He lives and works in Kent and is married with two children.

Wrecks

Bill Hallas

CORONET BOOKS
Hodder and Stoughton

First published in paperback in 1994
by Hodder and Stoughton
A Coronet paperback

10 9 8 7 6 5 4 3 2 1

British Library Cataloguing in Publication Data

Hallas, Bill
Wrecks
I. Title
823.914 [F]

ISBN 0 340 61321 1

Typeset by
Letterpart Limited, Reigate, Surrey
Printed and bound in Great Britain by
Cox & Wyman Ltd, Reading

Hodder and Stoughton Ltd
A Division of Hodder Headline PLC
338 Euston Road
London NW1 3BH

Thanks to David Brouard
and Barbara Darby

1

I heard them talking about me when I went to the bar. Two big men, wearing blazers and regimental ties. I'd never seen either of them before in my life.

I stared at the menu of sea bass, flatfish, and shellfish and hoped not too many people in Anton's could hear what the men were saying. I ordered two martinis instead of one and drank one while Carl Martin, the barman, was pouring the other one out of the shaker.

'Is that true, what they're saying, about you being found on a film set, unconscious, with a used condom up your arse?' he asked me.

'Very funny,' I growled at him.

Someone plucked at my elbow. I turned to see a woman with a moon-shaped face, with too much make-up on a coarse skin. She had a glass of white wine and a cigarette, and was trying to hold a menu under one arm.

'You're Sam Breaker, aren't you? There's been an accident.'

'Where?'

'You are Arthur Brouard's partner?'

'Yes, I am.'

'The fireworks,' she said.

'What sort of accident?' I asked, thinking of a late start, or the wiring failing on the aerial bombs, the rocket fuses getting damp, or a Catherine wheel coming off its post. The Brew was supposed to be putting on a summer evening display from Castle Cornet across the harbour, and now that it was dark, I realised I should already have seen the display on the skyline.

'A serious accident,' she said. Her face was creased with anxiety. her fingers were trembling. She spilt some of her white wine, dropped the menu to the floor. I bent down to pick it up – it was a struggle; the damned thing was the size of a door. She smiled at me, a twitchy, ghastly grin which showed large teeth stained to the colour of beeswax by cigarette smoke.

'You'd better get down there,' she said. 'Arthur said he wanted to see you.'

'How do you know?'

'I'm Sergeant Spooner's sister. He was there, so I heard about it.'

The men's voices rose. They were talking about me being impotent; but while everyone must have had the old limp collar every now and again, I couldn't remember the last time it had happened to me. That doesn't mean it hadn't happened – but how come they knew about it if I didn't?

'Do you know anything about an accident?' I asked Carl Martin.

'Only what she said. She said something about it just now, asked if you were the Brew's partner.'

'I'd better get down there,' I said. 'But if it was serious, the Brew would have phoned, wouldn't he?'

'It was serious all right,' the woman said.

'Why don't you order?' Carl asked me. He was wiping down the bar with a towel, moving with exaggerated care, as if he were watching himself on video; he was a big, slow-moving man. He was expecting trouble, bracing himself for the fight I was about to get into. But the last time I'd been hauled up on a public order offence I'd given an undertaking that I wouldn't fight any more, so perhaps he was banking on that.

'Carl, do you know those bastards? Because if you don't do something about shutting them up, I will.'

'You can't fight both of them.'

'Why can't I fight both of them?'

'Don't worry about them, they're just drunk. They don't mean any harm.'

I should have gone then. I don't believe in fate, or luck, I don't believe in anything, but something held me there. I might have stayed because I wanted another drink, or because I was hungry. But I stayed. Just long enough to have another drink, I told myself. Then I'd go.

The next time I saw the woman she was sitting with Milliner, a squat figure in a blue suit. She started talking animatedly to him, about the accident, I supposed. They both looked at me. Milliner nodded in my direction, but I couldn't see any reason to acknowledge him, so I didn't. He was a business-man, the kind who wielded a lot of local influence, who sat on committees, who had his finger in half a dozen pies. He'd been trying to get me thrown out of my scrapyard and off the Island for two years.

I ordered another martini. Carl took his time making it, his eyes bulging with care, his tongue flickering over the blue star tattooed on the inside of his lower lip. I waited for the drink, watching the shaker. It was just what I needed. I waited for it as patiently as a dog.

3

The two men were talking about my marriage now, about me and Evelyn. Whatever they said about that, I wasn't going to argue with them because I'd been drunk for a lot of my marriage. I'd had a few good years in Hollywood before my partner had run off with the money from the stunting business Evelyn and I were running, and I'd ended up back in Guernsey, broke. Before that, after leaving Guernsey and telling my family to fuck off, I'd been in Australia, which is where I started in film work. Recently I'd hit bottom. I didn't like thinking about it.

'She's another one,' Carl said. 'Margaret Milliner.'

'Another what?'

'Another arsehole, like her husband. She's gone up in the world since I went to school with her, eh?' He smiled. 'She's opened her legs for a few in her time, including me. Before she married that little prick and got too high and mighty to say hello to her old friends, eh? Her husband drags her here. Do you think she ever told him I once had her in the garage of a deserted house in the Vale? When I was fifteen and she was eighteen? She married into money, and now look at her. You wouldn't think her brother was the biggest bastard in the police force, eh?

'That's the trouble with Guernsey these days,' he went on. 'I remember the place before there were traffic lights, when everywhere looked as if it needed a coat of paint. But we knew where we were then, we knew who we were. Then the new money came in, the big money, the big cars, and everything changed. A lot of strangers arrived. Nothing's been

the same since, eh? Money's all anybody can think
about these days.'

If he was referring to Milliner, he must also have
meant me – my father at least, who'd brought us to
Guernsey when I was a boy.

'Do you know, when I was going out with her, we
used to stand up when the national anthem was
played at the end of the film at the Odeon?' Carl
said. 'Those were the days.'

He poured the drink. I drank half of it. He started
wiping the bar again.

'I knew your father. He did my old man out of that
scrapyard you live in.'

'I'd heard,' I said, beginning to wonder if I was
going to have to fight Carl as well.

'Yes, I knew your father all right. And your
mother.'

'My mother never went out. If you knew her, you
must have been delivering drinks for the off licence.'

The men's voices brayed across the room. I didn't
want to listen to them any more. I'd finish my drink.
I'd go. Every Saturday night I came to Anton's; it
was the one stable point in my week, the one event I
could set my watch by. The food was good, and they
left me alone. But tonight was different. I'd have to
skip the meal and go and sort things out with the
Brew. The accident meant that I had an excuse for
walking out of the place without smacking them.

I finished the rest of the drink and started to go
out to the lavatory, and it was then that I saw
Evelyn, sitting at one of the tables which had the
best view over the town and the harbour. I saw her
yellow hair first, that glimmering cloud of hair. She
wasn't looking at me but out at the sea. It was almost

dark and the sea was dark, and you could see the lights of the town through the picture window. She'd left me in California and I hadn't seen her for three years.

But I didn't stop. I kept going. I went towards the lavatory, across the room and up the steps on my way there.

Then I knew it as I went out of the room; I could feel it as the hairs on the back of my neck rose as I stood there unzipping my fly, and then heard the door open and felt the warmer air, and heard the noise from the restaurant, and their feet coming in quickly. I pulled the zip back up and began to turn, and then one of them hit me. He was in front of the other one – they were both well over six feet tall, and they looked like rugby players who fancied themselves but who didn't know what they were doing, because the first one masked the second one, and I was able to shake off the first punch, which had surprised me less than he'd thought. Stepping sideways as he punched at me again I was able to hit him on the side of the jaw as he overbalanced. But I had to take a punch from the second one, a clumsy haymaker which smacked me on the forehead. The first one was slipping to the ground, off balance, and I jabbed my fingers into the eyes of the second one to keep him unsteady, then turned my attention to the first one. I kicked his legs from under him and he went down in the urinal. Something hard seemed to break as his face hit the porcelain, and I stamped on his kidney region, which made him utter what must have been a scream into the slop he was lying in. I stamped on the hand which was scrabbling on the ground near me and still had time to deliver another kick to the side of his head before the second one could have another go at me. But by this time, he was backing out of the door. No one jumps me in my favourite restaurant, I must have thought, because I went out after him.

The people waiting by the bar scattered. He backed across the old gold carpeting with me after him, towards the yards and yards of glass, indigo with night, sprinkled with the lights of the town, the men and women at the tables staring at us, all with those frightened or embarrassed expressions people have when violence breaks out in front of them. And I saw Evelyn standing against the wall with her hand to her mouth.

He was staggering down the wide steps past the bar as I caught up with him. He hit me with his elbow before I was ready for it, then with his fist, and I got that woozy feeling and began to see the town lights jumping around inside my eyes instead of through the window, which gave him a chance to hit me again. Even so, I was getting the better of him somewhere over on the right of the bar, a couple of chairs breaking under us, and then Carl jumped on my back. I threw him off and laid him out with an uppercut which must have been the best I've ever thrown – his legs went the second I hit the point of his jaw and his eyes rolled up into his head even before he began to drop.

I'd been hit quite a lot by then, and I was running out of steam. The stranger was big; I'm six foot two, and he was two or three inches taller than me. But he wasn't seeing too well, so I had a chance. All or nothing. I took a run at him with my right fist brought back as if I was trying to king-hit him, and he leaned back ready to take me, but at the last moment I dropped my shoulder and shoulder-charged him in the midriff. I caught him off balance and he went backwards out through the panorama window, falling God knows how far – four feet, ten, twenty? I'd never looked in all the time I'd been going there. I watched the glass fall in slow motion out of the window after him, lights catching and twinkling in the shards. Then I realised that the wailing in my ears was more than just concussion: the police car must have been just around the corner.

Evelyn was screaming something, and I was going towards her when the first policeman caught me, and then another got me from behind. There was a terrible bang, and the lights came back on again, then another bang, and everything went black.

I must have surfaced soon after arriving in the cells. Inspector De Jersey was looking down at me.

'You stupid bastard,' he said. 'You never learn, do you?'

I wasn't going to argue with him. I looked around for something to be sick in. There wasn't anything. My vomit hit the floor, splattered his shoes.

I remember lying in the cell during the night some time thinking that if I hadn't been half drunk I could have hospitalised both my attackers without having to resort to cheap tricks, and then I remember thinking that perhaps they wouldn't have tried it on with me if I'd been sober. I should have hung on to this thought more firmly than I did.

In the night, Spooner came and said coldly into the cell, 'We've got you this time, Breaker, you bastard, you and Brouard, you're out of business.'

It must have been him who hit me with the truncheon he made a point of carrying in his car. He'd have enjoyed that.

2

The police doctor came to see me early next morning. He manipulated my neck and shone lights into my eyes.

'You're concussed, but you'll live,' he said, staring at me, his thumbs under my ears. He levered my jaw open, peered into my mouth. 'You made a mess of the men you assaulted. One of them has broken fingers, a broken nose, concussion, a possible fracture of the skull. There was blood in his urine this morning, so we can assume you damaged his kidneys. The one who went out of the window has a broken arm and shoulder, four broken ribs, and some damage to his spine. He's wearing a body cast. And on top of that the glass carved him up like a Christmas turkey. When he arrived at Casualty he looked like a badly painted sunset. Lucky it wasn't worse.'

He jerked his thumbs. My neck clicked. Ouch.

'I'm going to have to sew you up.'

'I feel like shit,' I said.

'Concussion. Did you have much to drink?'

'No.'

'That's not what I heard.'

'What about the barman?'

'Carl's all right.'

Earlier that year, I'd found myself at the scene of a fatal hit-and-run accident, and the doctor had looked a lot happier then than he did now. He clearly thought my injuries were my own fault, and a waste of his time.

'Take that shirt off. You're going to start bleeding again when I sew you.'

The blows from the truncheon had broken my scalp open, and I'd bled like a pig. I'd slept in the blood-soaked shirt and now it was as stiff as cardboard. I stripped it off and propped it in a corner, and sat bare-chested while he stitched my scalp wound. He didn't waste local anaesthetics on criminals, so I sat there grinning at him on principle, while the skin tightened up all over my face, the grin getting wider with every face-lifting stitch. He grinned too.

'Now clean yourself up,' he said. He fastidiously peeled off the gloves he'd used and disposed of them in a plastic bag. 'A pity I couldn't sew the head back on the character who died last night.'

Because I'd been punched in the throat, my voice was croaky, as if I hadn't used it for a month. I felt it gingerly.

'Where did that happen?'

'I thought you'd know.'

'Why should I know?'

He didn't answer me, just went on packing up his things.

'I heard you attacked the men, started the fight. That they went into the toilet and you jumped them.'

'I didn't. They provoked me, and then it was either me or them.' I didn't want to argue with him. I felt sick and my head ached ferociously. 'I wasn't trying to kill them. It was self-defence. Two against one. I need witnesses.'

'You've got a bad reputation here, Breaker. They'll murder you in court.'

'Why should they? Carl will speak up for me. There wasn't anything I could do about it.'

'Oh yes, Carl will speak up for you all right. He didn't like you in the first place. Now you've damned nearly broken his jaw.'

'What did you say about sewing a man's head back on?'

He closed his bag, looked at his watch, stepped round the pool of blood on the floor.

'Have you seen your friend Arthur Brouard lately?' he asked on his way out.

He wouldn't answer any more questions; no one would. But during the afternoon, the cell door opened and the Brew came in. He threw a clean shirt and some underwear at me and sat down on the only chair. He looked depressed. His hands were shaking. The smell of sweated-out whisky slowly began to replace the smell of the doctor's disinfectant and the smell from the lavatory.

The Brew was five foot six inches tall, neat, dark and muscular. He had thighs like an Olympic fencer, and the knobbly, powerful hands of a professional fisherman. He had an Adolf Hitler hairstyle, eyes as bright as black eyes can get, and a jowl he needed to shave several times a day. He was generous and good-humoured, and uncomplaining with everyone but me. I think he thought I often behaved like a prick. He was probably right.

'What happened to you, Brew?'

'Didn't you hear?'

'How could I? I've been stuck in here.'

'Fine time to pick to start fighting, eh?'

'I didn't start the fighting.'

'With enough drink in you, you'd fight an empty bar.'

So I gave him my version of what had happened at Anton's. He didn't believe me.

'Spooner says you're in a lot of trouble, eh?' he said, his sing-song Guernsey accent turning statements into questions.

'I'll get off. Self-defence. Two against one.'

'With your record?' the Brew said. He lit one of his cigarettes, home-rolled and as thin as a knitting needle; he held it in trembling fingers.

'Have you been on the booze?' I asked him.

'Saturday night last night, eh?'

'No need to get yourself in that state.'

'What state?' he snarled. He looked up at me resentfully from under his overlapping black wing of hair. 'I had a few drinks. I was in the pub, eh? So would you have been. Some silly bugger threw a match into the safety box before the display started. Blew everything sky high.'

'Christ.'

'Len Le Page was leaning over one of the launchers when it happened. You know what those launchers are like, eh?'

The launchers were oxy-acetylene tubes, one end sawn off, either buried to the muzzle in the ground or packed in earth-filled drums. They launched the aerial bombs we imported from Japan, the ones that went off like shrapnel at the beginning and end of the show and which could be heard miles out at sea, spinning two or three hundred feet up into the air.

'Was he hurt?' I heard myself asking.

'Hurt? Took his fucking head clean off.' He clicked his fingers. 'Like snapping a melon from a stalk. He started running round like a chicken. Blood all over the place. Like letting off a bottle of champagne. Was he hurt?' He laughed, then sat back, grinning. His grin was as ghastly as Margaret Milliner's had been.

The last time I'd seen Len Le Page, I'd given him two pounds for a drink. He'd always been short of money, in and out of prison, permanently on the Black List which was supposed to stop him buying any alcohol at all. He was a bum, a drunk and a petty thief, but I couldn't imagine anyone wishing him dead. And I couldn't get my mind round the thought of him being carried away in two pieces.

The Brew said, 'They're going to take my licence away. They're going to put me out of business.'

'Isn't there going to be an inquiry? Surely they'll find out it wasn't your fault.'

'I can tell you what the result of that's going to be. The bastards have been waiting for this, eh? Spooner said he'd just been looking for an excuse.'

'Spooner?' I thought about that; Spooner was a policeman, not a judge and jury. 'Don't take any notice of Spooner. He's just trying to get under your skin.' But I couldn't help asking, 'Weren't the fireworks covered?'

''Course they bloody were! What do you think I am?'

'Then how come someone managed to throw a match into the safety box, Brew?'

'How the fuck do I know? If I'd known, I wouldn't have let it happen.'

The cell door was kicked open and Spooner appeared in the doorway with two cups of tea. He put them down on the washstand.

He was a big man, solidly built, with a red, round, tight-skinned face, as expressionless as if it had been clumsily facelifted, or burned. I could never tell what he was thinking or feeling. I just assumed it was unpleasant.

'What a pair,' he said, in his grating voice. 'You're a dead man, Breaker. Assaulting a police officer. You'll spend next Christmas watching your cellmate shitting in a bucket.'

'I never touched you.'

'You lying bastard, that's not what they're going to say in court. As for you, Brouard, that's the end of your business. Criminal negligence? Manslaughter? No one will miss old Len, of course, but it looks bad on our statistics, eh? I don't remember that happening the last time the Queen went out on fireworks night. What was it, the big finish?'

'I test the fireworks, I check the safety box, everything, every time, eh?' the Brew said. 'There's fifty yards between the safety box and the display, at least fifty yards. Everything's locked up safe. I always check the wiring and the fuses. Every single display, I check everything. I always do it,' he said to Spooner. His eyes were burning. 'I wouldn't have got a licence otherwise, eh?'

'Licence!' Spooner's frog eyes bulged at us as he chuckled in his throat. 'It was an accident, I suppose, Brouard? I mean, you didn't do it on purpose, did you?'

'Of course it was a bloody accident! It's not my bloody fault, eh?'

16

'We're going to take your fireworks, Brouard, build a bonfire of them, and put you on the top as the guy.'

'I've got some big shows coming up, thousands of pounds' worth of fireworks, eh?'

'Tough,' Spooner said.

He went out, whistling.

'Bastard,' the Brew muttered after him, but the Brew I was used to would have reacted more aggressively than that, might even have gone after Spooner and thumped him; he never had cared much about consequences. But now he seemed defeated. He handed me one cup of tea and began to sip the other. 'They say bad luck comes in threes, eh? First the accident, now you. Is what they say true? Spooner told me he'd been looking for a chance to close me down – to close us down. That he was just looking for an excuse.'

I was thinking perhaps Spooner was persecuting the Brew because of his dislike of me.

'He's got one now,' I said.

The Brew was a professional fisherman, but he didn't own his own boat. He spent a lot of his spare time crewing for me on the *Lady Day*, which meant he acted as captain, navigator, meteorologist, fisherman and engineer while I paid him a few pounds a day and acted as cook and skivvy. Eventually, he'd moved his fireworks into the moribund scrapyard I lived in, I'd backed him financially, and he'd taken out some shares in the *Lady Day*. I rented her out for fishing and diving, but even though we stayed afloat that way, the money hardly paid for the diesel fuel we used. It was the fireworks that gave us big chunks of income; with that gone, and with me in jail, and with the Brew trying to run the scrapyard and the boat together, when with both of us working they hardly broke even, we were finished. It was going to be a long summer without money coming in.

'I don't know what I'm going to do,' he said.

'We'll think of something.'

'If you hadn't got in that fight last night . . .'

'I didn't mean to get in any fight. They came for me. I don't know why they did but they did.'

'Oh, balls,' the Brew said. 'You're just a walking fucking disaster area. I don't know why I ever got mixed up with you. Biggest mistake of my life, eh? They told me I was crazy.'

I grinned at him, 'They were right. You were crazy.'

The hand holding the cigarette folded it in half and flicked it away, and then formed into a fist. He stared at me, bright-eyed. We'd fought once, eighteen months before; he was eight inches shorter than me, and we'd still ended up in Casualty having the hands we'd broken into jigsaws on each other fitted back together again. No National Health Service on Guernsey. It had cost us most of that summer's fishing profits. I didn't want to go through that again.

So I held my hands up as if pushing him away. 'I meant nothing by that, Brew. I've just been sitting in this cell with nothing else to do but wonder not why things happen in threes, or even why they happen in twos, but why they happen at all. Do you ever think about that?'

He began to chew his thumb. The cigarette he'd

flicked away smoked in the corner.

'What are we going to do for money? With you in the nick, what are we going to do? We've got thousands invested in the fireworks. We can't afford to lose that money. They told me when they've finished with the stuff in the courts, they're going to blow it all up, eh? We'll lose the lot.'

'Give them half of it, hide the rest. Then we can sell it to someone on the mainland, or in France, get some of our money back. They won't know the difference.'

'Where am I going to hide it?'

'You'll think of somewhere,' I said.

'You need to get a bloody job,' he grumbled as he went out, and I was left to think about looking for work, some better-paid work than taking tourists fishing. Next year, when I got out of prison.

The next time Spooner came into the cell, I was lying down. My head hurt every time I moved. He sat down. He'd come to comfort me.

'I just wanted you to know there are a lot of witnesses to what happened at Anton's last night. I just wanted you to know, they're all hostile to you.'

'Witnesses?' I mumbled.

'We've got some good ones. Like your wife. She's left you, so she can't like you very much. Then there's Mr Henry Milliner. He doesn't like you at all.'

Milliner was filled with crusading zeal against those who sapped the moral fibre of the community. Degenerates like me. He thought my scrapyard was an eyesore and kept trying to get me to clean it up. He didn't think I was using it to run a proper business. He'd got the police to raid the *Lady Day* looking for drugs. He'd delivered a paper to the States blaming Hollywood and the film industry for the moral decline of society, of which there was evidence everywhere. And in his spare time, he'd brought a private prosecution against two teenage girls for sunbathing topless on a public beach. He'd be a hostile witness all right.

Spooner said, 'If you were going to beat up a couple of your wife's friends, why didn't you wait till you could jump them in a dark alley somewhere, one at a time? More your usual style, I'd say – here, watch it!'

He moved back suddenly, but all I'd done was sit up. The movement struck a gong in my head. I groaned, felt my skull.

'You were the bastard who hit me, weren't you?'

'I'd do it again if I had half a chance. Just doing my job, Breaker. But it wasn't the worst part of it.'

'You didn't have to hit me. I'd have come quietly,' I said. And I would have done. My fight was over by the time the police arrived. I might have started after Evelyn, but I didn't have violence in mind; I can't remember what I'd been thinking.

'You've never gone quietly anywhere in your life,' Spooner said.

'Who were they? They're not local. Where are they from?'

'You don't think I'm going to feed you information about your victims, do you, so you can chase them up and terrorise them? Innocent victims you tricked into a fight.'

'Victims? I'm the victim,' I said, but I gave it up; my head ached too much to argue with him. I lay down again. The doctor had given me some aspirin, but all it was doing was burning a hole in my stomach. Spooner stood grinning at me, red face shining. I began to wonder how I was going to get out of there.

With my record, and my reputation, I couldn't see me getting out on bail while there was any chance I might meet up with those two men again, or even with my wife. And even if I did get out, what was I going to do? There was some cash under my bunk in my cabin on board the *Lady Day*, but that was it, that was all there was, and the rucksack it was in was getting so light I hadn't dared count the money lately. The only weight in there was in the plastic bag which held the Colt .32 automatic I'd picked up in America to defend myself with. I forget what against. Nightmares, probably. The kind you have when you come off a drinking session you've been on for three months.

So there I was, washed up, my career as a stuntman as broken as my marriage, everything falling apart around me. Sitting in the white light of that nice, clean, disinfected police cell, with nothing to do but breathe in the smell of my own mortality and wait for the night when Spooner, with two or three of his friends, would come round to teach me the lesson he kept promising me.

But next day I was free.

3

In court, an advocate I hadn't briefed spoke up for me, and a man I'd never seen before was told to keep me out of trouble. Simon Sedley Breaker, released on bail. George Baxter was going to look after me.

His address was on Millionaire's Row at the back of St Peter Port. Middle-aged, with grey blow-dried hair, grey casual jacket with the sleeves rolled halfway up forearms covered with curly grey hair, a darker grey shiny silk shirt, and cream trousers and shoes. He had a gold Rolex watch and gold rings and a massive gold necklace above his open-necked shirt. Even from where I was standing I didn't like him.

The advocate's name was Richard Guilbert. He'd drawn up my will less than a month after a friend of mine had been killed in an air crash working on a film. It can't have been a difficult will to deal with, me leaving everything to Evelyn, but Guilbert had overcharged me. He'd been doing legal aid work at that time and he'd probably needed the money, so I didn't begrudge it then, though I did now. In the years since then his career had picked up. I wasn't going to pay him for defending me when I hadn't asked him to, even though he got me released on bail.

I was blinking in the sunlight outside the police station, where I'd picked up my old shirt and what

Spooner had found in my pockets – an Opinel knife, handkerchief, condoms, comb, three or four pounds in money – when Guilbert came towards me, brief-case in hand. He was a tall man, as gawky as an ostrich in his grey suit, with sloping narrow shoulders and large hands, and with a nose like a bird's beak. An injury above his left eye had left a pit I could have fitted most of my fist into. Right now, I felt like trying.

'It's been a long time, Simon, good to see you again,' he said in his smooth, cosmopolitan voice, but I noticed him looking up and down the street hoping no one from the Yacht Club would see me talking to him.

'You should have come to see me before you stood up in court for me.'

'Why? Aren't you satisfied with the result? They've treated you very kindly. You're lucky we're going to be able to hold the trial in a week's time instead of having it hanging over you all summer. We were able to negotiate an arrangement with the police and with the court. You can go back to your boat, and when you get there, stay on it.'

'What do I do, float around in the sea until they sentence me?'

'You've been placed in the hands of someone who's agreed to help make sure you keep out of trouble until the trial. The court was sympathetic to us, and was very flexible. People here are proud of the way the legal system on the Island provides justice for one and all.'

'Who's paying you?'

He pushed his face a little closer to mine. I'm tall

but he was taller. He looked down at me. He had an Adam's apple the size of a golf ball. It jerked as he spoke.

'You know very well who's paying me. George Baxter is offering you a contract to work for him for an unlimited period of time. He won't pay you a lot, but it will help to pay your bills. And there is talk of bonuses.'

'What if I don't want to work for him?'

'You must be joking. He's employed you to work away from the Island, but you'll be within the jurisdiction of the States of Guernsey, and the police can keep an eye on you too if they want to. And he's going to pay you for this. You're not telling me you aren't going to agree to his terms, are you? It's a miracle you aren't inside.'

He was full of probity; I was feeling pissed off, with him and with everything else. We stared at each other across an unbridgeable gap.

'There's a catch in this,' I said.

'There's no catch. It's straightforward. He's trying to help you.'

'Why should he?'

'He has his reasons.'

'Oh for Christ's sake, tell me where he wants me to work. Not on Sark, I hope?' He shook his head. 'Or Herm. Or Alderney.' No. 'That only leaves a load of rocks . . .'

'That's right,' he said. 'He wants you to work on the Hoummet.'

I opened my mouth. The jerk sent a crack of pain through my battered jaw. 'The Hoummet?'

'Yes, on the Hoummet,' Guilbert said. 'Baxter has hired your boat.'

'I don't know anyone called Baxter,' I growled at him.

'I'm surprised you don't,' he said. 'He's having an affair with your wife.'

Evelyn had left me three years before when I was recovering from a broken neck in hospital in California; a fortnight in the dark, and when I woke up a female nurse had put a whoopee cushion under my backside. 'April Fool's Day, 1991!' she'd shouted into my ear. After that, three months in traction. During this time, my partner, Theo Bradley, disappeared with all the money from the stunting firm Evelyn and I had been running. When I got out of hospital, I discovered she'd disappeared too. No one could prove what had really happened but I suspected she'd gone after Theo to get her share. They'd certainly ended up in the same place: Monaco. I hadn't seen her since. Our marriage was over.

Evelyn and I had lived together on Guernsey for a while soon after we were married. I'd come back because I have roots on the island; Evelyn must have come back because Guernsey is a tax haven. We were still married because our accountants in the States were trying to work out who owned what; the case was rumbling on in California. Why should I care about her private life? I don't suppose she cared about mine.

The Hoummet is an ugly collection of rocks north-west of the Alderney Swinge. There'd been talk of drilling for oil there, more talk of developing it as a centre for research into natural history. I was surprised, to say the least, that Baxter wanted me to take him out there, but I certainly needed the money.

'Did Evelyn talk him into this?'

'I really couldn't say. I don't know any details about your private life, or hers, and I don't want to know them.'

'What does my wife's lover want me to do?'

'Baxter is going to do some building work on the Hoummet for the States of Guernsey. Landing rights are restricted for a number of reasons, but they have to maintain the beacon, and the pier has suffered storm damage. Baxter has won the contract to repair it. It means shipping building material out there, and then doing some construction work. You can do that, can't you? This will also allow natural history experts to monitor the wildlife there.'

'All that, just to watch seagulls fucking each other,' I said.

He ignored that. 'There's Mr Baxter now.' I saw the man with the blow-dried hair dance down the steps towards a silver-grey Jaguar saloon, pausing just long enough to flap a hand at us before climbing into the back. The car door shut like a wallet closing on a fat bankroll, the exhausts kerfuffled at us, and with a squeak of tyres the car took off round the block. Someone else was driving; I couldn't see who.

'Baxter is all right; you'll like him,' Guilbert said. 'He'd been thinking of hiring your boat for some time, because he'd seen your advertisement in the *Press*. When the fight in the restaurant happened, I feared the worst, but he seems to want to believe your story. For what it's worth, you may as well know I advised him not to employ you. I didn't think you were the right man for the work. I still don't.'

'Thanks. Then who did?'

Guilbert shrugged. 'He must have made his own mind up.'

'And he's having an affair with Evelyn?'

'I don't really want to talk about that.'

'Where's she living these days?'

'I've seen her in Baxter's office. And on his boat.' He looked at me, waiting for me to react. 'He's got you out of the cells. You ought to be grateful to him. Don't cause any trouble.'

But I wasn't feeling grateful; I was hungry and I was thirsty and I was tired. 'You wouldn't know why those two bastards who jumped me were after me, would you?'

'I don't know anything about them.' He moved his Adam's apple around with his strong fingers, adjusted the knot of his tie. 'You've had a bad weekend. If I were you, I'd spend the rest of the week trying to stay out of trouble.'

'I'm going to find out who those bastards were.'

'Leave it to the police. You're legally bound to keep the peace, and that means keeping out of the way of everyone associated with the case. That's the deal we made with the police. Stay clear of the victims of the assault. And your wife, just in case, because of her possible, her alleged, association with those men – she was having dinner with them. The court is not aware of your wife's association with Mr Baxter,' he added, slyly amused, 'and I don't advise you to tell anyone about it. You're in Baxter's care; he doesn't want any adverse publicity. If you don't behave yourself, you'll find yourself back in the cells. Of course, if you want to go back into the cells, that's up to you.

'Here, you may as well take this,' he added, and

thrust that morning's paper into my hands. 'Read all about it.' Whether it was a joke or not I couldn't tell. I was hoping he'd give me a lift home, but he sloped off without giving me another glance.

Rather than take a bus I walked up to the restaurant to pick up my car. On the way, I caught a glimpse of familiar faces on the TV screens in an electrical goods shop, and then realised that the faces were mine, sprayed across a dozen TV sets in the shop window. Someone must have been filming my exit from the courtroom because the footage could only have been taken minutes before, and now I was on the news. With two days' growth of beard on my chin, with dried blood sprinkled over my trousers, and with the weal on my head rising up proud and red among the short-cut stuff I have for hair, as bright as a cockerel's crest, I looked like a maniac.

My car was a Morris Traveller which I'd found in my scrapyard. The salt sea air had got to it years ago and parts of it were brown lace, and three kinds of fungus grew out of the woodwork, but on Guernsey, a traffic jam with bays around it and greenhouses in between, there was no point in driving anything better, even if I could have afforded to.

I must have lost the car keys in the fighting, but I never locked the car, so I hotwired it and started it, and then noticed I was being watched from a downstairs window. I saw the face of Carl, the barman, and I waved to him. He didn't acknowledge me, but I didn't blame him for that; he was holding a towel to his chin. I drove out along the front to the south, and then turned left towards the Aquarium and parked there while I looked at the paper.

'BRAWL IN RESTAURANT'. It was all over the front page. There was a photo of me taken when I was playing the part of a psychotic GI in a Hollywood bloodbath; my face was smeared with boot polish, there was a knife between my teeth, and rape in my eyes. The text described my victims as law-abiding, ex-officer types, members of the Rotary Club and of good golf clubs; I'd been in court before, for fighting and drunkenness. I'd lost my stunting business, my marriage had been a disaster, and I was broke. No decent club would ever have me as a member, and I couldn't play golf. It was a good article, just on the right side of actionable libel. Reading it, I couldn't help laughing.

I sat in the Traveller and thought about what Guilbert had told me, and about what had happened in court, and then about what I could remember of what had happened in the restaurant. I couldn't remember all of it – parts of it came back much later – because Spooner had rearranged my short-term memory with his truncheon, but I could remember enough to be puzzled.

I should have sat there and done the crossword, or I should have gone into the Aquarium and looked at the fish. But Guilbert had already done the crossword, and I was sick of looking at fish, so I went to see Baxter instead.

4

Baxter lived in the most exclusive street at the back of Town, with half a dozen new homes fighting the old ones for the view over the harbour. The residents wanted to provide their own uniformed guard and steel gates across the entrance to the cul-de-sac. Fortunately, the States hadn't yet given them permission, so there wasn't anyone there to throw me out.

A rear wing fell off as I was driving the Traveller over one of the sleeping policemen that barred the street. I stopped and got out and went back for it, and chucked it in the back, and drove the remains of the car between palm trees and high walls with wrought-iron gates, and with not a sign of life. I found the house and parked outside the gates. They were eight feet high, with wrought-iron peacocks on them. I went through a side entrance and up the winding drive past the chalet-style three-car garage to the house, past the 'Beware of the Dog' signs and then past the Dobermanns which barked and snarled at me a few times and then stared sullenly at me from their kennel under the trees.

The house was just high enough on a knoll of golf-green grass to catch the sea breeze at any time of day, and to show the extravagance of this piece of planning the house had been constructed in a U shape to provide a shelter from the very breeze you were trying to catch. That allowed you to use the swimming-pool, a huge oval reaching right into the heart of the U. If you fly over Guernsey, the Island looks as if it's been splattered with turquoise paint, swimming-pools built by the rich – the famous live on Jersey – even though they live within walking distance of some of the most beautiful seas in the world.

There were palm trees along one side of the garden ending just by the gates, and holm oaks along another side, and nearby there was a pond in which koi carp glinted in the sun. But not as brightly as the red Mercedes convertible parked under the trees.

I stood there on the drive looking at the house and thinking it was a lot of land on an island where land was scarce. Even bigger than the house I used to live in in California. Not bad going for my estranged wife.

I was wondering how Evelyn fitted into this when I turned and saw her, walking around the corner out of the shadow of the house into the sunlight two yards away from me, naked except for white high-heeled sandals.

She stopped when she saw me. Every inch of what I could see of her body was the same honey-gold colour, a few shades darker than her hair, than the fluffy triangle between her thighs. It was as if the suntan had been spray-painted on.

'What are you doing here, Sam?' I was gawping like a fish. I closed my mouth and mumbled that they'd let me out on bail. 'I thought you weren't allowed to see me.'

'They can't tell me what to do.'

'You don't change, do you?'

'Neither do you,' I said, giving her a leer. 'How

32

did you know what happened in court?'

'I picked George up from the courthouse.'

'So it was you driving the Jaguar?'

'He doesn't like to drive. I'll get some clothes on.'

'You don't have to.'

'I wouldn't like to embarrass you.'

'You're not embarrassing me, Evelyn.'

She pursed her lips. 'This isn't the time, Sam.' She turned and walked away, taut and firm and wonderful to look at, while I stood and watched and tried to remember what it was I'd ever seen in her.

The house was white, post-modern, with shutters and balconies and deep eaves, and with a serrated roof I finally worked out was supposed to seem unfinished; it looked like a cruise liner getting a refit. I sat on a white sunchair in the shade of a mint-green umbrella and tried to pretend I was the captain.

Opposite me across the swimming-pool, big french windows opened on to the end of the pool, and I could see Evelyn moving behind them. I thought I saw something or someone move in one of the upstairs windows behind the balcony above the french windows, but I couldn't swear to it, and it might have been the breeze moving one of the ivory curtains which massed against one side of the window. Baxter? I was jumpy.

She came out wearing a short ivory-coloured wrap of washed silk. She was carrying a cooler bag, but even with that in her hands she moved across the green and white paving-stones around the pool like a dancer. She parked the bag, then leaned over me where I sat and examined the dark bloody scar on my scalp.

'Is that what the police did to you?' she asked; she'd patched me up too often in the past to have much sympathy. 'I saw Spooner hit you. He doesn't like you much, does he?'

'I don't like him.'

Her arms rested on my shoulders as she leaned over me. I could smell body lotion, a tang of sweat, and something else, the smell of her body, like a distant note of music in the air. Her arms dropped away. The physical contact was nothing – nothing to her, she'd only been looking at my wounds; but I found myself remembering the last time I'd touched her sexually.

She set down the cooler bag, opened it, and picked chilled glasses and two bottles of lager out of the ice.

'You are drinking, aren't you?' she asked as she sat down alongside me on a sun bed and handed me one of the beers. She emphasised the second word. People often did, ever since I'd fallen into an empty harbour and had ended up in hospital for neurological repair.

'Yes, I'm drinking.' I took a mouthful of the beer. It had been in the freezer before she'd put it in the ice; it was so cold it was barely moving. I drank some more, and felt a stab of pain in the forehead. 'Where's Baxter?'

'Not here. I dropped him off in town. He's either on his boat or in a bar.'

'Doing what?'

'Doing what rich people do on boats. If they're not screwing, they're drinking.'

34

'He's not at sea, is he?'

'George couldn't get that boat out of the harbour.'

'I'd like to talk to him.'

'He'd like to talk to you.'

We drank beer and looked at each other. She hadn't changed, not to look at. I probably had. Slacker, more relaxed, less fit, but probably more sober.

'What do you do here, Evelyn?'

'I work for George Baxter.'

'Richard Guilbert told me you were having an affair with him.' She smiled a slight, wary smile.

'Does that worry you?'

'No, it doesn't worry me.'

'I started off as his personal assistant. We all have to start somewhere. I progressed, that's all.'

'You're going in for older men these days?'

'After living with you, I need some stability.'

Touché.

'And he pays you?'

'You don't have to sneer.'

'I didn't think I had.'

'I've been thinking about you and me lately.'

'Nice thoughts, I hope,' I sneered.

'Terrific. You're different when you're not drinking.'

'I'm drinking,' I said.

'Not as much. You're not unhappy any more.'

'Probably because I'm not living with you.'

She coloured, slowly. She'd never shown her feelings much, ever. I realised I'd hurt her. I hadn't really meant to.

'Evelyn . . .'

'Don't worry,' she said. 'I had it coming.' She lit a

cigarette, tilting her head sideways as she did so. 'It was bad luck you getting involved in that fight,' she said sarcastically. 'Like the time before that. And the time before that.'

'It wasn't my fault. Who were those bastards, Evelyn? Spooner won't tell me. But you were sitting with them; you must know who they are. Are they friends of yours?'

'Friends of Jerry's, not friends of mine.'

'Who the hell's Jerry?'

'Jerry Rossetti produced one of our films,' she said drily, her tone reminding me she was the businesswoman, the one who'd understood money, while I never had. She'd encouraged me to set up an independent stunting business when I'd been turning over around a million dollars a year; I'd been too busy crashing aeroplanes and jumping out of blazing cars to notice I was spending everything I earned.

'They were visiting the Island. Jerry had given them my phone number, so I met them in the restaurant. They came on to me, and I was fending them off when they saw you; they went up to the bar, and I don't know what happened after that. Then the fight started.'

'So you don't know why they started on me?'

'No. It was nothing to do with me.'

I drank the rest of the beer and she took out another bottle. Real Czech Budweiser. She liked the best of everything; she always had. I opened the bottle, poured some, drank it. Cold. The headache sharpened. I felt light-headed.

I tried to keep my mind on what I'd come for; I didn't fancy spending the summer inside, but I didn't fancy begging her to plead on my behalf either. But she surprised me.

'By the way, what happened in the restaurant wasn't your fault. If it had happened to anyone else, the police wouldn't dream of even bringing a prosecution. After they'd arrested you, I did point that out to the police. But it's you. You've been in so much trouble, people just assume you're to blame.'

'What trouble?'

'You were in the papers earlier this year. For fighting.'

'I was jumped,' I said. I thought back. That was in the spring. 'How long have you been living here?'

'Three or four months.'

'Can't you get the police to drop the charges?'

'I'm just following Richard Guilbert's advice on what to do. But if the police are pressing the charges, they're not going to take much notice of me. I wanted to go to court today to speak up for you, but Richard said he wouldn't need me. But I did tell him I'll say anything that will help you.'

'You might be in court sooner than you expect.'

'I'll be ready,' she said.

That ended the conversation for a while. She settled back, and I sat and drank the beer, and then found another bottle in the ice, and started on that. In the hot sun, there was a light beading of sweat on her neck, dampness on the collar of the wrap. She'd rolled up her sleeves. Her limbs had an alien sheen, heavy and golden, like reptiles in the sun. I remembered a light golden fluff on them. Not now. Her arms and legs were as smooth as the squabs in the Bentley I'd once owned. Apart from her eyelashes and eyebrows, the hair on her head, and the neat fluffy triangle between her thighs, there couldn't have been a hair anywhere on her body.

I felt the old familiar excitement in the pit of my stomach. Between Evelyn and me, whatever else was wrong, there'd always been sex. There might be again.

I've never been good at hiding what I was thinking, and she knew; her eyelashes moved on her cheeks.

'I'm with George Baxter now,' she said. 'Don't get any ideas, Sam.'

I tried to smile at her, but I could feel my mouth going dry. The sunlight was glittering, glancing off the swimming-pool into my eyes, and the beer was going straight through my empty stomach into my head; I was getting drunk, but with sex as much as with alcohol. I could see between her legs, smooth golden lips under the hair. She covered herself absent-mindedly, but in those seconds the blood had started to pound in my temples. That glimpse of her vulva, the memory of her standing naked in front of me, was making me boil. I've never had a lot of self-control with women. Another of my spectacular faults. I was as stiff as a board.

'Evelyn,' I said, my voice coming out throaty and ludicrous, the blow I'd taken in my throat making me sound like a rapist in a vigilante film. 'Can anyone see us? I thought I saw someone upstairs, moving the curtains. Was it Baxter?'

'There isn't anyone. I told you, he's on his boat. And if you're going to make a pass at me, Sam, forget it.'

'If it's the cleaning lady, tell her to draw those curtains she's hiding behind. It might not stop her looking, but I'll feel better. Mind you, it won't be the first time we've done it in public.'

'There isn't anyone upstairs and we're not going to do it. Start anything, you'll be doing it on your own. I didn't ask you to come round here, you know.'

I reached out towards her. She hesitated, looking at me, before I pulled her gently towards me and kissed her on the lips. She kissed me back, but not for long, then pushed me away.

'For Christ's sake, Evelyn,' I said. 'I am your husband. If you're playing a game with me . . .'

If.

She reached out a hand. It closed softly on the back of my neck. It might have been drawing me closer to her, but it might just as well have been holding me away.

'There'll be a time and place for that, Sam. But we can arrange it better than this.'

But then her eyes left mine and flicked past me, and I saw something unreadable and surprising on her face. I heard something behind me, a voice called out, and I turned around to look. There was Spooner, walking up the drive.

5

Spooner was walking round the far end of the swimming-pool towards us, and behind him I could see a police Granada with go-faster stripes along the sides parked outside the gates. He was in his shirt sleeves and pulled his uniform cap from under his arm. He put the hat on, pulling the peak low down over his forehead, then reached for his notebook from the top left-hand pocket of his blue shirt. The beer trickling down into my stomach was as cold as guilt.

'Got you,' Spooner said, grinning humourlessly, but when he got closer his smile disappeared. He was looking at what he could see between the wings of Evelyn's wrap, her cleavage gleaming in the heat like the glaze on a Danish pastry. Spooner was married to a woman who looked as if she modelled dresses for the oversized. He couldn't have come across women like Evelyn very often.

She smiled at him, a ravishing, contemptuous smile. 'Are you all right, Sergeant? You look a little hot. Would you like a cool drink?' She shifted a little, showed another bulge of breast. 'Sam, get him something long and cool.'

'Not for me,' Spooner said. He swallowed. I watched his throat working. 'You aren't supposed to be here, Breaker. Weren't you listening in court?'

'I asked him to come,' Evelyn said. She pulled her wrap around her body, picked a cigarette from a

41

packet, made a fuss about lighting it. Sunlight glittered all round me, and I smelt the sharp, unpleasant smell of the smoke. She smiled at me, amused.

Spooner came close enough to cast his shadow over me. 'Weren't you listening in court, Breaker? You were warned not to have anything to do with your wife. Are you looking for trouble?'

'He can't be in trouble because he's come to see me – little me,' Evelyn said.

'The only reason they let him out was because Guilbert gave an undertaking Breaker was going to stay away from people associated with the case. I could put him back into the cells for this.' He turned to me. 'That's all I want, Breaker, an excuse.'

'I asked him to come over as soon as he could,' Evelyn said.

'I don't understand how you could have asked him to come up here, unless he'd . . .'

'He rang me up from a call box to apologise. And when he rang me, I asked him to come round here. To talk things over.'

'You feel safe with him?'

'We are married, Sergeant.'

'But you don't live together.'

'We're still friends. And whether we're friends or not, that isn't any of your business.'

'But if you're living apart, what's he doing round here? Sitting out here, drinking beer . . .'

He didn't go on. He'd been looking forward to getting his teeth into me; now I think he'd decided not to push it any further.

'I followed Breaker when he left Town, and he never went near a telephone box, Mrs Breaker.'

'I didn't see you,' I said.

'You didn't look.'

He was right; I hadn't.

'If I were you, I'd be careful who you're associating with,' he said to Evelyn.

'Do you mean those men who tried to rape me? Or Sam? He did protect me, you know. He saved my skin on Saturday night.' She laughed.

'I came round to tell you what happened in court today, to warn you to keep away from Breaker. And if you need help, telephone us, not him.' Spooner turned to me. 'You shouldn't be here, Breaker. You've got away with it this time, but don't ever make the mistake of thinking you can do anything you like. Not on this island. I'll be back looking for you.'

'Don't worry, I'm just leaving,' I said.

Evelyn laughed again.

'Don't mind him, Sergeant. Or me. You're just doing your job.'

He turned and walked away, stiffly, his back and every muscle of his body showing how conscious he was of being watched. It took him a long time to reach the gates.

'What do we do now?' I asked.

Evelyn was tying the wrap more firmly around her waist, body language that excluded me.

'Not that, Sam. It's about time you met George.'

She finished what was in her beer glass, stood up and made for the house. I watched Spooner's Granada back up beyond the wrought-iron gates, skid on the gravel, and tool away. I drank my beer slowly. The sun was bright on my forehead, the breeze cool on my cheek. I thought about my boat, and about the scrapyard which was supposed to be a business but which wasn't, then I looked at the house; Evelyn had done pretty well, to end up living in a place like this. But Evelyn always had done well. Before I'd met her, she'd been training as a pharmacist in London, doing some part-time modelling to pay her way. Then she'd gone to the Cannes Film Festival, had taken her bikini off in front of the paparazzi, and within a month she'd turned up in Hollywood looking for film work. I saw her first arguing her way into a film studio past a security guard; half an hour later I was admiring her all-over tan in the privacy of my mobile home.

A year after that, and after she'd taken the stunting standards tests herself, she was helping me run the firm she'd encouraged me to set up: no point in paying fees to an agent if the film producers could come straight to me, she'd explained. She'd persuaded Theo Bradley to run the finances, and within eighteen months, we were turning over three or four million dollars a year. Then came my cracked neck. After that, my departure from Hollywood had been made certain when I'd broken the jaw of a producer who was soon to wave an Oscar over his head on worldwide TV. We'd had an argument about money.

She came out of the house with a portable phone cradled against her cheek, lighting a cigarette with her head turned sideways against the breeze. She was wearing an old pair of jeans, white sandals, and a shirt of soft eau-de-Nil silk which must have cost more than I'd earned all summer.

'George will be waiting for us at the White Rock,' she said. She tucked the phone back into its leather sling. 'We can go out in his boat, if you'd like that. If you've got time.'

'I've got time.'

'I'd heard you'd got time,' she said. 'Out of work again, I gathered. No more firework displays. I read about that too.'

I let that pass, and we began to walk towards the gates and the garage. Stiff from the beating, I limped alongside her. There'd always been something competitive in our relationship, an edge.

'What do you have to do to pay the rent on this place?' I asked. 'Just sunbathe?'

'If this weren't Guernsey, I'd be sunbathing naked on the beach.'

'You can do better than George Baxter. He's twenty years older than you.'

'At least he's got money. He owns half a dozen companies, a helicopter, four cars, a boat you could land a jump-jet on, and three houses: this one, one in London, another in Gloucestershire. That's a little better than you can do, Sam. What do you expect me to do, kiss and make up with you? You're not going to say I'd be better off with you, are you? I like to eat, you know.' I didn't rise to that, so she said, 'Three years ago, I was living in Beverly Hills with the owner and star of a very successful film stunting company. You. I had a swimming-pool, a Jacuzzi, an XJS, and my own masseuse. Then you broke your neck. A good career move, Sam. I told you not to make that goddamned jump. Remember?'

I couldn't remember her telling me not to make it, but I remembered that fall all right because I'd cracked two of my vertebrae trying to break the world record for a high fall from a tower, and in every bout of cold weather it played up, the memories lodged deep in the bone. Now it was playing up again, thanks to Spooner.

I said, 'I remember where the money went. On your masseuse and your XJS.'

'Some of it. You spent your share.'

'What on? Drink? Not even I could spend a million dollars on drink. That crook we had as a partner was what happened to the money. Did you have an affair with him?'

'Don't be bloody stupid,' she said. 'Theo wasn't my type.'

'Where did you meet Baxter?'

'In Monaco.'

'You weren't looking for Theo, were you?'

'No, I wasn't.'

'What were you doing?'

'Trying to sell a film script. A European producer I'd made contact with had an office there . . . and I hoped he'd be interested.'

That made sense; there'd always been a few scripts lying around that we'd bought or had options on – I still had a couple in a drawer on the *Lady Day*.

She spoke more softly. 'I was trying to find some security, Sam. I was out of the film business. What else could I do? Go back to modelling? Open my legs so some dirty bastard could shove a camera between my knees? Come on, Sam!' She turned to me. 'You don't honestly think that – sshh, you brute!' she murmured to one of the Dobermanns as it tried to get at me through the wire mesh of the fence. Ever since a stunt dog waited till shooting was over and then tried to rip the back of my leg off, I've never liked working with animals, and I've never liked guard dogs, Dobermanns least of all. I stood well away, until at the sound of her voice it settled back.

'It's all right, you're safe,' she said. 'George keeps these because he's afraid of being burgled. They're not used to you yet. Don't worry. You don't think you can live with someone for any length of time without feeling something for them, do you?' she added softly.

The conversation had changed direction, so quickly I had no time to react. I didn't know what the hell she meant; I didn't know whether she meant Baxter, or me.

'Let's take it easy,' she said. 'Let's not spend all the time ripping strips off each other.'

We moved into the shadows of the palm trees which made blue starfish shapes on the asphalt and on the red Merc. The doors of the double garage opened automatically at our approach. There was an off-road vehicle with two rhinos humping on the vinyl over the spare tyre, and the silver-grey Jaguar. She climbed into the driver's seat of the Jaguar, started it, and gunned the car backwards out of the garage. The electric window on my side wound down.

'Get in,' she said.

I did. She dropped the clutch before I'd closed the door, which slammed it shut and jerked me backwards into the leather. In the wing mirror, I saw worms of black rubber on the tarmac, wisps of blue smoke in the air. She stood the car on its nose in front of the gates, which Spooner had left partly open, then decided she could get through and hit the accelerator again, clipping wing mirrors on both sides as she went through them. She went over the sleeping policemen in the road so fast the car took off. She drove venomously, expressively. The sound of the V12 engine batted back off the walls.

'They were good old days, Sam, when we used to do this for a living!' she shouted above the squealing of tyres. She swerved to avoid a cyclist, mounted the pavement at the end of the street, and braked so hard at the yellow stop line that the tyre smoke arrived around the car a few seconds later, like a police car drawing up alongside.

She threw her cigarette out of the window, and sat there, fingers drumming gently on the steering wheel, while the engine burbled.

'This place is like a prison. With these speed limits I can hardly get this car out of first gear. Do you know what that does to my peace of mind?'

'You were doing sixty up the fucking drive,' I said.

Five minutes later, we were stuck in the traffic jam that wound around the Island like a chastity belt. We stayed in it for the three-quarters of an hour it took us to get down to the marina. It seemed criminal to waste all that power on an island where the speed limit and the congestion reduced driving to slow motion. It would have been quicker to walk. I said so.

'You're all class, Sam,' she said drily.

I was still feeling light-headed, but it was pleasant enough to lean back in the comfortable seat and study her profile. She was certainly beautiful, and she had that classic bone structure of high cheek-bones and smooth jaw which photographs so well. Even so, in spite of her figure and her flawless skin, she hadn't made it in films; she wasn't great at acting, though that hadn't mattered to most of the big stars I'd worked with. But she wanted success. She wanted to stand there in front of a hundred million viewers accepting the plaudits of the Academy. Being a good stuntwoman wasn't enough; she wanted to be a star. And at the last, just when everything was ready to go right, it seemed as if things had gone wrong. Why? Not because she'd married me: that had given her the start she needed. I'd decided long ago that we probably shouldn't have married each other, but that didn't mean I hated her, or that I wanted to harm her in any way. My anger had gone. The marriage belonged in the past, so much so that it hadn't even seemed worthwhile to get divorced. But I didn't feel that I needed to blame myself for anything that had happened to her.

We said nothing for a while, until she asked, suddenly, without looking at me, 'Are you ever lonely, Sam?'

I wasn't, but I wasn't going to tell her that. 'It depends what you mean by lonely.'

'I suppose you've had girlfriends?'

'None of your damned business. Oh, I expect I have. I can never remember what I've had for breakfast, but I know I've eaten something.'

'I'd forgotten what a joy conversation with you could be. Promise you're going to be on your best behaviour when you meet George. He's done you a big favour already. You must know that Richard Guilbert doesn't work for nothing. George has already paid out a lot of money on your behalf.'

'Guilbert told me Baxter had paid him. I wondered why.'

'Because I asked him to.'

49

'You asked him to employ one of the top legal firms in the Channel Islands to defend the husband you don't live with any more, and he agreed?'

'He needs your help for what he's going to do on the Hoummet. I'd seen your advertisement in the papers, and I pointed out to him you'd be cheaper than anyone else, and that your boat was perfect for the job. He obviously decided that if he kept you out of jail he'd be saving himself some money. And he likes to save money. He's that sort of man. And he's doing me a favour.'

'He'd be doing you a favour hiring me?'

'Yes, Sam. I've thought a lot about the past recently. It's over, but we ought to forget the bad times. We ought to try to be friends, if nothing else. There's no point in kicking each other to pieces any more. It's all over.'

I didn't disagree with her – I'd been regretting the tension between us – but I was surprised.

'He'll want to discuss the business arrangements with you. Just make sure you behave yourself,' she repeated. 'Don't get drunk, don't start teasing him, and don't make a pass at me. There are some things he hasn't got a sense of humour about.'

'So he knows a lot about me, does he?'

'What I've told him. And what everyone else knows. The drinking and fighting,' she added, smiling. I was about to say, 'What fighting?,' but she stopped me. 'Don't be grateful, just be careful. Don't get into any more trouble. And don't make any fuss about us being married and all that. You mustn't spoil things. Promise me you're not going to make any trouble.'

'I promise,' I said.

6

The boat Evelyn drove me to was moored by the White Rock, so I assumed her draught was too great for the Victoria Marina. She was built rakishly of white-painted metal and smoked glass, a sea-going version of Evelyn's house. She had a flying bridge above two decks of five-star housing, and a comfortable, partly covered cockpit in the stern. She was called *Venus*. She made the *Lady Day* look like something I played with in my bath.

Evelyn led me down the gangplank. I followed her to the stern of the ship through an open cockpit underneath the flying bridge and went in through a door that said STATE ROOM in gold letters. Inside, music was playing softly: James Last. There was a polished wooden floor. If you wanted to hold a party, put in a big band, and serve a smorgasbord for twenty people, there wouldn't have been much room in there for the dancers.

A thick-set man in a flashy shirt came towards me. Baxter. My benefactor. He kissed Evelyn, possessively squeezed fingers into her rump. Then he held out his hand to me. I found some flesh between the rings and pressed it.

Close up, he had the bright, darting, complacent eyes of a man who'd been on the make all his life. His grey hair had been curled, bolstered by Vitalis, and blow-dried. He'd changed his clothes since I'd seen him in court, but not much: he was wearing a

51

shiny grey shirt patterned with lines of small white motifs, and grey slacks. He was of medium height, with broad shoulders, his body tapering all the way down to tiny feet. He was proud of his feet; his hand-made moccasins had laces made of gold chains with white leather tassels, and he moved with the short steps of a man showing onlookers that he knew what real dancing was.

'Come in, Breaker, have a drink,' he said. His North Midlands accent sounded affected, as if he felt he needed it to prove he was a hard-headed businessman. He put his arm around Evelyn's shoulders, squeezed the flesh of her upper breast.

'Evie said on the phone you called at the house. Found her sunbathing.' He grinned hotly. He wasn't jealous but he thought I was. 'She likes to walk around without her clothes on. Don't you, love?'

She smiled at him, but there was an edge there which he seemed not to notice; or if he did, it amused him. He gave her another friendly squeeze; for my benefit, not hers.

He led me over to the bar in the corner, and Evelyn disentangled herself and began stirring champagne bottles in a gold-plated ice bucket the size of a dustbin.

Baxter said, 'I've heard you're a malt whisky man. Well, there's whisky, gin, vodka, all the spirits. Cognac, Armagnac, Spanish brandy. There's three makes of martini, sweet, dry and bianco, Fernet Branca, Pernod, Ricard, both strengths, Campari, St Raphael, Dubonnet and Ambassadeur. Every liqueur you've ever heard of. We've got a roomful of wines forward of here. And if you want a cocktail, Evelyn can make you anything you want.'

'Tequila and beetroot juice. It's called a Cystitis Sunrise.'

'Eh?'

Evelyn gave me a warning look as she liberated a bottle of champagne from the ice bucket and poured three glasses. Baxter drank one while she was catching the drips with a towel. She poured another.

'A what sunrise?' Baxter asked me with interest.

'It's a joke, George. Sam likes to make jokes,' Evelyn said.

Baxter grunted at me, 'Start with champagne. I always do. For a start, it takes the edge off the hangover.'

'I can't afford to drink champagne every time I have a hangover,' I said.

'If you can't afford champagne, you shouldn't be drinking.'

With my lecture over for the day, he walked me round the state room. The polished wood floor was inlaid with a huge nude Venus made of different coloured woods. The floor alone would have bought the *Lady Day* ten times over. Baxter lit a Punch Corona and dropped the match on to Venus's navel. He manoeuvred around me.

'You're not the sort of man to let jealousy intervene in a professional relationship, are you, Breaker?'

'Jealous? Me?'

'I've teamed up with your wife. In more senses than one, you might say.'

'Christ, you wouldn't be the first.'

'Sam!' Evelyn said warningly from the bar.

'Sorry,' I said. I smiled at her, a smile she didn't return, so I turned the smile towards Baxter and said, 'If you can give me work, I'm grateful. Don't worry about me. Evelyn and I haven't stayed married because we're in love with each other, we're married because our accountants in America told us it probably wasn't the right time to get divorced. I don't give a damn what she gets up to in her spare time.'

He tried to look as if he was thinking hard about things, but he was just playing at it; he'd made up his mind before I'd arrived on the boat. 'Fair enough,' he said. He nodded towards Evelyn too, as if agreeing a business deal. She put her half-finished glass of champagne down on the bar and left the room. A moment later I saw the liquid tremble in the glass, felt something vibrate through the soles of my feet. She'd started the engines. Starting the diesel on the *Lady Day* made pint mugs hop across the table.

He said, 'From what I've heard, you need the money.'

'What have you heard?'

'You earn your living hiring your boat out and putting on firework displays, and now your firework business has gone down the sink.'

'It was an accident, no one's fault.'

'Accidents don't happen in a well-run business.'

'They do in mine.'

'Like what happened on Saturday night, in the restaurant?'

'That wasn't my fault,' I said, but I'd said it so often it was beginning to sound unbelievable even to me.

'Another accident?'

'Another accident.'

'Were you drunk?'

'I'd had a few drinks. I wasn't drunk.'

'Evelyn tells me you used to have a drink problem.'

'Yes, the problem was I couldn't get enough of it. I'm not an alcoholic, if that's what you mean – at least, my doctor doesn't think I am. An alcoholic is someone who drinks more than his doctor.' He didn't see that joke either. He sniffed at me, a noisy, contemptuous sniff.

'Not your fault, then, you say.' He dragged at his Punch Corona as if it was someone else's joint. 'Just an accident.'

'I don't know whose fault it was,' I said. 'I just know it wasn't mine.'

I didn't know why he was going on about it. I heard the engines of the *Venus* roar distantly in the background, and the bottles on the bar trembled. What was he trying to do? See how angry I got?

But then his tone changed, as if he'd made up his mind about something.

'I need you, Breaker. And I need your boat. She has a big hold and a shallow draught. That's what I need. A good working boat. That story I told the States is a blind, it's all balls. I'll repair their pier for them, but that's only the start of it. There's something else there I want. That's why I want someone who can keep his mouth shut. Can you?'

'I can keep my mouth shut.'

'There're a lot of wrecks around the Channel Islands, especially around Alderney and the Race. A lot of those wrecks are around the Hoummet. There're some nasty currents there. They run at eight or nine knots in the spring tides. Some of the strongest currents in the world,' he said with relish. 'What do you know about the place?'

A year before, I'd taken a husband and wife spear-fishing around Alderney. Currents can flow in opposite directions only a few yards away from the main tides, and while they were diving they'd strayed into one of these maelstroms. I'd lost them, and when I found them on the surface half a mile away, they were about to sink for good.

'It's hell, if you really want to know,' I said. This seemed to be what he wanted to hear.

'That means a lot of these wrecks haven't been properly investigated, Breaker. And there's something else that stops people looking too closely at them.' He pointed to a chart framed on one of the walls. The areas north-west of Alderney were marked 'Dumping Grounds (Explosives)'. 'A lot of ammunition was dumped around the Hoummet after the war.'

'That's old stuff,' I said.

'The older it is, the more unstable. The Hoummet is off limits except for routine maintenance; people don't fish the area much because of the currents, and they keep away from the wrecks. We're going to dive on those wrecks. And on one in particular.'

'That's what you want me for? To dive on a wreck packed with explosives?'

Baxter laughed. 'There're no explosives on this wreck.' He went back to the bar to fill up on champagne, still chuckling. 'In the end the key to it was a consortium trying to buy the rights to drill for oil around the Hoummet. There's oil there all right, but it's probably uneconomical to get it out. The States of Guernsey were frightened by the thought of the environmental problems. I didn't tell them the consortium was a front for my interests.' He looked at me, expecting me to be impressed, but I don't understand business ethics any more than I understand business techniques, so I said nothing. 'When I said I'd protect the area against exploitation and keep it as a nature reserve, they backed away from the consortium and fell right into my lap. I said I'd open the area up to scientific research for naturalists and so on, and if there was anything any of these scientific people wanted, I'd see that they got it. And I'd preserve the natural beauty of the area.'

'You didn't tell them about this wreck?'

'There's something we want to get out of there which I'm not keen on the customs people finding out about. Nothing illegal, nothing criminal, just something I don't want them to know. You know what customs officers are like: very small-minded. But I'm a businessman, not a criminal.' He drank his champagne. 'I'll pay a thousand pounds a week for you and your boat, for the duration, and three hundred for that man of yours, Brouard. I'll pay your bonuses, two thousand pounds if you manage to do what I want, another three if I find what I'm looking for. And I'll pick up all the bills,' he said when I tried to interrupt. He made an expansive gesture. 'Food, drink, smokes – girls if you want them. After all, I've got your wife, and girls are easy to get if you've got money.' He chuckled and put an arm round my shoulders and squeezed me the way he'd squeezed Evelyn. 'You'll never get a better offer than that, Breaker. What do you say?'

'I'll never get a better offer.'

'We'll shake on it. I don't believe in written

contracts for a job like this. I'll take your word and you'll take mine. A gentleman's agreement.'

'Now, that is a risk,' I said, but I shook his hand again. It looked hard, but the flesh between the rings was as soft as a baby's.

The blue granite harbour wall slid past the panoramic cabin windows. The engines that powered the *Venus* were of turbine smoothness and I'd hardly noticed them increase power. But we were soon at sea, and moving up the Little Roussel, which is the area of water between the islands. Evelyn must have been at the helm. Speed increased and the floor of the state room began to tilt. Conspicuous consumption: twin diesel motors which could have powered an aircraft carrier.

Baxter produced documents from a case, spread them out on the table.

'The Hoummet is shaped like a crescent. The wreck is in the bay of the Hoummet, right up against the rock at the back of the bay, and that's the wreck I want to get at.' He showed me some photographs of the bay. He lit another cigar; he'd only smoked a quarter of the first. He drew out the shape of a boat on the surface of the water under the big rock, which was freckled with bird droppings, and as large as a house. 'There is a problem. The problem is, the boat turned turtle when it sank. It's upside down. What I want is underneath it.'

'What do you want me to do?'

'It's hull-down in the mud at the moment, so I want you to turn it over, so we can get out what we want. That's what I'm offering the two-thousand-pound bonus for. So we can get at what's inside. Use a crane or something. Evelyn tells me you've got some sort of powered derrick on your boat.'

'I'd need more power than the derrick has, and a firmer base for whatever I use. Perhaps the island itself – I could put a crane of some sort on a base on the rocks. It can probably be done. It depends on the shape the wreck is in. Anything that isn't protected will be scrap iron with all that water moving around.'

'As far as I know, it's all right,' Baxter said. 'We sent in the inflatable the other day and had a quick look at it, to locate it.'

'You went in close, then.'

'We left the *Venus* outside first time, but then we found we could have taken her in, even though it's tight over the rocks. Evie went down with a snorkel and face mask. By God, that girl can swim.' He gave me a look of pure lechery. 'And we flew the helicopter in, too. You get a good look at the wreck from the air when you know what you're looking for. I own a helicopter,' he said in case I'd missed it. 'Picked it up from the Yorkshire Health Authority for a fraction of what it was worth. They used to fly them up and down the motorways looking for road accidents until someone noticed how uneconomical it was. I bought two helicopters for cash after a man I knew had reported them as being in a dangerous state of repair. I repaired them, sold one for more than I'd spent on both, kept the other, and made a profit.'

Another scam.

He said, 'The bay seems to have protected the wreck against the currents. Evelyn said it's made of alloy, or aluminium or something, so it hasn't deteriorated much. It's German, World War II, a big

59

motor boat. I do know the men who took it out there and scuttled it weren't sailors.'

'Then what do you know about what's inside?'

'That's my business, not yours.' He grinned at me, patted my shoulders. 'I'll tell you all about it, Breaker, all in good time.'

'What happens if I end up in prison after the trial?'

Baxter chuckled, a rich sound deep inside his chest. 'You needn't worry about that, Breaker. You haven't realised yet who you're dealing with. There's no way you'll end up in prison, no way. That's already taken care of.'

We went up on deck, through the cockpit, and up to the flying bridge. Evelyn handled the boat as if it were a small car. We made big waves in the water, engines growling, while the sun beat down on us.

7

All Evelyn had to do was tweak the throttles and the *Venus* rose in the water like a seaplane, wings of spray opening on either side of us. Other vessels dropped away. Twenty minutes or so later, we came in towards the Hoummet in a great curve. The same journey would have taken the *Lady Day* about four hours.

Evelyn knew enough about the seas around there to keep well away from the Hoummet itself. You could be speeding along in the *Venus*, drinking champagne and admiring what looked like open sea, then a change in current could slide you over a rock with a back like a razor, and the next thing you'd know, you'd be sitting in your expensive inflatable watching the Decca navigator disappearing into the sea. So we circled the Hoummet from afar while I studied it through binoculars.

The Hoummet is a crescent-shaped island of blue granite near the edge of the continental shelf. It's a wilderness of currents and standing waves, and rocks, some visible, some just below the surface, some visible only two or three times a year, or once in a decade. The Channel meets the Atlantic there, cold water meeting colder, so there is often mist, always haze, sometimes Grand Banks fog. The Hoummet sits there in the heat and haze, facing towards the Channel and brooding. The white beacon rises out of the rocks, a concrete fez on the head of the half-crouching man people claim to be able to see there. I've never been able to see it. I see an up-ended duck with a white tail.

It's a lonely place. Ships keep well away. Two or three of the local fishing boats fish nearby, but never in winds above force three or four. Even the Germans had given up in the end. When they invaded the Channel Islands during World War II they'd turned them into part of Fortress Europe, and their fortifications – sea walls, breakwaters, watch towers, pillboxes – are part of the landscape. They'd even put a gun emplacement on the Hoummet, but in the end, because of the weather and the loneliness and the danger, they'd abandoned it.

Through the binoculars, I could see the pile of rocks with its white-painted beacon, the concrete disc of the gun emplacement, and a rock the size of a medium-sized house at the head of the bay. Some of the rocks had had some cement poured between them to provide a primitive pier for the men who came every year to repaint the beacon, but the pier looked messed up compared to the last time I'd been there. For a moment I could visualise men, in field-grey uniforms, half a century ago, huddled there.

'That's as close as I'm getting,' Evelyn said to me, reversing the engines. They began to growl irritably. Water boiled astern.

'More champagne?' Baxter said into my ear.

With the sun going down, Baxter and Evelyn and I sat around the formica-topped table in the cockpit stern of the *Venus* under a striped awning. Baxter was using the wheel in the cockpit to steer with, the

Venus circling slowly in open sea, the engines ticking over. Guernsey lay along the horizon like a low cloud.

Evelyn sat with her back to the setting sun, her hair a glowing halo. I shivered in the suddenly chilly air. I was getting drunk, and trying not to. Baxter had produced a bottle of twenty-one-year-old Springbank. It's one of the finest malt whiskies there is. In the days when I had money I used to have crates of it shipped out to California. I hadn't been able to afford it for three years.

'There's plenty more where that came from,' Baxter said, watching me enjoy it. I took a large glass of the stuff and turned it in my hands like a jewel. The light caught in the bevels of the cut glass. I inhaled the smell. Peat and seaweed, malt and wet rock and iodine. Smells and flavours I'd almost forgotten. I loved the stuff.

'This is straight from the special vats in the distillery on Campbeltown,' Baxter said, his voice sinking to a suggestive whisper. 'Costs me over thirty pounds a bottle. By the time I've had it shipped down here it's more like thirty-five a bottle. What do you think of it?'

I drank some more. It was sixty per cent alcohol and I'd had four glasses. My lips were going numb.

Baxter said, 'Take a bottle with you when you leave tonight, so you can have a nightcap and think about our arrangements. Have it with your hot milk.'

He went on talking. The price of the whisky was him telling me how much it would cost me to belong to his golf club, or to go to his hairdresser's so I could get my hair turned into a soufflé. I struggled to keep my eyes open, then I caught sight of Evelyn, suppressing a yawn behind her hand. Baxter was telling us how to get laid in Reykjavik.

Then he said, without breaking stride, 'You must have guessed there's more to this than just diving, Breaker. We're a syndicate, me and Evelyn. She told me you could handle all the sub aqua side of it. Is that true?'

'I've done some diving; I used to do a lot more. What about you, Baxter? You're not an old man. Why don't you do it?'

'I can't swim.'

I sat there, my back warm from the seat I was reclining in, my forehead and forearms prickly with cool sea air. I saw Evelyn yawning openly now, and I asked, out of the blue, 'Why doesn't Richard Guilbert do the diving?'

'You've seen that dent in his forehead. He's got a silver plate in there the size of a twenty-pound note. A butane gas bottle blew up in his face.'

I was going to say, 'Then what about Evelyn?', but I didn't, I bit it back. Instead, I said, 'If you're worried about what's down there, because of the explosives marked on the chart, why don't you get an expert on underwater demolition? Find an ex-SBS man.'

'We don't want underwater demolition. We want someone to lift the wreck and get what we want out. You know where the wreck is, right up close to the rock, lying in not much water when the tide's low. We know she's upside down, and we could cut her apart with oxy-acetylene lances, but that'd take a month. All you've got to do is attach hawsers, and then pull her over. As I said, we want someone who'll keep their mouth shut. You want your bonus, don't you?'

'Of course I want my bonus. But I don't want to risk my neck for nothing.'

'You'll be risking your neck if you tell anyone else what I'm telling you,' he said, and laughed as he leaned back in his chair to show a gape with enough gold fillings to pay my mooring charges for a hundred years. Evelyn caught my eye, as if she thought I might have responded to the threat. And the alcohol was beginning to work on me; I was feeling irritable. I smiled at Evelyn, and saw her face freeze as I said:

'You didn't arrange that fight, did you, Baxter, to make sure I did what you wanted me to do?'

He looked surprised. 'Arrange that fight? I'm devious, Breaker, but I'm not that devious. I've never seen those two characters before in my life.'

Evelyn's smile was fixed – that poised, careful smile.

'You're not going to be difficult, are you, Sam? Sam has had his moments of jealousy in the past, George. Usually when he's been drinking.' She smiled at him, the big smile. 'All teeth and tits', she used to call it, the one that had got her as far as the big HOLLYWOOD sign on the hillside.

'You don't think he's jealous, do you?' Baxter asked, chuckling because the question was ridiculous: of course he thought I was jealous, that was the point. He leaned over and squeezed first her arm, then mine, his voice dropping as his warm fingers closed over my forearm. 'Jealous? You're a pussycat, aren't you, Breaker? Isn't that right?'

'That is absolutely right,' I said blearily, grinning like a fool, and I saw Evelyn relax. He laughed.

'Thirty-five pounds a bottle,' he said, watching me enjoy the whisky. 'I'll slip you a bottle when you leave. Don't let me forget. Here, I'll show you something to be jealous about.'

It was another toy, a large screen which had been hidden behind curtains at one end of the state room. He played me a video of a party that had taken place on board the *Venus* in Monaco the previous summer. There was Baxter, wearing shorts his belly bulged over, mirror-lensed sunglasses, and a ludicrous yachting cap. And there were half a dozen girls playing the kind of games those kinds of girls are expected to play at those kinds of parties.

'See that one there?' Baxter growled, pointing with a thick finger. He stopped the video, then reversed it. A large naked bust was pulled away from the camera and sucked backwards into the cups of a bikini, a woman flopped backwards into the sea, silver water crawled up her flesh to her face as she sank down into it. He stopped the video again. I saw the crown of her head, an island in the sea. Slow motion brought her jerking and flickering up into the light. 'That was my last PA, before Evie. Fiona Maugham. Lady Fiona Maugham,' he said, pronouncing the title with lascivious pleasure. 'I'll tell you all about her one day. Do you remember her, Evie?'

'I certainly do,' Evelyn said. She stood in the middle of the room, legs apart, drink in one hand, cigarette in the other, riding the gentle rocking of the boat in the swell as she circled. Because she was wearing shorts, I was free to admire her legs. To admire almost everything about her.

'Weren't you at that party?' I asked.

'I was holding the camcorder,' she said, with a voice poised between enthusiasm and irony – half for Baxter, half for me, I thought.

The party on the screen was getting wilder. Baxter was spraying champagne over a girl who avoided capture by jumping over the side into the sea. Two girls were oiling each other on the deck. A close-up of Baxter's sunglasses, with a naked woman reflected in the lenses.

'Very artistic,' I said.

'The party was in Monaco, where George and I met, and I was thinking films. It came naturally.'

'I forget what you were doing in Monaco. Do tell,' I said, the drink beginning to make me want to rile somebody.

'I told you, I was trying to sell a script to a producer, but I couldn't track him down, and no one else was interested. Could I get any money? Could I shit. Ever heard of a worldwide recession, Sam?'

'What was the script?'

'*Blue Body.*'

'I don't remember you buying that.'

'You don't remember anything of those days, Sam. I bought it while you were playing ship in the bottle – or was it shit in the bottle? I forget which.'

Baxter was chuckling at the screen. There was footage of him nude, bending away from the camera in a darkened room. A light went on. He was humping some girl, I realised, on a bed in the corner. I looked away. At my feet, Venus rose from the waves on the floor, leering up at me, one wooden hand fluttering near polished beechwood breasts with fruitwood nipples. Renaissance erotica turned into pornographic kitsch. I felt vaguely disgusted, a nasty taste in my mouth.

'I think that's enough of that, Evie,' Baxter said throatily. 'I don't suppose your husband wants to see too much more of that.'

'Now isn't really the time, is it?' she said drily. The video went off. 'There's food,' she said.

She brought a feast through from the galley – lobsters on plates the colour the lobsters had been before they'd been cooked, veal stuffed with truffles, salads of endive and tomato and radicchio, goats' cheeses covered with mould as thick as club moss, caviar as black as sump oil.

We ate, and drank a chilled Chardonnay of the sort I taste once in a blue moon, then with Evelyn steering, the *Venus* began to circle back towards St Peter Port.

Baxter restarted the video. I watched the figures on the screen, not taking much in. I sat drinking and thinking about Evelyn, then started trying to remember how many malt whisky distilleries there were in Scotland, from the west coast to the east. I started on Islay. Bowmore, Bruichladdich, Port Ellen, Bunnahabhain, Laphroaig, Lagavulin, Ardbeg, Caol Ila . . . I could name perhaps fifty more, but there must have been a hundred or so. Springbank isn't that common. I tried to work out the statistical likelihood of a man like Baxter, who didn't drink whisky, having bottles of Springbank lying around by accident. He'd bought it because he knew I liked it. That must have been Evelyn's doing. She'd told him a lot about me.

Then I thought about Evelyn looking for finance for a film script in Monaco; I decided I believed her.

I was in hospital with a broken neck, Theo Bradley had pissed off with our money, she must have been desperate. She didn't seem that bothered whether I believed her story or not, which made me inclined to believe her. Something else bothered me, though.

Why me? Why pick me for this little set-up? Why would Evelyn, who might have had some good reasons for having nothing more to do with me, get me involved in something that might do me some good? Evelyn, who had done the swimming standards to qualify her as a professional in stunt work, and who was a better free diver than I was.

When we circled back towards the White Rock, the bottle of malt I was drinking was as good as empty, so I reminded Baxter about the bottle of Springbank he'd said he was going to let me have. He made a great fuss of looking for it, only to find that he hadn't got any spare. I finished up with a bottle of Johnny Walker Red Label. I was grateful for that. And he was happy; he'd made me ask for the Springbank, even beg for it. And then he hadn't given it to me. I was just what he'd been told I was. I wasn't going to give him any trouble.

8

I'd had quite enough to drink by the time I left the *Venus*, but not as much as Baxter, who'd gone to sleep in front of his video machine, champagne glass dangling from his fingers, while the blank screen fizzed and glared.

In the Jaguar, I settled back in the leather. It was late evening, dusk, but still light enough to see the islands across the Little Roussel. Lights were going on along the Esplanade. Evelyn drove smoothly, and the lights went silently past the windows of the car. Like magic.

She lit a cigarette. I didn't like the smoke in the confined space of the car, so I opened the window. Past her profile, I could see a darkening sea, the islands of Herm and Jethou in the background, lights going on in scattered cottages over the sea. It reminded me of something, a moment I must have forgotten till then. We'd been driving my car down the Californian coast after I'd drunk too much wine to drive. I'd known her then for a week; we'd been driving south, looking for somewhere to stay where we'd be alone. It seemed a long time ago, a lot longer than the few years it was. I didn't have much in common with whoever I was then.

'Well, what do you make of him?' she asked.

'Does it matter? I can't afford not to like him. He's paying my wages. Is that why he started having

71

an affair with you, so he wouldn't have to pay your wages?'

'Don't get nasty, Sam.'

'Feel like a drink?'

'I'm driving. Hadn't you noticed?'

'I meant at my boat. I have a boat too, you know. I can cook you a meal, we can have a drink.'

'Forget it,' she said. More traffic. I sat and thought.

'Do you know Richard Guilbert?'

'I've met him.'

'Does Baxter employ him for other work?'

'I wouldn't know. I drive the car, I cook for him, I do some secretarial work for him, I steer the boat, but I don't arrange his life for him. And I don't read his mind.'

'What does he want a helicopter for?'

She sighed. 'He likes helicopters. You ask an awful lot of questions, Sam.'

'If I'm working for the guy, I'm bound to be interested in him.'

'You can get too interested,' she said.

She parked between the legs of the cranes on the South Side, got out and walked me to the *Lady Day*. I don't think she'd seen the boat before and she wasn't impressed. She looked down at the clutter on the decks, rolled a cigarette between her fingers and fiddled with her Zip lighter.

'You are going to behave, aren't you, Sam?'

'Of course I am.'

'This could be important for both of us. Just don't bug him, don't spoil things.'

'Me?'

'Yes, Sam. Don't get any ideas. I'm going out with him; I'm not trying to rekindle an old passion with you.'

'Just for a minute, by the poolside there, I thought something might have been going on.'

'You were wrong.' She lit her cigarette. 'I'll see you tomorrow.'

She walked away from me. She put each foot exactly in front of the other, like a tightrope walker. What this did to her hips made me regret what I'd said. She climbed into the car and let the power of the Jaguar rip up the tarmac as she took off.

I ate some ham and eggs and drank some fruit juice, then went to the scrapyard, forty yards away from where the *Lady Day* was moored, behind the cranes and the oil tanks. It was a wilderness of wrecked boats and broken cars and rusting metal I couldn't sell, the yard enclosed by three-metre-high blue granite walls that made it as forbidding as a prison from the outside. Inside, there was a wooden shed which was the office, the only building on the site apart from a warehouse with a pit and lifting gear, the warehouse choked roof-high with old cars. There was half an acre of waste ground on the other side of one of the walls which also belonged to the yard.

BREAKER'S YARD was written up in large pink letters on a grey board over the steel gates, which were always open so I could sit in my office and look out and see whether or not anyone was going to steal the *Lady Day*. The pink paint was a cheap undercoat and it was weathering off now, so you could just see the name of the previous owner, MARTIN AND SONS, underneath; and to one side the Brew's sign,

BROUARD FIREWORKS, was still there.

The light was on in the shed I called an office. The Brew was sitting reading the racing pages of the *Sun*. He'd rolled a thin cigarette and was smoking it. The ashtray was piled high with stubs, like a plate of broken spaghetti.

'You took your time,' he said. 'I sent a taxi to the police station for you, but they said you'd gone, eh? When you come back, you turn up in a smart car.' He pretended to smell my breath. 'Pissed.'

'I've had a bad day. Did you read what the bastards wrote about me in the papers?' He didn't hear me so I came round on his good side – he'd been deaf in one ear ever since one of his step-fathers had smacked him with a whisky bottle. Genetically, the Brew's large family were a bunch of almost total strangers – his mother had travelled around the world a dozen times without ever getting off her back in her own bedroom. The Brew's father had been a merchant sailor from Leghorn.

I showed him the local newspaper with my picture in it. He wasn't interested. He flicked over another page of the *Sun*.

'I've been in the cells, Brew, I've been in the bloody nick. I deserved a couple of drinks. I've been entertained by a multi-millionaire. He's given us a job. What do you think of that?'

'I think you're clumsy, eh?' he said, in his lilting Guernsey voice. 'I read the papers this morning. You didn't tell me you'd pushed one of the poor sods out of the window. That's cheating, eh? You told me you'd been in a stand-up fight.'

'I had two of them to deal with. At the same time.'

'They were from the Mainland, eh? You should have been able to deal with a pair of Englishmen without pushing the poor bastards out the bloody window, eh? Through the glass, eh? If they were Guernsey donkeys, I could've understood it, but they were bloody Englishmen. Soft as shit, eh?'

'Fuck yourself,' I suggested. 'Want to go for a drink?'

'The police have been around.'

'To do what?'

'To take the fireworks away. Our fireworks.'

'Well?' I asked.

'I gave them the rubbish. I'd already stowed the better stuff, the imported stuff.'

'Where?'

'Under tarpaulins in the hold of the *Lady Day*. Just don't light any matches in there. I had to hide them somewhere, eh?'

'All right,' I said. But he hadn't finished. I waited. He turned another page of the newspaper, but he wasn't reading it.

'That was your wife driving that car. Her hair's grown, but I recognised her.'

'That was my wife,' I said.

'You told me once you got into trouble when you were around her, eh?'

'I was probably drunk.'

'Things have changed, eh?'

'Things have changed.'

'I can get some fishing work. We can earn enough to pay for fuel, we can get some diving contracts on the Brittany coast. That'll keep us going all summer.'

'Baxter is paying us enough to clear all our debts. I

don't think Evelyn is going to stop me taking the job.'

'You won't be getting involved with her, eh?'

I laughed at him. 'Involved? Not a chance.'

'That's easy to say.'

'Then I'll say it again,' I said. 'Not a chance.' But the memory of her body in the sunlight by the swimming-pool came back hauntingly. I could hear music again. I grinned at him.

'We've been accident-prone lately,' he muttered.

'I don't think Saturday night was an accident. I think someone decided they didn't like me and wanted to beat the shit out of me.'

'Not your wife trying to get her own back, eh?'

'If she wanted me crippled, why would she get me a job afterwards? Anyway,' I added, 'in a street fight like that I can handle two amateurs. Evelyn knows that. She knows what I can do.'

I showed him a loading manifest Baxter had given me, building materials ordered from Norman Piette: timber, cement, concrete blocks.

'There's a couple of lorry loads,' the Brew said. 'We'll shift it from the yard tomorrow morning, eh? What kind of a fucking job is this? We'll have to stow some of it on deck.'

'You're on a big bonus. And you're not telling me there isn't enough room in the hold, with all those fireworks in there?'

'Very fucking funny,' the Brew said.

The sun coming in through the porthole was like an arc of light from a welding torch. I didn't use curtains, or ever close the port, except in a heavy sea. If the passers-by on the harbourside wanted to crouch down and peer in to see me snoring on my bunk, or trying to have the stand-up whore's bath which was all the plumbing arrangements on the *Lady Day* allowed, good luck to them. I'd never had any complaints.

I rolled out of bed and hit the ground. The headache was serious, not just because of the blows I'd taken on my head on Saturday night. I'd over-dosed on Springbank. I'd had this theory that single malts couldn't give you a headache, but that morning I gave it up.

I went up on deck. The sunlight was only margin-ally less intense up there but the porthole had seemed to focus it. I vomited over the side into the harbour. The tide was out and the harbour was dry, the *Lady Day* resting securely on her flat bottom on the mud. Half a moment later, gulls were fighting for what I had thrown up. It was only then I noticed I was naked.

The galley was on deck between the wheelhouse and the deckhouse which I used as a living-room. I made myself a cocktail of ginseng, minerals, vita-mins and fruit juice, and managed to keep that down. Then I began to follow some meditation exercises I'd learned from a Chinese woman in Los Angeles. Wonderful exercises, to relieve tension, ease pain, remove stress, or postpone orgasm. Especially to postpone orgasm.

I'd spent some months learning to control my breathing while concentrating on eternity – a hole in a blank space, a hole you could climb through towards an infinite three-dimensional plane. It worked pretty well if you'd been smoking grass all afternoon, even better if you'd spent years exercising the muscles in your perineum. I'd tried that for a while, stopping peeing halfway through and all that, doing it often enough to build up a muscle there where most men don't even have muscles. I told the Chinese woman that with the drinking beginning to interfere with the stunt business and my marriage on the rocks, I might take up being a gigolo. She'd laughed at me. 'You like women too much,' she'd said. 'And you're too ugly.'

I'd given up the exercises when I found she'd abandoned her ascetic principles, and had brought out her stuff on video. The last I heard of her she was living as a multi-millionaire in Beverly Hills.

There were prayers in Mandarin I'd learned to help the meditation, and I said some of them now. But then I started to think about the Chinese woman, and about the few silky black hairs she had on her neat pudendum. Then I got a hard-on and stopped thinking about eternity altogether. There might have been exercises to postpone orgasms, but she'd never been able to teach me any to postpone erections.

So I did some stretching and easing exercises, and then put on some trunks and took a towel and drove the Traveller round to Bordeaux Harbour where I swam in cold sea water for most of an hour. After that I was beginning to feel better, and the shakes had gone. I didn't need a drink any more. Things had seemed black last night, but now the sun was shining. I was beginning to feel all right.

9

When I got back to the *Lady Day*, one of the cranes on the harbourside was lowering a cement mixer into the hold. The hold was already half full of timber. Four pallets piled high with cement bags were on the harbour side, with all kinds of other junk.

The Brew was supervising all this, shouting instructions up at the crane driver. 'Want some help?' I asked. He waved at me dismissively.

'You'd only be in the bloody way, eh?'

I only owned the boat; he was the boss. I shrugged and went into the deckhouse and made a leisurely breakfast. I heard the banging, the sound of the crane moving and the shouts of the men, but I didn't watch them. I read a week-old newspaper and listened to the radio.

The Brew came in to look for something to sign the manifest with. The smell of his sweat overcame the smell of scrambled eggs and coffee. He didn't look at me. Something had upset him. I wondered what I'd done wrong this time, apart from being a drunk, a wastrel and a lazy bastard who left him to do all the heavy work while I sat in the deckhouse and drank coffee. He hadn't liked the way I'd had to fight in the restaurant on Saturday, but that was my business, not his.

'Our passenger's arrived, eh?' he said, still not looking at me.

'You didn't tell me we had a passenger.'

'You didn't ask.' His body language told me it was a woman before I saw her. It was Evelyn. Although she'd said she'd see me that day, I hadn't expected to see her on the boat; what surprised me was that I was glad to see her.

'Sit down and have some coffee,' I said to her. 'Brew?'

'I'll join you in a cup,' he said, but as I began to make it he left the deckhouse and went off to do something in the hold.

I felt her watching me. Checking up.

'I'm going to the Hoummet,' she said.

'Why?'

'George wants me to keep an eye on you.'

'To make sure I don't run off?'

'No, to make sure you do what you're supposed to be doing.'

'Who'd ever doubt that I would?'

'Almost everyone who's ever met you. I have to check the cargo, Sam. Can I get into the hold?' She had a clipboard of the kind civil engineers stand around writing on. She was playing a role, impressing the Brew, I guessed; she wasn't impressing me.

I took her down into the hold by the ladder that hung down into it and left her there. Back in the galley, the coffee-maker did its work. In the deck-house, I poured three cups. Evelyn reappeared soon afterwards.

'What's all that explosive you've got down there?'

'Those are my fireworks,' the Brew said, appearing in the doorway. 'Want to see some fireworks?'

She looked angry. 'Fireworks? Are you crazy? There are things down there they could have used in the Gulf War. If anyone sets light to that lot, we'll go into orbit.'

'Who's going to set light to it?' the Brew asked pugnaciously.

She was irritated. 'What the hell's the matter with you? Do you two like living dangerously?'

'We need to store them somewhere,' I said. 'Those fireworks matter to us. We've been put out of business, and we need to sell them for what we can get.'

'George won't like this,' she said.

'Then don't tell him. And whatever you do, don't tell the police.'

'Why not?'

'They think they've confiscated them, that's why not.'

'When I read the papers, I couldn't understand how a man's head could get blown off by a firework. Now I can.'

She had a small leather bag which she picked at with her fingers and found a packet of cigarettes inside. She lit one. I liked the smell of the cigarette mingling with the smell of the coffee, such a reminder of cool French cafés in the early morning that I found a bottle of Calvados and poured three shot glasses. She sat looking at the glasses.

'You're starting early, Sam. I thought you were drinking less.'

'*Un trou normand*, that's all.'

Her expression showed she didn't like that, but why should I justify myself to her? I didn't bother.

She said, 'I really was trying to raise some money to finance a script I wanted to film in Monaco. But I got into debt. Four thousand dollars in debt. George paid the debt off. I owe him. So I came with him to Guernsey.'

'You must have been good,' I said, with what I hoped was healthy cynicism.

'I've always been good.' She spoke matter-of-factly, but then she smiled at me, and I felt something stirring inside me: hope. I tried not to look at her below the neck. It was difficult.

'George likes having me around. That's all.'

'It was your idea that you come here?'

'It was his.' She widened her eyes at me. 'And I do everything he says.'

There were a lot of questions I wanted to ask, but it wasn't the time to ask any of them. I stuck my head out of the door to call for the Brew. He came striding back along the deck towards me, the wing of black hair flopping over one eye. He pushed past me into the deckhouse but wouldn't sit down. He stood looking at the three cups of coffee and the three glasses of Calvados, not at Evelyn, who after smiling at him gave up and looked out of the window.

'Nobody told me about the passenger,' he said. 'They should have told us.'

'She's coming with us, Brew.'

'Women are bad luck,' he said. He meant it: crossed knives, open umbrellas, and women in any form on board the boat, and he felt threatened by them.

'Don't be bloody ridiculous,' she said unexpectedly.

'I skipper this boat, and I don't like having women aboard,' the Brew said.

'I won't get in your way. You won't have to worry about me.'

'Then don't come,' he said rudely. 'And if you are going to come, don't smoke any bloody cigarettes anywhere near the hold.' He pointed to the NO SMOKING sign on the lip of the hold.

She sighed. 'I promise,' she said, and made a face at me.

'Take the weight off your feet, Brew, and join us,' I said.

He shook his head, rubbed his dark, stubbled jaw. 'Got work to do. Work for the wicked, eh? Work for idle hands.' He picked up the coffee cup and cradled it, and he stared at the Calvados with morbid interest. He wanted it, but he disapproved of anyone drinking at sea. He was always telling me how many accidents at sea were caused by drunks.

I sat down and sipped my coffee and put my shot of Calvados down in one piece. Evelyn did the same. I sat looking at her with watering eyes. The Brew looked at her too. She was wearing shiny black cycling shorts and a white tee-shirt that was moulded to her shoulders and breasts.

'I'll save mine for later,' the Brew said. 'For when I'm ashore.' He stood there, clumsy in his green Hawaiian shirt and in the yellow oilcloth apron he wore to work in, scratching his chin. 'Nothing wrong with my bloody fireworks,' he muttered. After a moment, he left the deckhouse and went forward. I saw him clambering down the ladder into the hold.

The first time I saw the *Lady Day* she was steaming up the stretch of sea between Guernsey and Herm. Backwards.

I was interested enough to stop the car and watch her. She was making a lot of smoke from her diesel engine, which blew forward and filled the drifting sail she had set, but she was moving steadily backwards against the backdrop of the white hotel on Herm and the green fields and the farm above. I should have started the car and driven off and never looked at her again. But I didn't. I tracked her down to St Sampson's Harbour and a week later I bought her from the Maltese businessman who owned her. After all, the currents in the Little Roussel are very strong, and there must have been an explanation for what I'd seen.

I paid fifteen thousand pounds cash for her, then I had to start rebuilding her, which cost me another fifteen thousand pounds. When I had her valued by the insurance company I found out that she was worth six or seven thousand pounds. If that.

The reasonable explanation for the *Lady Day* steaming backwards up the Little Roussel the first day I saw her was her engine, a four-cylinder two-stroke diesel, which on a good day gave 140 bhp at 360 revolutions a minute if you could get her up to that, and which wasn't powerful enough to guarantee you'd ever be able to overtake the current.

She'd been built in 1932 as a motor-powered, wooden-hulled drifter, ninety feet long with a beam of twenty-three feet. She had a foremast stepped into a tabernacle so it could be lowered to rest on the roof of the wheelhouse, which was aft of the hold, and there had been a mizzen mast behind the wheelhouse. Some rich man had bought her after that, and had got rid of the mizzen mast and rebuilt the deck-housing, so the wheelhouse was moved two yards further forward and a deckhouse was built aft of that, a fair-sized room with windows all around, and enough room inside to have a snooker table, a dining table, or a double bed with a running track around the outside. The hold was reduced, the rear of the boat below the deckhouse and aft of the engine room turned into cabins.

With brass railings on the wooden gunwales, scrubbed wooden deck, gaff-rigged foremast and bowsprit, black hull, white deck-housing, red and white lifebelts, red and white striped awning over the poop deck, she was a picture – tourists took photos of her in the harbour. But the weight of the wooden foremast made her roll like a barrel, her shallow draught and U-shaped bottom made her hard to steer, and she took in spray even in a light sea. I'd carried sheep to Herm, beer to Sark, a grand piano to a millionaire's house on Alderney; I'd hired her out to deep-sea divers and local fishermen, and to businessmen who wanted to be alone with their secretaries; but by the time I'd paid mooring charges, insurance, maintenance, and the Brew's wages, the *Lady Day* was what a boat always was, a hole in the water to throw money into.

I took the *Lady Day* up the Little Roussel north of the Platte, and then the Platte Fougère, which marked the deep-water channel. The horde of yachts and small boats around Guernsey faded into the distance, the haze began to grow, and there were fewer boats. I sat in the wheelhouse in the sun, as sleepy as a wasp in a sweet-shop window, the two-way radio burbling every now and again as it picked up the traffic between fishing boats in the area. Evelyn was in the deckhouse out of my sight. The Brew clattered around in the hold and the engine room, then came up on deck, checking the mast and the rigging.

Two hours later, three or four miles away from the rock itself, the smell of the gannet colony on Ortac hit us like a wall: rotting fish and bird shit. The Brew laughed and gesticulated from the bows. A rocket whizzed snaking across the water and went fizzing into a wave, one of his fireworks he'd set off for fun. The biggest Catherine wheel I'd ever seen suddenly started spinning on the foremast, spraying gold and silver into the sea.

He came into the wheelhouse, grinning, wiping his hands: cheerful again after the work.

'All right?'

'All right,' I said.

'She's a pig to steer with all this cargo aboard her, eh?'

He took the wheel. I let him; it was difficult sea from now on. I went into the deckhouse, picked up Evelyn's clipboard and looked at the loading manifest, trying to decipher the faded print-out. I poured the undrunk glass of Calvados back into the bottle and recorked it and put it away, and then climbed up on the roof of the deckhouse and sat looking around, trying not to look as if I was looking at Evelyn, who was leaning over the stern of the boat like a child on a river trip. I was thinking about something, I forget what, and it was a while before I realised I wasn't looking at the sea any more, but at the shape Evelyn's hips made in the shorts she was wearing, bent over the stern rail.

I could feel rather than see the Brew sitting in the wheelhouse behind me, hear the radio hissing. He was talking to someone about a bet he'd put on a horse.

Seagulls were floating in the air above the mast. The sun was on the water, I could smell the sea all around me. I wish this would go on, I found myself thinking. This must be what it's all about. This is living.

For the second time in two days I stared at the Hoummet through binoculars. Gulls swirled around it, crying. The currents around it made the water seethe. The same currents made a broken wave at the foot of the beacon. The Hoummet looked like a ship steaming at full speed into a rough sea.

I could see standing waves four or five feet high standing up out of the dead calm sea on a day when there was so little wind the shags could hardly get off the water. We were a lot closer than we had been in the *Venus*.

'God Almighty,' Evelyn shouted from the bows, almost losing her footing as the *Lady Day* began to pitch and roll in the waves.

'There're undulates on the sea bottom there, big ripples of sand,' the Brew said, grimly amused by her alarm. 'They cause the overfalls – the big waves there. But they keep moving around. Those waves will always be there but they'll shift their position. Half-tide's running, and rising.'

We came in through the waves and I heard as well as felt the old boat shuddering as the waves hammered and twisted her, and spray broke over the bow and hissed along the scuppers.

Evelyn scurried back along the deck, eyes wide. She came into the wheelhouse. Grabbed a cigarette out of her bag hardly before she'd got through the door. Now she looked nervous.

'Fuck this,' she said, grabbing my arm for support. 'It wasn't like this the last time I came this close in the *Venus*.'

'The tide's running. We'll be all right, the Brew knows what he's doing,' I said. I put my arm around her to steady her, feeling a line of surprisingly firm muscle down her back: surprising because I'd forgotten how firm.

I could see the crescent shape of the Hoummet forming a half-sheltered bay in the lee of the big rock rising up at the back of the bay. The Brew brought the *Lady Day* up towards it and then disengaged the diesel and let it rattle away under our feet while he went out of the wheelhouse and went and stared over the side into the calm water of the bay.

'What's going on?' I asked.

He pointed towards what was left of the pier. Storm damage had made its outer wall fall into the bay. 'We can't go in there on those fallen stones, we'll rip the bottom out of her, so I'm looking at the depth of water,' the Brew said. 'If we moor against the big rock there, we'll be able to lay a gangplank and unload there to one side of it. If you look at the chart, you'll see we're supposed to be able to push into the back of the bay. But I don't trust charts much.'

'I thought you said you'd been here before?'

'Not this close.'

He came back into the wheelhouse and pushed the gear lever with his knee. The *Lady Day* wallowed forward a few yards. Gulls rose crying from the rocks as we approached. He left the wheelhouse and went and looked over the side again, leaving me holding the wheel. He came back, wiped the back of his neck with a handkerchief, pulled the gear lever back into reverse so that the boat slowed, stopped, began to turn a little. 'Have a look at that chart,' he said. I did so. Charts weren't my strong point, but I don't suppose they were the Brew's either; his knowledge of the Channel Island seas, the huge three-dimensional model of the seabed with all its variety of current, tide, weather, was carried inside his head. 'What's the depth at the back of that bay?'

It was an old chart, the depths marked in feet. I couldn't remember whether the heights referred to high tide or low tide.

'About thirty feet,' I said.

'That's never thirty feet,' he said. 'It's not even fifteen.'

I went forward to have a look. As I did so, I heard the gearbox crunching and the beat of the engine slowed as the Brew began to ease the *Lady Day* forward again.

'We're going to go in close to that rock and moor there,' the Brew shouted to me. The boat edged forward; the wall of rock came closer. Leaning over the old-fashioned bowsprit looking down into the water, I saw the indigo water suddenly reveal pale seaweed, which seemed to jump up at me. Jesus, I thought. I couldn't remember whether I'd kept up with the insurance payments on the *Lady Day* or not. Probably not. I felt rather than heard the keel scrape on something underwater. I looked back at the wheelhouse. The Brew grinned at me. There was a moment's hesitation, then we slipped forward again.

'There's your wreck!' he called out to me as he reversed the engines in the slack water of the bay. 'Another ten seconds lying on it, we'd have broken her back, eh?'

He came along the deck towards me, wiping his hands on a rag, pushing the wing of black hair out of his eyes. 'I don't like it, Sam. I don't know what this bloke Baxter's up to, eh? But I've got a bad feeling about it.'

'You're a superstitious bastard.'

'You ought to listen to me,' he said. 'I'm usually right.'

10

I dropped anchors fore and aft. Then we laid a gangplank to the rocks and made it fast to the iron stanchion set in concrete in the blue granite of the northern, right-hand arm of the bay.

The dry part of the Hoummet is the size of a football pitch. Beyond the wall of rock it climbs to what was a beach several thousand years ago, a ridge of pebbles well above the waterline, the stones the size of cannonballs. Beyond that is a thatch of rough grass, scrub and sea holly, which is what makes the Hoummet an island rather than a rock. Some oyster-catchers were nesting there, and some things which I thought were rats until I realised they were petrels living in burrows.

When we started the repairs to the pier, we were too awkwardly placed to use the derrick arm of the *Lady Day*, so that meant carrying bags of cement and gravel and buckets of fresh water across to the shore, enough for the Brew to start mixing the stuff with a shovel on a piece of hardboard, then carrying the planks across for him to build the shuttering while I ferried more cement across. The gangplank had a rail on one side only and bent like a bow whenever any real weight was put on it. There was enough breeze to disguise the heat of the sun, and I started to burn.

I retreated to the deckhouse for a while and had a beer. The Brew came in after me. He drank water from a plastic bottle. He had a photocopy of the chart of the Hoummet on which someone had drawn another outline, bigger than the pier we were supposed to be repairing.

'Take a look at that,' he said. I looked at it while he rolled a cigarette and lit it. 'Well?'

'Well what?'

He pointed to the words written at the top of the photocopy. 'It's never a pier,' he said. 'It's too big.' He pointed to the island. He'd marked the new outline on the rocks with tin cans. I looked at them, and looked back at the plan.

'Baxter, or whatever his name is, would've submitted a plan to the States of Guernsey, but this isn't it. They're building it bigger than they need to. We'll have repaired the old pier all right, but by building all this around it. Are we going to do as he says?'

'He's paying us to do it.'

'What if the States want us to dismantle it after we've finished?'

'He'll be paying us then too.'

'What's he going to do with all this space?'

'Play badminton,' I suggested. 'How the hell do I know?'

The Brew shrugged. I'd told him about the wreck. 'You'll never turn a wreck over with a crane on the *Lady Day*. You'll sink the bloody boat, eh?'

'That's what I said to him, Brew. What do you suggest we do?'

'I'll set a couple of steel rings at the edge of the concrete. There's an old donkey engine back at the yard. Diesel. If we anchor that on the rings, that'll put the wreck over.' He drank more water. 'Visitors, eh?' he said. 'They're all bloody mad. There must be a score of wrecks round here. If he's got some idea about one of them, good luck to the bugger. But he's paying my wages. That's all that matters, eh?'

I tied a rag over my head to keep the sun off and went back to work.

The first stage was to rebuild the wall of the old pier. I collected loose rocks for aggregate and helped lift up the stones, and I did the carrying. The Brew chose the sites for the stones, placed them, and began to construct the wall.

I started shifting shuttering and bags of cement up out of the hold, across the gangplank to the shore. The sea breeze had dropped and the sun was overhead, and it was murderous down in the hold. I was standing there, resting, one hand on the sun-warmed rungs of the ladder, when a shadow covered me and Evelyn called down to me.

'You need any help?'

'I need help shifting these bags of cement,' I said, but that didn't seem to put her off. She came down the ladder.

'I'll help you.'

'I've got to carry the cement up the ladder, across the gangplank, over the rocks. You'll never do it.'

She said, 'You lift them up the ladder, I'll carry them over the rocks. I need the exercise.'

'Are you sure about this?'

She rolled the short sleeves of her tee-shirt up over her shoulder and flexed her biceps. 'Feel that,' she said. I did. Under the soft skin it was hard as steel. 'I didn't stop working out when I stopped stunting, Sam.'

So we did the donkey work together, while the Brew drove stanchions down into the rocks, built the shuttering, mixed the cement and poured it in, and then laid steel mesh on top of it as a primitive reinforcement. The pier began to spread outwards from the spine of that arm of the bay. Several times the Brew left me to go on board the *Lady Day* to look at the plans, which left me standing there in the sun sprinkling handfuls of fresh water from one of the plastic barrels we had brought ashore to stop the cement from going off too quickly. Evelyn went to get iced drinks, and came back with a cigarette. Sweat had soaked through her tee-shirt.

I hurt as much as if I'd spent the time boxing, the aches of Saturday's fight rekindled by the exercise. 'You've done bloody well,' I said to her.

'And you're a patronising bastard,' she said. We stood there grinning at each other.

'Which fitness programme did you use?'

'My own. In Monaco, I hung around with a sports coach for a while, when I was trying to sell the script. He dealt in medicines for sportsmen, most of them legal. He wanted me to go in for film roles as a strong woman, Arnie Schwarzenegger without the balls. Just before I met George, I found out the bastard was spiking my fruit juice with steroids. I was growing hair on my hands and my tits were disappearing.'

'They've come back.'

'You're not exactly subtle, are you?'

'You know I'm not; you wouldn't have me any other way,' I said.

She turned and walked away, her back towards the boat, peeled off her tee-shirt and used it to wipe sweat from the back of her neck and under her arms, then, after crossing the gangplank, she laid the tee-shirt to dry over the section of the rails that we'd opened like a gate.

She'd had her back to me all this time, and the look she threw back at me over her shoulder was hard to read. But the drying tee-shirt looked like a flag of surrender to me.

The shuttering was still in place, most of it held there by iron spikes wedged or hammered down in the rocks – a pool of drying concrete the size of a tennis court. The Brew had fixed the rings he'd been talking about along the edge of the concreted area.

'I tell you, it's far too bloody big,' he said. 'What's he up to, eh?' He shook his head in angry despair. 'We'll cover it with a tarpaulin to keep the worst of the sun off it and call it a day.'

We did that, and then he went off to the *Lady Day*, and I stripped to the skin and put on the goggles I kept in the wheelhouse for swimming, and I dived into the bay. The water was liquid silver on my skin.

I swam for a while, drifting round behind the boat and floating face down to peer into the depths of the bay. There was a garden of seaweed underneath me, ochre and umber and red, and a shoal of fish, mullet probably, pushed in there by the tide, and not much sand. Near to the rock that backed the bay a long shape lay in the water. The wreck? It had to be. The anchor chain of the *Lady Day* went down into the water, brown with rust above it, as green as spun glass below.

I was just floating up when something exploded in the water in front of me, and my heart leapt as if it had been kicked.

I don't know what I was thinking of, what fear had been lying at the back of my mind, of explosions underwater, bombs lying in the wreck, but a mine might have gone off in front of me. For a moment, I thought I was going to die.

But then I saw a limb flash in the mass of bubbles and realised it was Evelyn, that she must have jumped into the water from somewhere high above.

She swam out of the bubbles into the green water, naked and gleaming silver, turned towards me for a moment. A bubble broke out of her mouth and went wobbling upwards, then another, her eyes dark holes in the silver mask of her face. Her whole body was silver, the light flickering on it, making it shimmer like a waterspout.

My heart was pounding with adrenalin and the strain of holding my breath. I swam upwards. There was a strange feeling of being reborn as my head and shoulders came up slowly into richly coloured air, then I saw a coil of gold in the water beside me, from under which the dome of her forehead appeared, her skin tanned again in direct light. She smiled at me, swam away with a powerful stroke. I watched her climbing out of the water on to the rocks. She straightened up and pulled the wet hair out of her eyes with a gesture which I remembered as belonging to her only. How much else had I forgotten?

I pulled myself up over the stern ladder of the *Lady Day*, went into the deckhouse to pick up a towel and towelled myself dry. I could see her walking among the rocky cannonballs of the raised beach, the oystercatchers bothering her with their piercing cries. I could hear the sea slopping against the rocks, and an aeroplane going over very slowly and very high. I stood there letting the sun warm me. I was shaking; it wasn't just the sudden uprush of fear, the shock of the exercise I'd taken on an empty stomach and with a hangover.

She lay on a rock, face down.

I heard something and turned to see the Brew in the wheelhouse. He was moving the binoculars out of sight under the compass binnacle.

He grinned at me, the quick, nervous grin of a boy caught spying. 'They're all Jonahs, eh?' he said, pushing his hair out of his eyes. 'You ought to tell her she'll have to cover herself. She'll burn in this sun.'

'No she won't. She's got a skin like a rhinoceros,' I said, trying to make a joke of it. But I was lying: I knew it was like silk.

'What's the matter with you?'

My hands were trembling. 'It's the drink,' I said. 'I've been drinking too much.' But it wasn't that.

'Bloody women,' the Brew muttered. 'They cause all the trouble in the world.'

'They cause half of it,' I said numbly.

You'd see as much on almost any beach in the world. And Evelyn was my wife. We'd made love a thousand times. But not for over two years, and I'd thought since that she was lost to me.

I wanted her. I could feel my blood pounding, relentlessly. Yesterday or the day before, or the day before that, almost any woman would have done, even in spite of what had happened at Baxter's house. But this was different. I wanted Evelyn now.

But nothing could alter the Brew's mind about having women on board, and I had to put up with his bad temper all the way back, and by the time we reached St Sampson's it was dark. Evelyn went off to her Jaguar, and drove back to George Baxter. I left the Brew clearing the decks and clambered up the ladder to the harbourside. Then I walked across to the public phone booth by the clock tower.

If anyone was likely to know about any one of the Island's sixty thousand or so inhabitants it was Jenny Mahy. She was a nurse, and was married to a man who'd spent much of his working life editing the *Guernsey Press* before multiple sclerosis had struck him down. Guernsey families being what they are, with four sisters and two brothers herself, with scores of cousins and a fistful of in-laws, she was probably related to a quarter of the people on the Island. And she had an obsessive interest in the rest. If anybody could help me, she could. I left a message on her answerphone.

The Brew was ready for a drink when I returned to the boat, and we settled down in the deckhouse and opened the Johnny Walker Baxter had given me. I put some in a cup of black coffee, sipped it, and watched him drink the rest of the bottle.

11

If the *Lady Day* were sinking, the first thing I'd save would be the Selmer Mark VI tenor saxophone I bought from a Chicago nightclub owner; he'd claimed it had once belonged to Wardell Gray. I didn't believe him but I was happy to pay, just in case. I spend a lot of time practising. I don't get better. I've reached my ceiling.

Early that morning, I played scales, exercises, blues, then some of the big tunes: 'Stardust', 'Misty', 'Easy Living', 'Round Midnight', the Lester Young solo from 'All of Me'. I was making a mess of the second chorus when someone came down the ladder from the harbourside and dropped on to the deck. Jenny Mahy.

I'd met her in hospital after my fall into an empty harbour had caused a clot on the brain. Briefly, just before I left, she'd shared the bed I was occupying in an empty ward. She was married, and her husband was ill; we'd never spoken of it since.

I put a cup of China White tea in front of her, and she settled opposite me across the table in the deckhouse. She was in her late thirties or early forties, had large brown eyes with very clearly defined dark eyebrows and eyelashes, wore more lipstick than a ward sister should, and had a glimmer of silver in her curly brown hair. I'd often suspected that the ward sister's uniform she wore had been tailored specially to fit her figure. It did.

'You're not drinking again, are you?' she asked.

'Not like the good old days.'

'You sounded drunk on the answerphone.'

'I was.'

'Well, then. Getting yourself into trouble, fighting visitors, fighting the police. What are you trying to do – get yourself thrown off the Island?'

'You don't have to believe everything you read in the papers.'

'You were lucky to have Richard Guilbert defending you.'

'I was lucky to have a lawyer at all.'

'Who paid him?'

'Someone called George Baxter.' She looked mildly impressed. 'I wanted you to answer some questions, not ask them.'

'I find you endlessly fascinating, Sam, you know that. I can't tear myself away.'

'I asked you here, Jenny, because I want to know about Baxter.'

'Oh, is that why you asked me here?'

'What other reason could there be?'

Her eyes twinkled. 'I can't possibly think.' Not for the first time, I had the feeling she was getting her own back on me for something. 'George Baxter is as rich as Croesus, I've heard – I've never met him. Made a big splash when he moved over here. Always opening and sponsoring things. Had his own junior football team for a while – that kind of thing. Kept cropping up on TV and in the press. Loaded. Play your cards right, Sam, you might get some of the money.'

'I hope to,' I said. I looked enviously at her sun-browned hand as it lay on the table. The gold wedding ring on her finger winked in the sun. 'Tell me anything you know. Anything. Hard fact, rumour, gossip. Innuendo. Anything.'

She smiled at me. 'The least you can do is make me lunch.'

'I'll see what I can do.'

'I'd like some sherry.'

I went to the galley and I made Haddock Monte Carlo out of lightly smoked haddock and eggs poached in milk. While Jenny toyed with her food and sipped glasses of the Dry Fly I kept especially for her, I ate enough for four men. When she lit one of the two mentholated cigarettes she allowed herself a day, I got her the bottle. She had a gleam in her eye as I poured her the next drink.

'Evelyn used to go round with my youngest sister Lizzie before Lizzie got married. You're not smitten with her again, are you? Didn't being married to her put you off?'

'I'm always being smitten, Jenny, you know that. She works for Baxter . . .'

'It's funny you should say that,' Jenny said, slipped from the leash. 'When Evelyn went to work for George Baxter, the one you're working for . . . ah. This is complicated, isn't it? Lizzie said they met abroad somewhere. Monaco, I think. Tax haven to tax haven. Then they came over here. It isn't just a business relationship, I heard. Do I know more about your wife than you do?'

'Richard Guilbert told me what was going on.'

'She is having an affair with Baxter. I heard they met about two years ago.' She drank more sherry, rolling it round her mouth, delicately puffed at her cigarette. 'Lizzie says Evelyn had told her Baxter lent her some money when she got into debt gambling in Monaco.' She smiled sweetly at me. 'Her collateral in that case was services rendered.'

I didn't say anything to that; she drank some more sherry.

'Lizzie is working for your friend Henry Milliner,' she said. My friend! When Milliner wasn't making money he spent his time and energy trying to get me and my scrapyard moved elsewhere – to Jersey, for instance. 'I read all about your fight at Anton's on Saturday. And I know Carl. He might have come out as a witness on your side if you hadn't punched him.'

'He jumped me,' I muttered, and I was going to add that it wasn't my fault until I realised it was wasted on her.

'That's what made me think about Milliner – he was at Anton's on Saturday, wasn't he? Lizzie says the pay is all right but there isn't the overtime she expected because Milliner does all the extra stuff, all the Land Use stuff, himself, takes the files home with him at night because he hasn't got time to do them during the day – he's on the Land Use Committee, you know. Things aren't going very well for Mr Milliner at the moment, Lizzie says. Lizzie went to work for him the same day I was taken on by Mr Poucher, when I started doing some extra work to try to pay the bills. We went out to dinner that night to celebrate. That's the last time Ray was well enough to come with us. Three years ago now.' Then she said, in a broad, self-mocking Guernsey accent, 'You know how Guernsey families stick together, eh?'

'I certainly do,' I said.

I followed her up the ladder to the harbourside to the special Rover Metro she drove, which had been built up to the height of a Range-Rover at the back so it would take her husband's wheelchair through the rear door. This allowed him to sit in the wheelchair inside the rear part of the car.

She stopped by her car. 'I'm giving up nursing, Sam.'

'Why?'

'Ray hasn't got that long to live,' she said, and shivered a little as if touched by cold air. I knew it was true. Multiple sclerosis had savaged him so severely he couldn't open an envelope or hold a pen any more. 'There, I've said it. There isn't anyone else I'd say it to.'

'What are you going to do?'

'I'm going into journalism – sort of. Writing an advice column for the *Press* from home. I've got Ray's experience behind me. He'll help me to get started, anyway. I have contacts; I might be able to branch out one day. I'm going to have to do something.'

I reached out and held her hand for a moment, but that wasn't what she wanted; she pulled away.

'Ray's all right; I think he's facing up to it,' she said, knowing I'd be thinking about him. Then she said, 'I'm worried about your drinking. Are you drinking?'

'Every now and again.'

'You shouldn't. A recovering alcoholic has to be especially careful.'

'I'm not an alcoholic. I'm a heavy drinker who saw

the light before it was too late. I'll be all right.'

'With your injuries and your record? Don't forget, I had a good look at you while you were in hospital.'

'Don't remind me,' I said.

'You've had quite a beating in your life. A lot of broken bones. You'll have a lot of arthritis as you get older.'

'I already do.' I rubbed my neck, hoping for sympathy. But I got the lecture instead, the one about cirrhosis and cancer of the liver and collapse of the pancreas, about portal haemorrhages and high blood pressure and the overloaded spleen.

'So take care of yourself,' she said when she'd finished, and kissed me on the cheek. A light professional kiss. She got into the car and I watched her drive off. I was just turning away when I heard a squeal of brakes. Somebody started yelling. She'd nearly hit someone who was standing in the middle of the road. She drove off again, and he yelled something after her. It was only when I saw that he was walking towards a theodolite on the pavement that I realised he was a surveyor.

I walked across to the scrapyard. The donkey engine the Brew had talked about was an old Perkins diesel which had been converted to wind in a pulley. I checked it over and started it up, and sorted out a hundred metres of hawser, chains and hooks, shackles and ropes. I had some heavy-duty underwater torches I'd bought as a job lot from a marine mining company, and I sorted them out. Then I started picking the bits of wire out of my hands, and thinking about Jenny. Her interest in life was other people, and other people's business, especially mine, but Jenny and I were more like friends than lovers. A lot of her animation came from frustrated sexual energy: apart from her skirmish with me, she'd told me she'd been faithful to her husband. She felt guilty about what had happened between us; so did I, partly because I liked Ray, even though he was too ill now for much of his personality to be apparent – just a blurring of previously clear out-lines, a wax figure melting in the heat.

Then I started thinking about the surveyor with the theodolite. I went out to talk to him.

While his partner chalked lines on to the tarmac, he sat on a bollard and smoked a cigarette. He was rubbing sun cream into his face. He had long hair and a bandido moustache.

'What are you doing up here?' I asked.

'I don't mind you asking,' he said, and looked as if he wasn't going to answer me. 'I'm surveying the road, what does it look as if I'm doing? I hope you've got a reason for asking. I'm having a bad morning.'

'I own the scrapyard. If you're going to alter the boundaries and encroach on my land . . .'

'We're not going to move the road,' he said. 'You must be Breaker. I've seen your name. We're putting in a cesspool on the other side of your land and we're tracing the drainage system.'

'A cesspool?'

'A big one. We'll have to close the road for a while, that's all. Then do you know what will happen?'

'No,' I said, falling for it.

'It'll fill up with shit.'

Back in the scrapyard I opened up the office and began to sort through the collection of bills I kept spiked on a hook on the back wall. I filed most of my post in the bin, but among a collection of police complaints about the state of my car, I found it. A letter from a man called Harkin, dated earlier that year, offering me twenty-three thousand pounds for the sale of the scrapyard; I'd kept it for its curiosity value. My father had tried to sell the scrapyard for years because the States wouldn't let him build on the land; apart from another scrap-metal merchant – Martin, Carl's father, who'd sold my father the land in the first place – no one else had ever made me an offer. Who wanted to buy a moribund scrap-metal business? Who could tell me who did?

The telephone in the office had been cut off for months, so I had to use the public telephone in the Southside Café. There wasn't a Harkin listed in the phone book. I got straight through to Richard Guilbert. An hour later I was sitting in his office.

12

Richard Guilbert's office looked out over the part of the harbour where his partners moored their yachts. Martel, Guilbert and Martel. At the top of the building was the big office with the picture window the width of the room looking out over the whole of St Peter Port harbour, from St Martin's Point to the White Rock. Guilbert had the smallest office and the smallest window in the building. The biggest yacht in the marina belonged to the senior partner; if Richard was willing to deal with someone like me, he probably didn't even own a dinghy.

I'd never been in his office before. I'd never had any desire to be there, and he hadn't asked me. Even now, I felt he was worried someone might recognise me as the man who'd been throwing people out of windows three days before.

His desk was the size of a snooker table. On it were several framed photographs of himself, one of him as a much younger man, wearing flying gear and standing in front of a helicopter.

He didn't look welcoming. Something had upset him. Me, probably.

'Nice place you've got here,' I said cheerfully. 'You must have had a partnership waiting for you when you got back from abroad.'

'I never had a partnership waiting for me because I don't have a partnership,' he said; what I'd said had riled him. 'The Guilbert in the firm's name is a cousin of my father's, it isn't me. It's because of him I got the job, that's all. These things happen – you don't look a gift horse in the mouth. But I spent the first four years here trying to earn a residency permit working for practically nothing, helping out with legal aid, working with the police. Squeezing legal work out of people like you.' He fingered his tie. 'What are you doing here? Come to change your will?' If this was intended to relieve the tension, it didn't, so he tried grinning at me; his wide, thin-lipped mouth twisted itself into a shape that could have expressed anything. He pushed the lapels of his suit up his chest with his thumbs, jerked his head, then leaned forward to say something to me; I thought he was going to say something in confidence and leaned forward too.

What he said was, 'You look awful.'

I was wearing a casual shirt of forest green, Abris shorts, my Spanish boots, and some Elastoplast over the cut on my scalp. I thought I looked all right. I said so.

'No, physically. You don't look well.'

'I've got nine stitches in my head, a handful of visible bruises and a bloodshot eye. The wound that's been stitched was put there by a copper who assaulted me when I was trying to defend myself. The bruises were put there by the men who were assaulting me at the time. I got the bloodshot eye because I drank too much last night and fell into the hold of my boat. Remember the line about the assault. You're going to defend me in court. You might need it.'

'Monday. And I won't need any help. Just don't go wandering off anywhere. What do you want?'

'I want your advice.'

'Then you'd better know my scale of charges.'

I ignored that and pushed the letter towards him. The desk was so deep he had to lean forward a long way to reach it. He smoothed out the letter and read it. He didn't react at first – at least, his face was expressionless, a mask. But I saw his Adam's apple jerk like a float struck by a large fish.

'What's this?' he asked.

'Do I sell?'

'Not my department.' But it had thrown him. He struggled for something to say. 'Just walking in here ought to cost you fifty pounds. Walk up a flight, it'd cost you three hundred. Another flight and they charge eighteen hundred for a consultation. I may be the bargain basement, but don't make the mistake of thinking I work for nothing.'

I ignored that too. I said, 'My father tried to sell the scrapyard and the land that goes with it years ago, but no one would buy it because they couldn't do anything with it.'

'This letter is months old. Why bring it round now?'

'Because a couple of States engineers are surveying the road outside my scrapyard. They're going to put a big cesspool in there.'

'What do you expect on Guernsey? Mains drainage? I wouldn't start worrying about details like that if I were you. Just concentrate on staying out of prison.'

'Cesspools mean housing.'

'So you do want to sell your land?'

'My father couldn't get planning permission, but that doesn't mean nobody can. What if someone already has planning permission? What if they're set to make a big profit out of the land I sell?'

'That's business.'

'I need professional advice.'

'Then you ought to pay for it,' he said. He fiddled with the letter. One of his hands strayed across the desk-top like a hunting spider.

'Twenty-three thousand pounds. What do you want me to do? Are you instructing me to accept this offer on your behalf? I don't deal with this kind of work.'

'Do I take the offer?'

He got up and walked to the window and looked out at the yachts, then came back and sat down.

'You didn't just come here to complain about not being offered enough money, did you?'

'You were the one who was complaining about money, not me.'

A remote expression crossed his face; I'd said something he didn't like. He opened and closed a drawer, moved one of the photographs on the desk.

I said, 'I can't afford to sell the scrapyard and you know it. I don't have a permit to live on Guernsey as a native any more. It lapsed while I was in America, and I'm only allowed to stay here because I pretend to be running a business. So if I sell the scrapyard, I'll become a UK resident again, and that means paying all that tax my ex-partner left hanging around my neck.'

'They might throw you out anyway, if you keep getting into fights in restaurants.'

'Are you on the Land Use Committee? They're the people who handle this kind of decision.'

'I'm not on the Land Use Committee,' he said.

'What business is that of yours anyway? You have to be on the inside to get on that kind of committee. I'm not on the inside. And they take their decisions in strict, honourable secrecy. They are the ones who make the final decision about planning permission and the like, yes.'

'Who's on the Land Use Committee?'

'Septimus Martel, who is the senior partner here, Henry Milliner, Munro Henderson, Jeremy Falla. A couple of others. The chairman changes every year. It's Milliner at the moment. Why?'

'If the Land Use Committee decided my business wasn't viable, and that the land might be used for building, could they buy it by compulsory purchase?'

He moved his head. I couldn't tell what the gesture meant.

'I'm telling you I don't know anything about it,' he said. He spoke slowly. 'You didn't answer when the first offer was made. You may have lost your chance. It looks as if the potential purchasers must have decided you weren't interested in selling. I'd chase them up if I were you. See if they'll make you a better offer.' He looked at the signature on the letter. 'Somebody called Harkin. I assumed you knew who it was.'

'I've never heard of him and he's not in the phone book. He claims to be the company secretary of a firm called GHH, Grande Havre Holdings, whose letterhead he's using. Who are they? I need to know.'

He looked at the letter as if it was a piece of shit on his desk. 'Normally I don't deal with this kind of thing. Why don't you go to someone who's qualified to help you. Like a psychiatrist.' He chuckled. 'I just don't handle this kind of thing. I'm an advocate, I stand up in court and put a point of view.' He became serious again. 'But I'll help you out. If that's what you want.'

He used the phone, and tilted his head back as if he was trying to drain his sinuses. He spoke to the ceiling. 'What if someone wants to buy your land simply because they want to buy a scrapyard? Have you thought of that?'

'I've thought of it. But I don't like it much. Carl Martin's scrapyard went out of business last year. That's why he works as a barman. It could be him.'

'Yes, it could be,' he said, as if the idea interested him.

'But it's more likely that the scrap business, as it used to exist on the Island, is finished. The small firms are closing, the bigger ones are thriving. It isn't you, by the way, is it?' I asked, following the shotgun policy of asking the first question to come into my head. His brow crinkled.

'No, it isn't me.'

'Would you swear that in court?'

'You seem a little paranoid to me, Sam. Too much drink?' He spoke into the telephone for a moment, then leaned back in his chair and watched the mail boat heaving into sight beyond the White Rock. Beyond it, a twin-masted yawl was furling a spinnaker, the sail white as snow on a distant mountaintop.

'Just this once,' he said, as if he was talking to himself. 'Just this once.' He didn't look at me; he'd already seen enough of me.

I looked at the things on his desk. The photographs. Young Richard Guilbert, skinny as a heron, with pimples on his cheek, wearing a flying jacket, helicopter in the background, looking pretty pleased with himself. In the years since then he'd turned into a middle-management stuffed shirt, sitting in a small office with a big view. He didn't have the money he wanted, he wasn't driving the Jaguar he probably felt he deserved. He spent his spare time looking at yachts he couldn't afford to own himself.

I heard a woman's voice through the phone. He saw that I'd heard it and covered the earpiece with a hand. He nodded and turned his back to me. I leaned forward to take a closer look at the photograph of him in front of the helicopter, and I realised then what had been bothering me about it. It was a French helicopter. It had French Air Force markings, and he was wearing military uniform.

He turned back towards me, put the phone down, wrote something down on a notepad, folded it carefully and pushed it over the desk towards me. 'Grande Havre Holdings. Registered as a company here on Guernsey. If you go through the right channels, you should be able to find out more details – who the directors are, and so on. You can do that yourself,' he added, before I asked him to do anything else.

He showed me the door.

'Well, it's been interesting talking to you,' he said sarcastically. 'Not very rewarding financially, but we all have crosses to bear.'

'I promise you ten per cent of everything I get,' I said.

'I'd rather have bugger all,' he said unexpectedly.

But then he wasn't listening to me, he was looking past me at someone who was getting out of the lift. Just before Guilbert pushed me out of sight, I saw who it was. Twenty years younger than Richard Guilbert, and wearing a suit which must have cost the best part of a thousand pounds. Septimus Martel Junior, the senior partner's son, fresh from public school, still wet from the shell. He walked silkily across the landing and through a mahogany door; he was built for the catwalk.

'He's going to have your job in a couple of years' time,' I said when the door had closed.

'The bastard,' Richard Guilbert said evenly. He showed me towards the fire exit and the stairs.

'Don't you want to be seen with me?'

'I have a reputation to keep up,' he said.

Once outside, I opened the piece of paper he'd given me. The name written on it, in his spidery writing, was Carl Martin, the barman I'd hit on Saturday night.

13

Information as well as money runs the film industry and there are agencies that deal in nothing else. These are detective agencies in all but name, but instead of the gumshoe and the .45, they use the computer and the fax machine. If you're looking for a cameraman or a script writer, for someone you've liked the look of in a blue video, or for a man with one eye, or for a woman with three nipples, they'll find them; if you want to know the financial status of a producer who wants to back you, or the real names in the exposé of Hollywood life that's on the best-seller list, or the sexual habits of a movie critic who's being hard on you, they'll find them. They'll find anyone.

My credit with the film business was all but used up, but I had one good contact left. Links, based in England in Wardour Street. The English end of it was run by a friend of mine, an American called Nathan Bernstein. Nathe knew more about Julie Garland and the divine Marlene than anyone alive, and researching them for the Friends of Dorothy had given him the skills to set himself up as the co-founder of Links.

I telephoned them, and after the usual problem of not having a credit card I could quote so they could oil the wheels of their machine, I got through to Nathe and told him I wanted a trace on Baxter.

'As far as I know he's never had anything to do

with the film industry,' I said.

'That won't matter,' Nathe said. 'If his head has ever shown above the parapet, old sport, we'll nail him. Just tell me everything you know. And how's the wife?'

Awkward bastard; he'd always told me not to marry Evelyn, but his interest in women was strictly seasonal so I hadn't taken a lot of notice at the time: Nathe once told me he had heterosexual impulses only in the spring.

I told him about the *Venus* and about the Hoummet, about Baxter's drinking habits, his appearance, his relationship with Evelyn, even his boast of how he'd bought the helicopter. Then I asked him about Jerry Rossetti. Rossetti had been in England until that weekend, but had disappeared into New Guinea to research a film; Nathe doubted I'd be able to get hold of him for at least a fortnight.

We'd drifted away from the subject and were chewing over old times when I had what in the end turned out to be the brightest idea I had all that week. I asked for a trace on Guilbert.

I went to the Freemason's Arms that night for a few drinks. A Channel Island Nosebleed, Special Brew and tomato juice, food and drink in one. Mixed together they make an opaque pinkish cocktail. I drank several, leaning on the bar, staring at the blue and orange shadows on the TV screen, thinking about Evelyn, and Baxter, and Richard Guilbert, and about the way they all combined to make a knot which seemed to have trapped me somewhere in the middle of it. Guilbert might have been right about

my drink-induced paranoia, but I didn't feel threatened, I didn't feel as if they were after me. I could
see why Baxter wanted me for the job at the
Hoummet: I was cheap and I could keep my mouth
shut, and he wouldn't have many sleepless nights if
something happened to me.

It was harder to decide why Evelyn wanted me.
But perhaps she wanted me back. Whatever Jenny
Mahy thought.

I finished my drink, went back to where the
Traveller was parked and drove up to Anton's,
parked next to some of the smart cars belonging to
the regular clientele and went into the reception
area. I stood, magnificent, I thought, in my shorts
and boots, with the fisherman's waterproof I wore
when it was raining, as it was then. I stood there
dripping on the old gold carpet before moving
towards the bar. People moved away.

'Don't worry about me,' I said. 'I'm not eating.'

The broken window was boarded up to the ceiling
and you couldn't see the sea, or the lights of the
harbour or the town. There weren't many custom-
ers. I could see Milliner and his wife sitting by the
window at the table I usually occupied. He was a
small man with short, greyish-reddish hair and half-
moon rimless glasses. He turned to stare at me,
outraged, a glass of wine frozen on its way to his lips.
And I noticed that, of all people, Richard Guilbert
was sitting at the table with him, head and shoulders
taller, and looking embarrassed by the whole thing.
Carl Martin looked at me as if I were dripping blood
rather than rain.

Milliner's presence there irritated me. Was it last
year, or the year before, he'd tried to get me to tidy

up the scrapyard, or if not, to keep the gates closed so the tourists couldn't see the mess? I smiled at him across the room; I couldn't help it, and I couldn't help the kind of smile it was, the kind that comes out just before I start swinging.

There was a barmaid there I'd never seen before. She came towards me with a welcoming smile.

'I'll have a double dark rum,' I said. 'Give Carl there a drink and have one yourself.' I threw a tenner on the bar. 'Where's the manager?'

'I'm here,' a frosty voice said behind me. I turned. Anton had got there fast. 'What exactly are you doing here, Mr Breaker?' he asked.

'I've come to ask you a question,' I said. The double rum was there on the bar and I took a small mouthful, rolled it round my teeth, swallowed it and breathed fumes all over him. 'I want you to tell me, have you ever seen those characters who attacked me before?'

'They were throwing rather a lot of money around earlier in the evening, but I'd never seen them before that,' he said. Anton had plump hands, plump cheeks, sad eyes. His English was better than mine: he'd learned it in Vienna.

'My wife ever been here before Saturday night?'

'Not as far as I know.'

'Who called the police, Anton?'

'I did,' he said. Then he hesitated and said, 'At least I was going to. They arrived before I could reach the telephone. Now, I want you to leave.'

'I'm sorry about the other night, it won't happen again,' I said.

'Of course it won't happen again. You won't be coming here again. I've barred you, Mr Breaker.

Your custom is unwelcome.'

'Anton, I've been coming here for years, without causing any trouble.'

'Alas, no longer,' he said with a courteous gesture. 'Will you please pick up your money and leave.'

Milliner had risen to his feet and he came bustling over towards me. I suppose he was sixty years of age, and seemed half my height, coming up the steps from the restaurant area towards me. He had to get involved.

'You shouldn't even be here, Breaker,' he said. 'You should be in prison where you belong.'

There wasn't a spoken answer I could give to that. I turned away from him towards the bar. 'Carl, I need to speak to you too.'

'Any time, Sam,' he said. 'But not now. Come round to the garage. Now isn't really the time,' he added with a weak smile that showed the star tattooed on his flabby lower lip. He gestured apologetically at Milliner. He looked sick.

'Mr Breaker,' Anton said warningly behind me.

But I'd had enough of being pushed around. 'Here,' I said to Carl, 'buy Anton a drink, and buy Mr Milliner here two drinks. He's not himself tonight, must be having his period.'

'I don't want a drink, Mr Breaker, I want you to leave,' Anton said. He took the ten-pound note from the bar and tucked it into the pocket of my shirt. 'Thank you for your custom in the past, I appreciate it, and I'm sorry that our professional relationship must end. But, sadly, so it must be.'

'Anton,' I said, trying to keep my temper, trying to be as reasonable as I could, 'what happened here on Saturday wasn't my fault, I haven't been tried yet. I'm not guilty. Was barring me really your idea?'

'No, it was mine,' Milliner said. His voice grated on my nerves.

'What's it got to do with you?'

'I have a financial interest in this business, as it happens,' he said, 'and on my instructions you are to be turned away, and in due course you are to be prosecuted so the cost of repairing the restaurant can be reclaimed.'

'It wasn't my fault,' I said, but it still didn't sound convincing. In spite of what I'd told myself about good behaviour and controlling my temper, I felt myself turning nasty. But I didn't want to hit anybody, I didn't want to start a fight. I took the ten-pound note out of my pocket. 'Take the money, Anton. I'll pay for my own drinks.'

He inclined his head.

'I'm sorry, Mr Breaker, I really am, but I have a business to protect. You're a nice man, but you shouldn't drink. I have to bar you.'

'If you don't leave now, I'll call the police,' Milliner said, forcing himself between us. 'And you know what that will mean.'

'I know what that'll mean, you prick,' I said. My voice had risen so everyone in the restaurant could hear me, and I hadn't meant to start shouting. I recognised some of them. They looked amused; I was on show again. I screwed up the note and threw it on to the bar, but it was a ridiculous thing to do, and I regretted it. 'I'm sorry,' I said. 'I'm not trying to cause trouble, I'm just trying to put my point of view.' But that didn't help, so I said, 'There's plenty more where that came from, Anton. I came round to buy you a drink to make up for what happened.'

'It'll take more than a drink to do that,' Milliner said, and laid his hands on me. A mistake, that. I grabbed him by one of his shoulder pads and pushed him away. I think he fell down the steps into the restaurant area somewhere out of my line of vision. 'You'll regret barring me, Anton.'

'That's all right, Mr Breaker, I'll fight that battle when I come to it,' Anton said, and began to usher me towards the door. Even Carl came out from behind the door to help him. I let them. Milliner was being helped up by the woman he was with. He shouted something after me.

The Traveller started first time, but I was in a hurry, and I was angry, and as I swerved out through the car park, I caught the front of a car parked there. A red Mercedes convertible. I stopped to look at the damage. The offside sidelight was smashed in. Sidelights are hard to replace on those SLEs. You have to take the bumpers off even to replace the bulbs. I got back in the Traveller and went jolting out of the car park, past the crowd spilling out of the entrance. I don't know what they thought they were going to do – lynch me, perhaps. Milliner was in the lead. He waved his glasses at me – he must have broken them – shouted and stepped in front of the car. Just for a moment I was tempted . . . But I've never killed anyone, I've just wanted to every now and again. I swerved past him and drove out into the road.

14

Next day, the Brew and I made the long haul out to the Hummet in the *Lady Day*, stripped away the shuttering and did some finishing off. Then I went to help the Brew with the engine because the injectors were playing up.

The *Venus* turned up not long afterwards, and this time Evelyn brought the inflatable with the outboard motor into the bay, and took the Brew out to the *Venus*. He brought her into the mouth of the bay and alongside the *Lady Day*. We made them fast, side by side. Then we went ashore to look at the cement. Baxter tiptoed over the rocks in gold-laced white kid shoes, then paced around the pier area looking grumpily satisfied. I explained about the donkey engine and the way I was hoping to turn the wreck, and then we climbed up to the top of the rock above the bay to look down into the water at the inverted hull. Fifty years in the water had furred its outline.

Evelyn had prepared a picnic and laid it out on the springy grass above the raised beach. We drank champagne and white wine and ate sandwiches: smoked trout and cream cheese, smoked ham, tuna and onion, prawn. There were seagulls' eggs, and more caviar. I picked over the food with oil-stained hands.

The Brew hardly ate anything. He sat there glaring at the sea, dreaming of hamburgers and chips.

Then he went off to tinker with the engine on the *Lady Day*. More his style. Mine too, I was thinking, listening to Baxter talk.

He showed me his latest toy, an over-and-under shotgun he kept shut away in a locker on the flying bridge. He started tossing empty bottles into the bay and blasting them. Then he threw a couple in the air and shot at those. Broken glass sprayed the bay. He let me play with it. It had automatic fire capability; it was the kind of gun the South African police use to keep their citizens in order.

'You load it with heavy shot and you could cut a man in half,' Baxter said proudly.

'You've got heavy shot, I suppose?'

'You've got to be careful these days. I've got a lot to protect.'

'Too much gun,' I said, but he didn't take any notice of my tone of voice. He raised the gun to his shoulder and took a shot at a seagull, missed, and fired again. A bloody bundle of feathers flopped into the bay.

'Gulls are only bloody flying rats,' Baxter said, as if he needed to answer something I'd said.

'Put the gun away, George,' Evelyn said. He looked offended.

'You do it,' he said.

She got up, took the gun from him, broke it open, and walked away down the sloping beach towards the gangplank and the boats with the gun hanging over her arm. I watched her. She was wearing a white bikini that made her honey-gold skin glow. My wife. Baxter's girl. I'd lived with her for years and I understood her less now than I had then.

Baxter began to drink. He talked and I pretended

to listen. A few minutes later I heard raised voices suddenly coming from down in the bay. I got up and looked down, and caught a glimpse of Evelyn in the cockpit of the *Venus*. The voices died away just as suddenly. I sat down again; I wanted an excuse to get away from Baxter. This didn't seem to be it.

He said, 'I've done some checking up on you. Your track record's been pretty bad over the years. I hope nothing's going to go wrong this time.'

I didn't rise to that, so he said, 'You haven't been talking to anyone about what we're doing, have you?'

'Everyone who reads a newspaper knows I'm working for you, but I haven't said a word to anyone about what I'm really doing. My business is my business. Your business is your business. It isn't anyone else's business. And you're paying me to keep my mouth shut. So I do.'

He liked this rubbish. He stopped scowling and grinned at me. I reached for the bottle of Spring-bank, which was jammed upright against a lump of granite in which the mica was glittering like dia-mond dust, and I poured myself another tumbler-ful. The sea air and the smell of the whisky combined.

'Do you know what I'm looking for, here on the Hoummet?' he asked. 'Are you telling me you haven't thought about it?'

'Of course I've thought about it. I didn't think it was my business to ask.'

But my silence tormented him; he wanted me to question him, he badly wanted to tell me.

I said, 'You'll tell me when you're ready. That's your way. You're the boss.'

'Okay, I'll tell you,' he said. 'I'm looking for early retirement.'

I drank some more of the malt, lay back and squinted up into the sky. Seagulls flickered past my eyes. When I looked back at him, he was still staring at me, his eyes glinting.

He said it again. The words meant nothing to me. He might have been speaking Esperanto.

'Early retirement?' I said. 'You're too old. You already missed it.'

This lessened the smirk, but not much; secrecy gave him power. I wanted to change the expression on his face, by telling him what I thought of him, or by throwing his bloody whisky in his face. Or throwing him in the sea. But I didn't. I just sat up and tried to look like a good employee. Servile to the last. I needed the money.

'I'll tell you more about it when it suits me,' he said. He was working himself back into a good humour again. 'You'll find out, all in good time.'

He'd said that to me before. I stretched, looking towards the boats. 'Thanks for the lunch, Mr Baxter. We've finished here. We'll be leaving soon, as soon as the Brew's checked over the engine.'

That didn't stop him. 'If this goes right, you'll be able to afford a new engine.' He grinned, felt his groin through his thin grey trousers. He shook himself and stood up and came over to me, lay down on the rocks closer to me. 'I suppose you think you're pretty tough, don't you? With your stunting and he-man stuff.'

'It's not a question of toughness, it's a question of timing,' I said, an answer I'd given hundreds of times

126

before. I wondered how much he drank. His eyes were red-veined, his face pasty under the tan. Something was smouldering inside him.

His voice dropped. 'That wife of yours is something in bed, you know.' His voice dropped even further. I could hardly hear him. He bent close and I could feel his hot breath on my cheek. 'I used to have a scene going with another girl besides Evie. I told you about her, her name was Fiona, Lady Fiona Maugham. She worked for me, used to live on the boat in Monte Carlo. I'll tell you what she was, she was an upper-class whore. Nicely spoken, but she sold herself. When Evie arrived from Guernsey, I met her in a bar and got her to come to the boat. I think Evie was jealous of her. You know what women are like.'

I did – at least I had an idea; I didn't say anything.

'I thought Fiona knew all there was to know, but she couldn't keep up with Evie. Evie's like an animal in bed, a fucking animal. You picked a good one there, Breaker, and you're a bloody fool for getting rid of her.'

'But she got rid of me,' I said innocently.

He grinned; he wanted everything about him to tell me that the same thing wouldn't happen to him.

He grabbed my elbow, pulled my ear almost into his mouth, and spoke with sudden, throaty excitement. 'I had 'em both one night. Had a few drinks, a few pills, a bit of speed, a bit of this and that. I was in bed with Fiona when Evie came back to the boat. She came into the cabin, saw us, she walked out with a face like thunder, and I thought that was it. But five minutes later she came back. She'd taken her clothes off and had picked up a couple of vibrators from somewhere. I can see her standing in the doorway as clear as I can see you now, nude as a fucking pin. I'd been at it half the night, but the moment I saw her, looking at the tits on her, I got a bone-on a dog could've chewed. She just walked over and climbed into bed with us. After that, we went through the card.'

'Amazing,' I said. Sexual jealousy has never been a problem of mine, but I didn't want to tell him that; he wanted to kick me while I was down. I let him.

'They both played along. It was like the Cup Final. Fiona, the deb, the whore from Cheltenham Ladies' College; Evelyn, from the other side of the tracks. "Laura Grady and the Colonel's lady are sisters under the skin," ' he quoted ponderously. 'Know what I mean?'

'I know what you mean.'

'Ever been sucked by two women at the same time?' he leered.

'I've had a bit of trouble with three once or twice.'

'Good joke!' he said, and laughed. He slapped his thigh, rocked backwards and forwards, his face twisted with laughter. 'They were good days, bloody good days. And I was hoping they'd go on and on. What a crew that was! But a week later, Fiona went down with food poisoning, and nearly fucking died. Silly cow, must have been something she ate. Always messing around with oysters. I sent her flowers.' He looked reminiscent, even nostalgic for a while, then drained his whisky glass, poured another from the bottle of Springbank. 'That wife of yours will do anything – anything – if I ask her to. I've reached the stage I think up things for her to do to see if she'll do them. Haven't found anything yet she wouldn't do.' He turned to look intently at me, even gripped hold of my arm. 'Was she the same with you?'

'No,' I said. He looked relieved, then complacent.

'I didn't think so. I didn't think she'd go all the way for anyone but me. I used to come all over her food. She'd eat it.'

I stood up, stretched my limbs.

'Where are you going?' he asked suspiciously.

'I'm going for a swim.'

'Oh. You want the exercise? Want to burn off some of the alcohol?'

'No, I want to get clean,' I said, showing him the oil on my hands.

We left Baxter and Evelyn on the *Venus* at the Hoummet. It was a long haul back to Guernsey, and afternoon was already turning into evening as we set off.

Soon after the Hoummet slipped out of sight, I heard the Brew call to me. I went forward to join him in the wheelhouse. He'd broken his own rule; he was drinking, a bottle open on the ledge by his elbow. His black hair flopped over his eyes. He scowled at the sea.

'What's the matter with you?' I asked him. 'You know you don't go in for this kind of thing. You're the skipper, Brew. You're in charge of the god-damned boat. Keep off the drink.' It was red-eye – Bucktrout's blended Scotch. I took it from him, screwed the top on.

'I was just thinking about that man who was killed at the fireworks,' he said. 'Old Len. I just can't stop thinking about him.'

'You're giving yourself a bad time for nothing. It wasn't your fault.'

'That's easy for you to say. You weren't there.'

'There was nothing you could have done. Stop thinking about it. Put it out of your mind.'

'I can't – I can't get away from it,' he said. 'It wasn't my fault, you know. What I can't work out is how it happened.'

'They'll find out at the inquiry,' I said.

'Somebody must have done it on purpose.'

'You're off your head,' I said.

'I was talking to your wife about it.'

'Why her?'

'It was after she came down here and accused me of listening to her talking on the R/T. Me!' He took the cigarette out of his mouth. 'When you were with Baxter on the island. I was looking at the engine on the *Lady Day*, then I went over to the *Venus* to get a light. I lit my fag in the cockpit, eh?, while she was up on the bridge using the two-way radio. Next thing I know, she jumped down into the cockpit, looking as if she'd seen a ghost, eh? I said sorry for scaring her, of course. But she swore at me. You expect me to have heard her, me being below deck?' the Brew said. He touched the side of his head, near his deaf ear.

'What was she saying?'

'I couldn't hear a bloody word, could I?' he said. He was acutely, aggressively sensitive about his deafness. 'Bloody women, eh? They cause all the trouble. But I did say to her I knew Len's death wasn't my fault. And if it wasn't my fault, it had to be someone else's. And I couldn't see how it happened by accident.'

'So who did it, Brew?' I said, to keep him talking more than anything.

'I told her who was there – she asked me. Fuck!' he said suddenly. Another boat was cutting across our bows.

'Fucking waste of time, this is,' he said. 'There's more to it than what they're saying. There's something else going on, isn't there?'

'I don't know, I really don't know. I've been trying to tease it out of Baxter the last couple of days.' I took the bottle with me when I left the wheelhouse. He'd had enough.

The western sky turned orange under a layer of petrol blue and then slowly went dark. Then the only light left was in the sea, in the phosphorescent trail we were leaving astern, on the horizon, and in the riding-lights of the boat.

The *Lady Day* reached St Sampson's Harbour around midnight; we came in past the light at the end of the pier and crept under the lights by the cranes, which turned off almost the moment we'd docked.

When the engine stopped and there was the sudden silence on board that is always quieter than anything, I heard the Brew coughing, then spitting over the side. He came towards me in the darkness, stocky and pugnacious. I could smell the drink on his breath, his sweat as he came close.

'You and I have been mates for two years, eh? Don't let this woman break it up.'

I made a joke of it. 'She is my wife, Brew.'

His face was pale in the darkness. 'Something's on your mind, eh?'

I said almost the first thing that came into my

head. 'I'll tell you this, Brew, I think she's in trouble. Baxter turns my stomach. I think she's trying to get away from him. That's the sub-plot. I might help her after I've turned his wreck over for him.' And then I said – or mumbled, because he could hardly have heard me, 'There's something about that wreck that bothers me. It oughtn't to. But I don't have the nerve I used to have.'

His hand closed over my arm. 'None of us have,' he grunted in the darkness. 'I thought you said it wasn't nerve anyway, it was planning. And you can plan, eh? Just don't do it for the money, that's all. We can do without the fucking money.'

I didn't answer that; but I was grateful for it.

'Do you want a lift home?' I asked.

'I'll take a taxi.'

'I'll drive you,' I said.

The Brew didn't own a car. He sat alongside me while the Traveller grumbled and whined through the dark streets. After a while he lit a cigarette, and the conversation I'd been trying to make died. I drove the Brew home to his place not far from the Esplanade on the way to St Peter Port.

When we got to his house, he invited me in for a drink. I went into the living-room. There were toys on the floor, a fireguard in front of an unlit fire. One of his sisters cleared a space on the table among the plates encrusted with baked beans and bacon rind. She was the mother of one of the children living there. I guessed she was about sixteen, perhaps seventeen. We exchanged a little conversation, but not much. I didn't like being too close to her; the Brew had been working in the sun all day and even he smelt better than she did.

There were thirteen other people living in that house, including the boyfriends of several sisters. The Brew supported all of them – worked for them, cleaned up after them, did what he could for them. There was never enough money and there was never enough time. The Brew's father and all the other fathers had gone years ago, and when his mother died and left him with the job of running the family she doomed him to staying with them for the rest of his life. I thought it was time he left them to sort themselves out. I'd often said so, and I said so again. But he was held to them by responsibility, and probably by guilt. Like a lot of families.

'They wouldn't know what to do without me, eh?' he said, as he always did. He sat there with the beer glass in his hand, bright-eyed and smiling at me, the way he usually did when we weren't at sea.

I had a beer with him, and then made my excuses and left. He might have wanted me to stay. He was going to relax, he said. I'd spent a couple of nights relaxing with the Brew. He'd have a crate of the local Pony beer and a stack of pornographic videos. I liked him, but not that much.

15

Jenny Mahy and I met for lunch at La Collinette Hotel. I ordered plaice and chips, she ordered turbot and salads. I paid.

The glove compartment of my car was full of the material about Baxter and Guilbert which Nathe Bernstein had faxed to a local chandler's on my behalf and which I'd picked up that morning; Nathe had waived the fee – I still had a few favours owing to me in the film business. It made interesting reading. After we'd eaten, I told Jenny some of it.

'Baxter doesn't have anything like the money he claims to have, and that boat of his, the *Venus*, is hired, just as he hired the *Lady Day*. His property company went bust last year. He can't sell the houses he owns in England because the property market has fallen apart. Evelyn isn't having an affair with Baxter because he's rich. I've got two hundred quid in a rucksack, and that's more than he's got. What he's got are big, big debts. So banks lend him more money. Until they call the debts in, he can keep on spending it.'

'She doesn't know,' Jenny said. 'Or she wouldn't still be around.' She lit one of her mentholated cigarettes. 'What's he paying you to do on the Hoummet?'

'We've been tidying the place up, that's all. Construction work. We're building a pier to make landing easier.'

'And he's paying you for that?'

'He's paying me for that.'

'Just that?'

'Just that.'

She didn't believe me.

I pushed my refolded napkin around on the table-cloth for a moment, smelling the flowers and the sharp, cool smell of the menthol.

'Do you know anything about Richard Guilbert?'

'Hardly anything. He's not a Guernseyman; he lived abroad for most of his life.'

'In France,' I said.

'Yes. His mother was French.'

'What's your sister Lizzie doing at the moment?'

'You know that very well, I told you the other day. She's been working for Henry Milliner for two years. Over two years. I know that because he prides himself on his sense of humour. She joined on April Fool's Day, 1991. And he hired the Jersey Amateur Dramatic Society to come over and pretend they were bailiffs closing the firm down, on her first day. It was very convincing, Lizzie said. Guernsey's answer to Jeremy Beadle.'

'Milliner keeps getting under my feet. What's he up to at the moment?'

'He's chairing the Land Use Committee this year. Lizzie is his secretary.' She hesitated, then looked at the watch pinned to her breast. 'I'm off duty this afternoon. I'd like a brandy with my coffee.'

She'd just made up her mind to tell me something she shouldn't.

When I came back from the bar, and she'd sunk half

the double brandy I'd bought her, she told me what it was.

'Milliner's in trouble. His business is on the rocks, and on top of that he's having an affair. I don't know who with. But Lizzie says she walked in on an argument between him and his wife. She couldn't help overhearing what they were saying. Mrs Milliner was very angry with him. Lizzie thinks the marriage is going to break up. And Mrs Milliner is going to leave the Island. She's booked a flight to Spain. Lizzie says he told her he wasn't going to give her any money to go away with, even ordered Lizzie not to endorse any money from his accounts, but Mrs Milliner is going to go anyway. There weren't any April Fool jokes this year.'

I remembered seeing Mrs Milliner at Anton's the last two times I'd been there. If she'd looked distressed the first time, I'd assumed it was because of the accident at the firework display.

'Milliner has business problems? I thought he was loaded.'

'He has a big house and a yacht, but he has four sons at private school too, and they're probably costing him thirty or forty thousand a year. He owed a lot of money in legal fees because of some deal he was involved in, but he's found some way of paying that off privately. But Lizzie says he hasn't paid last term's school fees. Why are you so interested?'

'I told you, he keeps getting under my feet. And people with problems, especially with financial problems, are likely to commit crimes.'

'Not Milliner. What does he want to commit a crime for?'

'What kind of car does he drive?'

'A gold Rolls-Royce. You must have seen it around the Island. A ghastly thing.'

'He doesn't own a red Mercedes sports car?'

'He used to. He gave Lizzie a drive in it once. I don't know if he still does. I know he put it up for sale some time ago. Why?'

'I'm trying to find a frame to fit Evelyn into,' I said. I'd stolen a spare place setting and was pushing the napkin, the knives, forks and spoons into various shapes. Looking down at the table, I saw that I'd made a box shape into which I'd put my hand, walled in.

'Carl Martin made me an offer on my scrapyard,' I said. 'But in the letter he sent, he used the name Harkin. As far as I know, Harkin doesn't exist.'

'Who told you he'd made the offer? Did he?'

I looked up at her. She'd pursed her lips tightly. She was giving me that look I seem to attract from some women – affectionate, and not critical exactly, but not exactly approving either. I said, 'Carl joined in the fight at Anton's the other night. The way he did it, jumping on me from behind, I don't think he was trying to keep the peace, I think he wanted an excuse to beat the shit out of me. I don't know why. Do you?' She shook her head, so I said, 'I know he owns a garage out at Grande Havre, and that he and his brother used to have a scrap-metal business there. He sold up last year. I wonder if he blames me.'

'I don't see why he should. Your business is no bloody good anyway. Everyone knows it doesn't make any money.'

'My father bought the scrapyard from his father a generation ago. Carl probably thinks it's still his.'

'Not if it was legally sold. He's not a barbarian.'

'He's a Guernseyman and I'm an outsider. Before the fight on Saturday, Carl was talking to me about newcomers coming in and spoiling the Island. In his thinking, I'm one of them. Certainly my father was. My father was the kind of businessman who'd have been a full-time crook if he'd had the luck and the nerve. God knows what he did to Carl's father. There may still be scores to be settled.'

'The last thing Carl would do is want to take over your scrapyard,' Jenny said decisively. She drank some coffee, then some brandy, and puffed at her cigarette. 'He hates the business. The best thing he ever did was sell up. You're out of date, Sam. Didn't you know his brother was killed last year when a car they were cutting up fell on him?'

'No, I didn't know,' I said.

'There's no reason why you should, I suppose,' she said. 'But now I've told you, remember it. Carl doesn't want anything to do with scrapyards.'

'Then why did he make the offer?'

'How do you know he did?'

'Because the lawyer who defended me last Monday told me he made it.'

'Are you sure he wasn't lying? You know what lawyers are like. They don't always tell you whose interest they're representing.'

There wasn't an answer to that, so I didn't attempt one. 'All right, tell me what Milliner is up to. Lizzie ought to know, oughtn't she? If Milliner is up to something?'

'What could he possibly be up to?'

'All kinds of things. If he sits on as many boards as he does, and on the boards of charities, and on the

Land Use Committee, which, as we all know,' I said sarcastically, 'is incorruptible . . .'

I was beginning to annoy her. 'You're an outsider, Sam, you don't know how things are done. You lived here when you were a teenager, but you've been abroad for too long. You've forgotten what things are like. There's less dishonesty in the domestic affairs of this Island than there is in any average local council on the Mainland. Ray used to say he was the only home-grown investigative reporter in the Channel Islands, and he spent twenty years trying to find something on Milliner and the Land Use Committee. He never did. None of us likes Milliner, but he's honest.' She stared at me. 'I know what Ray would say to you, Sam, I can hear him saying it. Don't you realise that what controls human behaviour is character?'

'Character is formed by circumstances, not just by genetics. Circumstances control people.'

'Milliner may be a shit, but he's never done anything dishonest in his life, never. If you're looking for a criminal, look for someone who's already committed a crime. If you're looking for a traitor, look for someone who's already betrayed you.'

I lifted my hand from the table-top, flexed it. It felt as if someone I didn't know and couldn't see had touched it intimately. And sitting there staring at the tablecloth with my head bent had started a twinge in my neck.

Stubbornly, I said, 'How would Lizzie feel about letting me know what the Land Use Committee is up to at the moment?'

'She wouldn't dream of it. Anyway, although she's Milliner's secretary, she doesn't usually work for the

Land Use Committee. I told you, he does the work himself. He takes it home with him.'

I tried again. 'Look, Jenny, what I'm asking for isn't *sub judice* or anything, it's not top secret, it probably isn't even confidential. I just need to know if any form of planning permission has been granted in the area of the South Side of St Sampson's, where my scrapyard is. And who's involved. It must be possible to find out something about it, somehow.'

'Of course it's confidential. Lizzie wouldn't dream of it. And I wouldn't dream of asking her.'

'I need to know.'

'I couldn't possibly ask Lizzie to do any such thing,' she said, and tried to look cross with me.

She'd tell me.

On the way out to the car park, in the hotel lobby, she suddenly stopped and faced me. We stood toe to toe, Jenny looking up at me. 'Have you started up with Evelyn again?'

'No,' I said, surprised.

'One of Arthur's sisters told me Arthur was talking about the two of you taking Evelyn out to the Hoummet the other day. She was sunbathing. Without her clothes on.'

'So what?'

'She's after you.'

'Don't be damned silly,' I said. I was annoyed; it was ridiculous. 'Evelyn is a good swimmer, an athlete, she's unselfconscious about her body. Don't tell me there's something special about sunbathing in the nude. What do you want her to wear? A diving suit? Anyway, she's with Baxter. What does she want with me?'

'You can bet your life she's not showing off that perfect body of hers just so she can get her claws into Arthur Brouard,' Jenny said sarcastically. 'She's quite something according to Arthur – I heard he couldn't sleep last night. The perfect woman. I hear the scar doesn't show.'

'What scar?'

'You know what scar. Oh, forget it,' she said, and turned and walked away. I followed her. Instead of feeling curious, I felt angry. I was being manipulated, I felt. I thought she had her own reasons for trying to put me off Evelyn.

'What are you trying to tell me, Jenny?'

'Mr Poucher flies his wealthier clients over from London to his nursing home in St Peter's after he's operated on them. Nothing but the best for Evelyn. That was the last time I met her. She had what they used to call women's problems. But I've said too much already,' she said. 'I thought you knew about it.'

She walked quickly, and I didn't overtake her until she'd reached her car.

'What are you talking about?'

'She had a hysterectomy.'

A car went past, horn blowing. I heard a squeal of brakes. The sounds went away. A window closed.

'Why?'

'She'd had an abortion when she was a girl, she always had dysmenorrhoea, and she said she'd lost a child – she told me about it. Three years ago, the first job I had with Mr Poucher was nursing her. He's a good surgeon. You could hardly see a thing even then.' She stared at me. 'Sam, you're getting yourself into a lot of trouble.'

'What do you mean? With the police?'

'No, with her. You were married to her, so I suppose you think differently about her than I do. You're probably still very fond of her. Do you think you're still in love with her?'

'No. I don't.'

'Don't be. You got out when you had the chance, now stay out. Be careful.'

'What the hell has this got to do with you?'

We were suddenly irritable with each other, I didn't really know why. And I didn't know whether the drinking had begun to get on top of me or not, but I felt leaden, cold. I could have done with another long swim, or a long run in the sun – anything to tire me out, get rid of some of the poison building up in my muscles; I could feel it sapping the strength in my thighs and behind my knees. And there was a cold knot in the pit of my stomach that hadn't been there a few moments ago.

We didn't speak for a while. Then it was her turn to reach out and touch my hand.

'I'm sorry, it isn't my business.'

'There's a lot of bad luck around,' I said, for something to say.

'You're not superstitious, are you?'

'Not exactly. Suspicious, perhaps. Christ knows why Evelyn should be screwing a second-rater like Baxter.'

'It shouldn't worry you, Sam. If a man has enough money . . .' Jenny murmured.

'Is that all there is to it?'

'Of course,' she said, and was disturbed enough to hunt out and light the second of the cigarettes she allowed herself a day.

'You don't really mean it's just a question of money?' I said, with the disbelief of a man who had no money at all.

'Of course it is.'

'It may be true of Evelyn, it's not true of everyone.'

'It's true of Evelyn,' she said.

I kissed her gently on the cheeks, and she leaned against me for a fraction of a second. Not as long as I wanted, and she pulled away. She smiled at me.

'Look after the Brew, won't you?' she said. 'And you be careful. You'll end up killing yourself. And you know what happens to drinkers. If you don't kill yourself, somebody else will do it for you.'

She was damned nearly right.

16

A friend of mine used to say, if you feel rough, put on a suit. My version of this is, if things aren't going well, cook. So I made a good breakfast. I skinned some tomatoes and fried them while I beat some eggs with a spoonful of rice wine, then poured the eggs into the pan with some vegetable stock. Chinese eggs and tomatoes. I drank China White tea and mineral water. It made me feel better.

I was sitting looking at the remains in the deckhouse of the *Lady Day* when I heard someone jump down on to the deck from the harbourside. It was the Brew's sister. She looked no better than she had the last time I'd seen her. But there was a white tenseness in her face, a kind of anger, that was new.

'You've got to come at once,' she said.

'Why?'

'It's Arthur. He's had an accident.'

'Just when I need him,' I said. 'You know we've got a big job on, worth a lot of money.'

She looked at me strangely. 'He's in hospital,' she said. 'They think he's going to die.'

We drove to the Princess Elizabeth Hospital in an old Ford Capri which belonged to a red-headed shot-putter, Jim Brouard, another of the Brew's brothers, once winner of the Inter-Island Elvis Look-Alike Contest and now earning beer money as a part-time worker in the abattoir. The girl smoked incessantly. She'd brought her children with her, one a few months old, the other about two. I sat in the front seat with the window open and listened to a Roy Orbison tape. Painful, ludicrous music.

The Brew was in a ward in the intensive care unit, a tube up his nose, another in his arm, his muscular forearms passive on the sheet. Unconscious, and he looked like a boy. One side of his face was a slab of minced beefsteak and there were bandages around his skull. For some reason a television on the wall was tuned into a children's programme, the sound turned down. His hair had been cut off and the blue of the screen shone on his domed forehead, now gleaming with sweat. I felt his face. It was cold.

'What happened to him?' I said to the doctor who'd taken me to look at him, as if it were his fault.

'Someone found him this morning lying in a gutter.'

'In a gutter?'

'Behind the White Horse pub. We think he was hit by a car,' the doctor said. He drew the curtains around the bed and we went out into the corridor.

'What's wrong with him?'

'Fractured skull, mainly. He has other bruises, breakages, but that's the one to worry about,' the doctor said. 'In layman's terms, he has a big clot on the brain. We've operated.'

'When did it happen?'

'He was brought in about six o'clock this morning.'

'Why would he have been hit by a car?' I said.

'Probably didn't look where he was going.'

'He lives on the estate about half a mile away from there. What would he have been doing walking down to the Esplanade? Before six o'clock in the morning?'

'Might have been drinking.'

'Who found him?'

'The police. They probably saved his life. If they have saved his life. If the life they've saved is going to be worth saving.'

I stood there and looked out the window at the neutral landscape which hospitals like to surround their buildings with. Grass, and flowerbeds waiting for something to be planted in them. It can't happen, I thought, not to the Brew.

'Is he going to be all right?'

'He ought to be dead now,' the doctor said. 'You're a friend of his, are you? Not family?'

'A friend. He works for me.'

'I don't think his family are going to be a lot of use.'

'I don't think I am either.'

'We have to make a decision some time today,' the doctor said. 'Either we're going to fly him to hospital in Southampton, or we're going to decide he's too ill to move and we're going to fly a brain surgeon in from London. Frankly, things don't look too good.'

'What was he doing walking around at that time of the morning?' I said. 'Down there, with no one to see him? He knew the state of the tide meant we wouldn't be leaving early in the morning, so he probably had a few beers last night, probably didn't get to bed before about two or three.'

'There you are, then,' the doctor said. 'He had too much to drink. Went for a walk, got hit by a car.'

'What caused the fracture?'

'Fractures,' the doctor said. 'Lord knows. But the injuries are commensurate with, say, falling, being hit by a fast-moving vehicle, hitting the kerb. You should ask the man who found him.'

'Who was that?'

'Someone driving to work. And a policeman on patrol in the area. Sergeant Spooner.'

I didn't like Spooner, but I had to admit he was fair about what happened.

'I'm very, very sorry about it, very sorry indeed. I liked the Brew, he was all right,' he said. He was wearing his uniform and was sitting facing me in the interview room of the police station. We were drinking tea. Spooner was smoking a cigarette; I didn't know he smoked. His round red face shone as if he'd scrubbed it. He kept shaking his head. His fingers trembled as he held the cigarette, but then, I thought, he'd had a nasty shock.

'Poor blighter,' he said.

'He's not dead yet,' I said.

Spooner looked at me as if I'd said I believed in little green men.

'He's nearly dead. Probably better if he were. When I found him, he had a dent in his skull you could have fitted half a brick into.'

I didn't say anything. The tea tasted of disinfectant. The other flavours in my mouth were unpleasant. I could see a woman through the half-open door of the room scrubbing the floor, but with her arms thrust to the wrists in the bucket she was using she seemed to be in the grip of something torturing her. I got up and went to the door and closed it and came back and sat down.

148

'What were you doing there at that time of day?'

'Driving,' he said, surprised and resentful, as if I'd accused him of something.

I said, 'There's something wrong with this. I don't believe the Brew was wandering around at that time of the morning down there. Why would he be? He doesn't have a car, but if he was going to work, at the Fisherman's Cooperative or on the *Lady Day* at St Sampson's, he'd have arranged a lift with someone and they'd've come to his house. Or he'd have got his brother to drive him in that death trap of his.'

'Perhaps he was meeting someone on the Esplanade.'

'Why would he do that? Everyone knows where the Brew lives. Why meet him on the Esplanade when it's only half a mile up to his house?'

'Perhaps he didn't want anyone to know who he was meeting.'

'He's the most straightforward man I've ever met. Isn't there going to be an investigation?'

'I've made my report,' Spooner said. 'I've talked to my inspector about it. I'm doing my job to the best of my ability.' He spoke defensively. He tapped ash into the ashtray. His fingers were stained gold with nicotine: the Midas touch. Why hadn't I noticed he smoked before?

'Were there any skid-marks, or anything – any evidence of a hit-and-run accident?'

'Nothing,' Spooner said. 'He was just lying in the gutter. If I hadn't picked him up at the last minute, I'd have run over him myself. I still had to swerve, bounced off the wall. I've bent the front bumper of the police car,' he said, as if that was the worst thing of all. I sat and thought about it and looked at

Spooner's scrubbed red moon face and at the cigarette smoke curling up towards the ventilator. I
knew the accident had happened on a blind corner; I
could visualise it.

'You were the only one there, were you?' I asked.
He nodded. 'But I thought the pigs usually travelled
in pairs.'

'I was on my way up to the station to start work, as
a matter of fact, so I was on my own.'

'You were on your own when you came to Baxter's house the other day.'

'I often work on my own,' Spooner said. 'I saw
him at the last minute, swerved, mounted the pavement and hit the wall. I stopped the engine, got out.
Someone coming behind me nearly hit my car, and
stopped too. He was a dock worker, on his way to
the White Rock. He got out to help me. He knew
me, he knew the Brew – everyone does. It was half
light, difficult to see anything. But I could tell he was
badly hurt. So I didn't move him, I called the
ambulance.'

I drank some more of the vile tea. Someone was
clattering outside the door. Spooner looked at his
watch.

'I've got my daughter in the waiting-room,' he
said. 'She's on her way to hospital for more treatment.'

'Sorry to hear it,' I said automatically.

'Spina bifida,' he said. 'Spina bifida is a wicked
thing. The therapy goes on and on. A lot of the
money comes out of my own pocket. It doesn't seem
fair, somehow, does it? It doesn't seem just.'

I said, 'The Brew and I have been doing some
work for my wife, and for Baxter. The Brew said to

me the day before yesterday that he'd overheard something she'd said, and they'd had a row of some sort.'

'What am I supposed to make of that?' he asked.

I said, hearing how foolish it sounded as I spoke, 'Do you think it's possible she hit him? Or arranged for him to be hit?'

He even seemed to take it seriously for a moment, then shrugged. 'Why don't you ask her? Sounds unlikely to me. If she was going to do it, and she's not the sort of person you'd imagine waiting around to clobber someone with a brick, why do it there? Why not knock him on the head on the Hoummet and chuck him over the side there?'

It wasn't the answer I'd expected. I stared at him. He smiled back.

'Where was she at the time?' he asked. 'That's the thing you've got to consider. Has she got an alibi?'

'I don't know. I expect so. I haven't thought it through.'

'And anyway, wouldn't she ask you to clobber him if she wanted him clobbered? Judging by how well you were getting on together the other day, by the swimming-pool? All friends together?' He grinned even more broadly. 'You don't know much about human nature, do you, Breaker? And here's something to think about. Don't start using the law to get back at your wife after you failed to do it with your fists. I know a man clutching at straws when I see one.'

'Is that what I'm doing, clutching at straws?' I asked. 'That man who was killed at the firework display. Do you suppose someone related to him got back at the Brew for that?'

'Ah, it's a line we might be following. I don't want to talk about that at the moment,' Spooner said. He looked at his watch. 'I've got to go soon. Don't get muddled up with police work. Leave it to us.'

'The doctor said you probably saved his life,' I said. 'I have to thank you for that.'

He looked embarrassed. He puffed at his cigarette, inhaled, blew out the smoke, and stubbed it out in his saucer. I realised he was upset, judging by the flushed, anxious look on his face. I didn't think policemen could get upset, least of all policemen like Spooner.

'I'd have done the same for anybody,' he said, 'because that's my job. But the Brew's all right. Perhaps we ought to do something for his family. Without him, well . . .'

'They're a bunch of redundant fuckers, it's about time they did something for themselves.'

'Look who's talking,' Spooner said.

The look I gave him was less than friendly; I wanted to strangle the bastard.

'Hey, it's not my fault this happened,' Spooner said, as if I'd accused him of hitting the Brew. His red colour darkened. He stood up. 'I've got to go,' he said. 'I've got to get my daughter to the hospital. Then I've got a job to do. You can go off and do what you like, I suppose.'

What I did was, I went to the desk and asked to speak to Inspector De Jersey.

17

De Jersey was stretched out in his chair. His shoes, the same shoes he'd been wearing on Saturday night, poked round the corner of the desk. They'd been cleaned, but not as well as he'd have liked.

'Did you hear about the Brew?' I asked.

'Saw the report this morning,' he said. 'Poor bastard.'

De Jersey had once hired my boat for a weekend's fishing, and we'd got on all right then, drinking a couple of crates of beer in the deckhouse, while the Brew steered the boat. He was a neat man, small, efficient, glossy. And bright. A well-groomed weasel. I loomed over him.

'Sit down,' he said. I did. 'So you want an informal discussion. Nothing about your case, I hope. I want to keep away from that.'

'I'm worried,' I said.

'I'm not bloody surprised.'

'The case of assault that's being brought against me is a frame-up.'

'I wouldn't expect you to say anything else, Breaker. You two-faced slippery bastard.'

'You've got it the wrong way round. They're going to get me off.'

That made him sit up. 'Who is?'

'Evelyn's going to testify on my side. She's going to say she was provoked and I was protecting her. It's not my idea, it's hers. I went to see her the other day.'

'You shouldn't have done. You were told to keep away.'

'Did you know I'd been to see her?'

'For fuck's sake, I've got work to do. Is this going to take long?' he said. But he was sitting up listening to me.

'The men who assaulted me have left the Island.'

'Assaulted you? One of them was flown home in a plaster cast. Call that assault?'

'Do you know where they are, what happened to them?'

'I'm not discussing this with you, Breaker.' He took out his snuff box and went through the rigmarole of sniffing some of it up his nostrils and wiping his nose on a large brown silk handkerchief. 'For what it's worth, they gave false addresses. The one in the plaster cast insisted on being returned to the Mainland, but when we checked the address it was false. We're trying to get some reaction out of the British police, but it's not easy. Needles in a haystack. And I'll tell you something that pisses me off, one of the bastards had the nerve to tip me, forty quid in notes in an envelope. "Give it to the police fund, if you don't want it," he said. Cunt.'

'Doesn't that mean you'll have to dismiss the case?'

'No, we'll press the case. You wrecked the restaurant and smashed the barman, remember? And it's Spooner's case; I'm going to let him bring it.'

'Is Milliner leaning on Spooner to bring the case?'

De Jersey frowned. 'Why would he? I know he part-owns Anton's but it's got nothing to do with him. We make the decisions here, right here in this police station.'

'I'd never seen the men who assaulted me before, but when I went to see Evelyn on Monday she told me they knew me.'

He sniffed, wiped his nose. 'What's Richard Guilbert doing defending you? You can't afford him.'

'I'm not paying him, George Baxter is. Do you know anything about Baxter?'

'He's got too much money, but so have a lot of other wankers on this Island. As far as I know, he's not involved in anything he shouldn't be involved in. Why?'

'You know I'm working for him on the Hoummet,' I said. I told him about building the pier. 'But not just that. Baxter's actually employed me to help him dive on a wreck in the Hoummet bay. He must have some idea there's big money down there. The pier's twice the size it ought to be. That means it can double as a helicopter landing-pad so Baxter can get his toy helicopter in and out when he wants to, with whatever it is he imagines is down there, so he doesn't have to call in at customs in St Peter Port. Or anywhere else.'

'He's got a boat he could use. What does he need a helicopter for?'

'He doesn't own the boat, but he does own the helicopter – he told me he bought it for cash. He might intend to leave the boat behind, making a quick getaway. There must be something on the Hoummet he doesn't want to declare.'

'I've never heard anything so damned stupid. What could be that valuable on the Hoummet?' he said. He stood up, went and glared out of the window.

I said, 'There are two possibilities. One is that someone is out to skim Baxter. The other is that someone is out to skim me.'

'The third possibility, of course, is that no one is out to skim anybody,' De Jersey said. 'Why don't you pull out? If you think there's something wrong with what's going on, why don't you get in your boat and sail away somewhere? After the trial, of course.'

'I can look after myself. I'm going to help them find what they're looking for, and I'm going to take the money they're going to pay me. The Brew needs the money I'm going to earn. He needs all the help he can get.'

'He may be past help, from what I've heard.'

Which is what Spooner had said. I seemed to be the only one who thought the Brew might have a chance; or I was hoping he might.

'Did Spooner say anything to you about me?'

'No.'

'Nothing about my movements?'

'No.'

'You didn't know I'd been to see Evelyn?'

'Why should I?'

'He does his job, does he?'

'Spooner's all right.'

'No, he's not, he's an arsehole,' I said. 'And if he wasn't a copper who worked for you, you'd say the same thing. Do you think he's honest?'

'Of course he's honest,' De Jersey said. 'What kind of question's that?' He took some more snuff. 'What are you worried about? About your scrapyard? About your boat? They're not worth anything.

Smuggling? It's not worth going to all this trouble for.' He hummed gently to himself.

'There's going to be an inquiry into Len's death at the firework display, isn't there? Wouldn't it be funny if it turned out to have something to do with Baxter.'

'Nothing is that funny. I've seen Spooner's report. Just a lot of people milling around where they shouldn't have been. Arthur probably threw away a cigarette end or something.'

'That's not like him,' I said. 'Is it possible that Len has a family who've got even with the Brew by trying to kill him?'

'No, it's not possible. Len Le Page was a bum, a drunkard. He hadn't got any family. He'd only been out of the Castel for three days. No one cared. If you wanted to kill someone and not start a vendetta, he was perfect.'

'Does Spooner know that?'

'Policemen do operate with an element of autonomy,' De Jersey said. 'I wish you'd piss off. I've got work to do. You know drinking can make you imagine things. I suppose you've considered that. All that high living might have got to you, Breaker. All that California sun and Hollywood cunt. Can't have done you any good. All that snow and shit you must have stuffed up your nose.'

'I've had a lot more shit since I left California. Especially here.'

'Just as a matter of interest, have you got anything they want?' he asked mildly.

'I've got a fucked car, a pig of a boat, and a scrapyard which is worth about what a bank clerk earns in a year. Someone's just made me an offer on it, but it's not worth killing me for.'

'Killing you, who's talking about killing you?'

'No one, it's a figure of speech. I haven't got anything they want.'

'You just don't think you have. Look harder. You'll find you have.'

'Are you serious?' He shook his head in a way that might have meant anything. 'All right, if you mean it, why aren't you doing something about it?'

'Because I don't mean it, and I can't be bothered, and you're a waste of space. I'd watch my back if I were you, sunshine,' De Jersey said. He chuckled. The telephone rang. He jerked it off its stand, spoke briefly into it, covered the mouthpiece and said to me, 'You were lucky, you got Spooner on a good day. He's just forked out a couple of thousand for an all-singing, all-dancing electric wheelchair for that daughter of his. He's in a good mood. Otherwise, he'd have bitten your balls off.'

'Isn't there going to be an inquiry into what happened to the Brew?'

'We'll look into it. But don't worry, we're all on your side – me, Milliner, Spooner, all men of the utmost moral probity,' he said, as if it were a joke. 'I've been a Freemason for seventeen years and Milliner's a steward in my church. Even Guilbert, for all he's a smart lawyer these days, used to work with Spooner a few years ago, counselling people who couldn't afford to pay for a lawyer. He didn't have to do that, he did it out of the goodness of his heart.'

'If there was any dispute about Guilbert's right to live on the Island, if he was trying to earn the right to live here, it wouldn't have done him any harm,' I

said. 'You know something like that can sway the
authorities if there's any doubt about residency
qualifications.'

'You're a cynical bastard – no wonder people
don't like you. But it isn't you they're after,
Breaker. Grow up, for Christ's sake. I'll take a bet
now, it's Baxter's money they want, not you. And
the accident to poor old Arthur Brouard was an
accident, that's all.' He was about to speak into the
phone, then covered it again. 'Sod off, Breaker,' he
said cheerfully.

But I went to a phone. I had to. I telephoned
Baxter's house, and got Evelyn. I told her about the
Brew. She was just as shocked, just as sympathetic,
as I would have expected her to be; but she wasn't
over-concerned. Why should she be?

'They're saying he's going to die, but I think he'll
pull through.'

'Optimistic,' she said.

'How would you know? Have you seen him?'

'Don't get nasty, Sam.'

'It wasn't an accident,' I said.

'What, you mean he was run over? Deliber-
ately?'

'I think he was hit by someone. He had an
argument with you yesterday.'

A pause. 'Yes, you're right,' she said. 'I hired a
maniac from the Mainland to knock his brains out.
What the hell are you talking about?'

'Nothing.'

'Is this another of your jokes?'

'What was the argument about?'

'He made a pass at me, for Christ's sake. You

want to know what happened? He put his hands on me.'

I remembered the Brew hiding the binoculars. His embarrassment, his anger. Then I remembered his blue films, the pile of pornographic magazines he kept under his bed, and his awkwardness with women.

'I'm sorry,' I said. I felt baffled.

'You were accusing me of trying to kill him?'

'No,' I said. 'No.'

18

After leaving Town, I needed petrol, but I made a point of driving out to Martin's garage just off the triangle of grass before the sprawling bay of Grande Havre begins. As I drove in, the Traveller began to stutter. A red Mercedes sports car was parked on the forecourt. I got out of the Traveller and went to look at it, saw the broken sidelight on the far side of the car.

Carl Martin was inside the garage, an old asbestos-roofed building that should have been demolished years before. He came out and started to use the petrol pump. Then he came over to where I was standing by the Mercedes, walking heavily, a big, shambling man. He was wiping his hands with an oily rag, and I saw from the way his trousers were soaked as if he'd pissed himself that petrol must have overflowed as he was filling the Traveller.

I shook his hand. The bruise I'd put on his jaw was the same colour as the blue star tattooed on his lower lip. He looked pale and irritated – because of the petrol, I supposed. He must have wondered what I was doing there.

'You were lucky to catch me open. I usually close early on a Saturday.'

'When they built the Traveller, they didn't design it for modern pumps. You should have stood out of the way,' I said.

'Oh, that? It's only petrol, eh? You all right after

that fight the other night?'

'I'm all right. I've still got a bit of a headache.' I batted him gently on the chin. 'Sorry about the punch, Carl. You shouldn't have jumped on me.'

'Oh, that's all right, eh?' He moved his jaw from side to side with his fingers. 'You throw a good one, I'll give you that. I heard about the Brew. Bad news, that. Lovely bloke, eh?'

'It's tough. But he's tough too. If anyone is going to make it, he will.'

He looked into the distance over my head, towards the Vale Church. 'I heard he was dead. Isn't he dead?'

'He was still breathing when I saw him this morning.'

'Well, thank God for that. Next time you see him, tell him I'll buy him a drink when he's out. When.'

I wanted to change the mood; I didn't want to deal with Carl's pessimism about the Brew. I nodded at the Mercedes. 'Nice car.'

'Not bad. Fuel injection's buggered, though. It's the Island, eh? You drive an engine like that around all day never going faster than thirty-five miles an hour, you're bound to wreck them. So I just take 'em out and blast 'em around in first gear, clean everything out.' He sniggered. 'I have a good drive round myself, then charge the punters two hundred quid for the service.'

'Who owns the car?'

'I can't remember his name, off hand,' Carl said. 'Nobody I know.'

'You do a lot of repairs?'

'Not a lot. Why? Do you want that Traveller of yours welded back together?'

162

'Couldn't be done,' I said. He laughed dutifully. 'How's business?' I asked.

'What do you mean, business?'

I leaned my head towards the boarded-up gates of his scrapyard. 'That business.'

'Oh, we've closed that one up.'

'Someone made me an offer on my yard.'

'Take it, there's no fucking money in scrap over here.'

'Have you ever heard of a man called Harkin?'

'Is that what you wanted to ask me? Is that why you came up to Anton's to see me the other night?'

'I wanted to ask you if it was you who was trying to buy my scrapyard.'

His reaction surprised me, but perhaps it shouldn't have done. He coloured, slowly. The anger stained his cheeks, then his forehead. The tattoo on his lip slowly turned purple. His hands squeezed the cloth he was holding.

'What gave you that idea?' he asked in a low, angry voice.

'Just an idea,' I said.

'I'm finished with the scrap business,' he said. 'I don't want anything to do with it. You can keep your fucking scrapyard. Fuck you.'

He walked away.

I went into Town to collect supplies, food, beer, a big crowbar, and two oxygen cylinders I'd had refilled. I loaded them into the back of the Traveller and drove back up to the hospital. There was no improvement. The Brew lay alone in his ward. The exposed parts of his face had the cold sweat of defrosting meat. In the waiting-room I found several members of his family, male and female, the air thick with cigarette smoke, horse-racing blaring from the TV. They looked at me as if they blamed me for something, and laughter died when I came in. But Jim, the shot-putter who'd driven me to the hospital the day before, came outside to talk to me. We stood outside the main door in the sunshine while he rolled a cigarette.

'Some of the others are blaming you,' he said, as if proud of knowing something I didn't. 'Arthur used to be at home more before he started working for you.' He glared up at me, as if he'd been told to accuse me, even as if he had something to settle. But his shot-putting muscles had turned to fat several years before, his shape blurred by over-indulgence and idleness. I didn't feel afraid of him, and I don't suppose I looked it.

'That wouldn't have stopped him from being run over.'

'That phone call, five o'clock in the morning. I answered the phone. It was you, wasn't it?'

'Me?' I look surprised enough for him to keep going.

'At least, it sounded like you. Mind you, that time in the morning . . . I'd had a few beers the night before. Friday night. I picked up the phone, called him downstairs . . . He just asked for the Brew, the way you do.'

'When I'm talking to the family I ask for Arthur,' I said.

'Well, it sounded like you.'

I told him about my conversation with De Jersey, even about what Evelyn had said to me about the Brew touching her.

164

'Dirty cow, he said she wandered around without her clothes on,' he muttered, but grinned knowingly.

'That is my wife you're talking about,' I said, and he looked up at me with sudden fear, as if afraid that Anton's might repeat itself all over again, with me deciding to defend her honour with my fists. 'Do you think Arthur might have been tempted to touch her?'

'It wouldn't surprise me, the way he talked about her. But she didn't run him over, did she?'

'No. Why would she? Sergeant Spooner is working on the theory that the man killed at the firework display might have had friends or family, that it was revenge of some sort.'

'If I ever get hold of them . . .' he said.

'It could just have been a hit-and-run.' I was thinking aloud, not getting anywhere.

'We'll find out who did it,' he said threateningly. But his tone changed as I began to move away. 'Here, you haven't got an advance on Arthur's wages, have you? We're all a bit short at the moment.'

I paid the Brew peanuts, unless we caught a lot of fish or hired out the boat, when I split the profits with him. Usually, there were no wages because I couldn't afford them, and Jim must have known that: it was charity he wanted. I found two twenty-pound notes in my back pocket and gave them to him. He didn't thank me; he pushed his way back through the doors.

It was Saturday, the night I usually went to Anton's, something I usually looked forward to. Not tonight. I wouldn't be going there again. Instead I went swimming for an hour, then went back to the

Lady Day, and spent the rest of the afternoon tidying up. Later that night, I bought a Chinese meal and took it back to the boat. I drank beer in solitude, listening to tapes. I listened to Lee Wiley's 'Street of Dreams' several times. That's where we were, in dreamland – or Evelyn was, and Baxter. I didn't know where I was.

Early next morning, I stowed the supplies I'd brought with me. I put them in the wheelhouse, alongside the snorkel, the goggles, the flippers and the rest of the underwater gear I'd sorted out from the hold.

There was a light haze, the kind you hardly noticed until you realised that not only couldn't you see the coast of France, you couldn't see Sark either, and that was only nine miles away. I couldn't tell whether it was a good omen or not for the kind of day I had in mind. I didn't want anyone watching me, but I didn't fancy navigating the waters around the Hoummet in poor visibility either. I felt tight, on edge.

I went down into the engine room, which you reached by going through a hatch and down four steps into an oil-stinking hole behind the wheel-house. There was a collection of nudes pinned up on the bulkhead, the Brew's collection. Glossy fawn breasts bulged at me from the photographs. Perhaps he had groped her, creeping up the steps behind her to find her standing in the wheelhouse. And then lied about it to me. Perhaps he hadn't.

I started the diesel and let the engine idle in neutral while I went forward and hauled up the anchor, then went back to the wheelhouse and put her into gear. I could hear a church bell ringing. I was going to the Hoummet, on my own, without the Brew, on my own and all grown up.

I hadn't told Jenny everything about what Links had given me; there was almost too much detail on Baxter, who had what Links called a high media profile. While it's hard to tell what someone as slippery as Baxter was worth, Links felt he might not have been worth anything at all any more. He was a once-rich man putting on a big front, believing all his financial problems would be over when he found his pot of gold.

What there was on Richard Guilbert was much more interesting. He'd spent at least ten years of his life working for French intelligence.

I couldn't see any sign of any other vessel at the Hoummet, but even so I was nervous enough coming in over the undulates. The chart described 'Strong overfalls' on one side, 'Violent eddies' on the other. This meant the waters could be almost unnavigable in a boat like the *Lady Day*. At that state of the tide the standing waves over the undulates meant it was like taking her down the Colorado Rapids.

Although there was hardly a breath of wind, spray kissed my face, then slapped it. Then the *Lady Day* rolled and heaved, and a wave broke over the prow. I saw the water hissing along the deck, and I was suddenly standing ankle-deep in sea water in the wheelhouse. I felt my chest tighten; I'm not cut out for this kind of thing, I found myself thinking. What the hell was I doing here without the Brew?

I took the boat into the bay, threw her into reverse

and then into neutral, and dropped the anchor smack in the middle of the pool. It wasn't pretty, and I didn't do it as well as the Brew would have done it, but it was all right. I was there.

I had another look at the chart in the wheelhouse, and thought about having a drink, and even took a bottle of whisky out of the cupboard under the compass housing, the bottle with the shot glass stuck upside down over the cap, the one the Brew had been drinking from, but I put it back. Drink for celebration, I thought.

I stripped and put on the flippers and looped the mask and the snorkel over a fender and then tied a knife to a loop of orange twine which went round my neck. I took a powerful underwater torch with me, and tied that to the belt of my trunks by another loop of twine. I stood staring over the side for some time. I tried to make out that I could see the shape of the wreck lying there, but all I could really see was seaweed.

I went in. The water was colder than I'd expected, and I had to struggle back to the surface to catch my breath. I reached up and took the snorkel and the mask and put them on, rolled over on to my stomach and floated, lungs inflated, looking down. The water was fairly clear. Most of the seaweed I could see was brown in colour and must have been growing on the wreck; brown seaweed grows deeper than green, but it still doesn't grow very deep.

I duck-dived down six feet or so, and hung there upside down in the water, Superman in space, then floated back up to the surface, cleared the snorkel and next time went all the way down. I stayed down half a minute or so, feeling my way among the seaweed, which came out at me rubbery and clammy, and then found the metal shell of the wreck roughened by barnacles and corrosion and rust.

I went back to the surface and clambered over the stern ladder on to the deck of the *Lady Day*. I put on the aqualung and the mouthpiece, which made me gag as I bit it. The straps dug into my shoulders. I grabbed hold of the crowbar and slid back into the water again and let air into the buoyancy chamber until I was just about neutrally buoyant. Then I floated down into the water. I had with me an undercover camera, a bright yellow high-tech number left over from the days when I'd had a lot of toys like that. I'd only kept it because the executives who sometimes hired the *Lady Day* liked to send photographs of themselves flapping about underwater to their girlfriends.

Deafened by the sound of my own breathing, I let myself slowly sink, minute by minute, down into the seaweed. My feet found something solid among the weeds. The hull. I bumped and scrambled down it to the bottom of the bay and found rocks underfoot. Fish squirted away from my feet as I landed.

The water wasn't clear enough for me to be able to take in the whole vessel in one, but I could see she was upside down, and I could work out that she must have been about fifteen metres long. She'd been protected from the worst of the tides, lying there at the safest, calmest part of the bay, and she was in better shape than I'd expected. And as I crawled along her side, I saw that the metal she was made of was probably a high-grade aluminium, like an air-craft hull. She must have rolled over almost as soon as she'd begun to sink. Whatever superstructure was left had prevented her from rolling over completely, but there wasn't much of it. The same currents that had half buried one side of her in tidal mud had kept the other side clear. There was a gap on the side nearest me between the gunwale and the sea bottom but it wasn't large enough to allow me to do much more than reach an arm under.

Then I saw something I couldn't make sense of, a metal wing sticking up out of the bottom of the hull like a knife stuck into a slab of cheese. Unlike the hull, this metal was rusted. Steel, I supposed, broken some time in the past, and shaped roughly like the blade of a sword.

I began to use the flash cameras. The probing beam of torchlight turned the black water under the hull into wine-bottle green; the flash made sheets of glass with weird images on them leap at me. Nearby I saw a nest of broken crab shells which must have meant an octopus living there, and the broken ribs of a lobster pot swept there by the tides. Then there were bent pieces of black steel, coils of wire cable fluffy with seaweed. And then rubbish, lots of it, for the deck had rotted through years before, and whatever had been in the hull had fallen to the sea bottom – parts of the engine, hawsers, junk, sludge.

I could see the cowling that had once protected the compass, and on it I could see what I was looking for, a brass plate which should have identified the vessel. I wriggled as far as I could and took a series of photographs, scraping away as much stuff as I could with my hands. Then I saw something else.

It was hanging over the stern of the upturned vessel, a twenty-foot-long cylinder, one rounded end raised up by the way it was lying on something on the seabed and pointing in my direction as if it was coming straight at me. I knew what it was even before I wriggled a yard nearer to get a better look. A beard of seaweed covered something on the rounded end. I pulled the seaweed away, but I already knew what I was going to find. The propeller that was the firing pistol of a wartime torpedo.

19

My first instinct was to get the hell out of there, fast.
My second was to stay where I was. I must have been
torn between the two, because I convulsed, and
found myself gasping in panic, and enough air boiled
out of the valve to make it impossible to see anything
for a moment or two. For some reason, I tried to
remove my mask and my mouthpiece, and as I
fought the fear, adrenalin rushed through me, as
virulent as a dose of poison. I did my best to bite
back the fear, stayed where I was until the worst of it
had passed. But I didn't know what I was doing; for
a few minutes, I was as scared as a child in a dark
house at night.

I crawled away, backwards, floated slowly to the
surface. I paddled to where the rocks sloped down
into the bay and moved up them, carefully, a
frightened man. I moved like someone edging across
a greenhouse roof. If there was one torpedo, there
might well be more. If any of them were armed,
there'd be enough explosive in the warheads to blow
me up, and the *Lady Day*, and most of the Hoummet as well.

Back in the *Lady Day*, I rinsed my mouth with
whisky to get rid of the taste of sea water, and
rubber, and fear. My face felt stiff and strange, as if I
were still wearing the face mask. I was scared. I
didn't like the thought of six or seven hundred
pounds of highly explosive warhead corroding softly

173

underwater for half a century, until some bloody fool came along and kicked it just enough to set it off.

I'd never liked explosives, never liked working with them, which is why I'd always left the firework displays to the Brew. Fire, horses, cars, high buildings, even guns. But not explosives. Three stuntmen I knew had died working with them. I'd seen one of them die.

In the half-hour or so I'd been underwater, the *Lady Day* had begun to turn on her anchor rope, and her stern banged suddenly against a half-submerged rock. The blow went through her timbers like a mistimed drive through a bat handle, and in the state I was in I practically jumped overboard and made for the shore. I must have thought the vibrations might carry through the water and strike the firing pistol. It wasn't rational, but I wasn't enjoying this any more – if I ever had. I was scared. Even hauling in the anchor made me imagine it swinging in the water and catching the hull of the wreck a blow strong enough to dislodge it, and . . .

No wonder they wanted me to do the diving. No wonder Evelyn didn't want to. I thought about it on the long haul back. Even the money Baxter was paying me was beginning to make sense, because I might not be around to collect it. He'd lured me into this because I was expendable.

Early next morning, I had my film printed by an express photographic service, then went up to the States Library at the back of town. I spent the morning in the reference section, finding out as much as I could about the German occupation of

Alderney. I went through what they had about German naval vessels, and the armaments they carried. Then the index system told me that what I wanted was hidden away in the back room. A small contribution to the research funds of the library – a twenty-pound note to the librarian – got me in.

What I was looking for wasn't secret, it was just out of date: information about the movements of German ships during the Occupation. I found what I wanted in a collection of journals, letters, files and assorted documents from the Harbourmaster's Office. And after fiddling around with the files, something literally fell into my lap. A series of photographs held together by a paper clip. They'd been taken in April 1945 by a German official, and had been confiscated after the Liberation.

I flipped through the photographs. What drew my attention to them was the picture of a half-submerged submarine anchored outside the break-water of Alderney Harbour, and a couple of MTB-type vessels alongside, smallish motorboats with torpedo tubes forward. These were variants of the vessels the Germans called *Schnellboote*, S-boats – the Allies had called them E-boats. These were metal-hulled, with round bilges and powerful Mercedes-Benz diesel engines. Writing on the back identified the submarine as research vessel U-2338. The E-boats were numbered ZB-181 and ZB-282, experimental variants on the coastal MTBs. They were too big for whatever was lying at the Houm-met. But in one photograph there was another vessel.

At first glance, it looked like a service boat of some sort, but when I looked closely I changed my mind. It was too rakish, its hull more like the hull of a rocket than of an S-boat, which had a World War I look about it. A single torpedo tube projected over the stern. I could just read the code number on the bows in the fuzzy photograph. VS 12. I looked at the photographs I'd taken. This was it.

More details followed, and a pencilled cross-reference in the margin of the papers led me to another file about security operations during the Occupation, as if whoever had put it there had been on the same trail I was on, and had forgotten to rub it out. In the new file, there was a pencilled translation of a letter from some high-up German official in Cherbourg informing the commandant of the occupying forces on Alderney that special vessels would be berthed there – Alderney, having been evacuated by the Nazis, was the only one of the inhabited Channel Islands with no prying native islanders left to find out anything about what was going on. The letter explained that it would be advisable for the vessels to be moored outside the harbour because there was some risk of explosion.

Another letter, dated a month later, was about the visit of the research submarine U-2338. The surface vessels on special assignment, moored for a month outside the breakwater, sailed away just before the Liberation. One had been sunk a week later by marauding aircraft, another had been scuttled. There was no further reference to VS 12. It had vanished. There was no trace of it except for the single reference in one of the letters, and the black and white photograph. But I had no doubt in my mind what had happened to it. It was at the Hoummet, and I'd touched it a few hours before.

I put the photographs in my pocket, then went back into the main part of the library, and spent two hours reading about submarine development, and the naval weapons the Germans had used during World War II. Then I went to see the Admiral.

The Admiral – Tom Baptiste – lived in the Vale in the north of the Island. He was nearly eighty, but he'd held his master's ticket for fifty years, and he had been the best small-boat builder in the Channel Islands. He'd supervised the work on the *Lady Day* when she'd been even more of a floating embarrassment than she was now, and he'd taught the Brew a lot of what he knew about navigation and fishing. We'd always got on, and I knew he'd undercharged me for the work his men had done on the *Lady Day*.

He was pure Guernsey – good-humoured, tough, superstitious behind the mask of reasonableness. He lived in a bungalow on the corner of Rue Robin behind Bordeaux Harbour, and now spent his days sitting in a conservatory in hundred-degree heat watching golf on television. He was tall, thin and teak-brown, wearing jeans, a blue vest, and a blue Breton cap on his bald head. Cancer had removed most of his right ear and part of his cheek. The ragged edges of the holes were the colour of tobacco juice.

We sat among the yucca trees and the weeping figs and exchanged conversation about this and that, drank the tea his daughter brought, and ate the Guernsey gache she'd made, before she left the room and I showed him the photographs. There'd been collaboration during the Occupation, under-standably on an island where there was nowhere to

177

run to, but there'd been resistance as well. Tom had stayed in the islands all through the war, and he'd done as much as anyone to make life difficult for the Germans.

He sorted through the photographs with hands hooked like an eagle's claws.

He said, 'Some of us were licensed to fish during the Occupation, as long as we signed our boat out every morning and back in every evening, and we were only allowed a small amount of fuel. My brother and I were allowed to go as far north as Alderney. With no one doing any fishing at all out there except for us, the fish we were getting by the Casquets and the Hoummet were the best I've ever seen. Crabs with shells the size of carving plates, and the crayfish we caught we had to cook in a tin bath, couldn't get them in a saucepan. It's an ill wind, eh? We kept the best of them for the local people, but the Germans were hungry by then, and I used to take some crabs in to Alderney a few times. That meant we could look around Braye Harbour a bit, eh?

'We saw this sub when they'd towed her into Braye Harbour.' He pointed to the picture of the half-submerged submarine U-2338. 'There'd been an explosion aboard, but she sank in shallow water so she could be salvaged. They pumped her full of compressed air, half floated her, and towed her behind the breakwater. They repaired her and she left some time in '45. It was the hydrogen peroxide that blew up.'

'Hydrogen peroxide? I though you put that on your hair.'

'You've probably used it as a disinfectant, and

178

seen it bubble when it mixes with blood – that's the problem with it, liquid makes it unstable.' He grinned toothlessly. 'I'll just go get a couple of books, Sam. You get the rum from the kitchen. Then we'll talk about it.'

The Admiral told me that the Germans had experimented with hydrogen peroxide as a fuel for years. A catalytic reaction breaks down peroxide into oxygen and water, generating the heat that is used for propulsion. They made some of the fastest submarines ever built, but hydrogen peroxide was so unstable that contact with sea water would make it explode. When the war ended, the Germans still hadn't commissioned any of the peroxide-powered vessels. But they'd been using peroxide as fuel in torpedoes for several years.

'Torpedoes?' I said. There wasn't much air in the conservatory. I gulped in some of what there was. It was about as easy to breathe as bath water.

Tom said, 'That was why this sub was moored outside the harbour, eh?, too dangerous to be moored inside. It was one of the torpedoes that blew up. It killed seven men. But they hadn't loaded the rest of the torpedoes and they transferred them to these motor torpedo boats.'

'What happened to the torpedoes?'

'They went on testing them. I remember seeing firing trials at dummy vessels out in the Swinge.'

'And this?' I pointed to the small, rocket-shaped boat. My boat.

'That's my footnote in naval history,' Tom said with a dry chuckle. 'I was the first non-German to see a Nazi hydrofoil and know what he was looking at. I even managed to get a radio message through to the Admiralty about it.'

'They didn't have hydrofoils in 1944.'

'The Germans did. They built their first in 1943, but the idea had been around since the turn of the century, and the Royal Navy experimented with them before the war. The Germans tested theirs by running them up and down the Berlin lakes. This one was the smallest, and the fastest. Fifty knots, I think. Fifty fucking knots,' he said, responding to my surprise. 'They'd brought it overland on a train for sea trials. They wanted to see if they could use them against an Allied invasion. A single torpedo tube over the stern of the boat launching these peroxide-powered torpedoes. If the trials had been successful, all those underground factories churning out Messerschmitts and Focke Wulfs would have been making these hydrofoils. They'd have blasted the troop carriers out of the water, and D-Day might never have happened. But the sea trials were disastrous. A lovely little boat, but she was too small for the kind of waves you get in the English Channel.

'First and only time I saw her at full power, it was a calm day and I thought at first a sub had come up under her. Then I saw she was up on four legs – five counting the screw, eh? And she was travelling like an aeroplane, wheeoo, no bow waves. I couldn't believe it at first, but then I did, I believed what I'd seen, and I remembered it.'

He flicked through my photographs again. 'So that's where she ended up, eh?'

'Do you know anything about how it got there?' I asked him. He shook his head. We were drinking Pusser's Rum by then. The dark brown liquid exploded in my stomach, and I blinked, and breathed out fire. I was sweating in the heat of the conservatory, the sun blazing in from the west, glinting on the blue and gold of the bottle.

He turned up the relevant pages for me: FAST ATTACK CRAFT, THE EVOLUTION OF DESIGN AND TACTICS; THE NAZI NAVY; NAVAL INTELLIGENCE REPORTS; GERMAN NAVAL WEAPONS OF THE SECOND WORLD WAR.

'Aluminium-hulled, with an engine built by Hispano Suiza. The engine's a beauty, vintage engineering. Pity it'll be too rusted to salvage. Sam, if she's got peroxide aboard, she's an underwater bomb, it's no wonder they don't want to cut into her with oxy-acetylene torches.' He ate a piece of gache, sipped some rum; he loved the taste of it, tilted his head back and let it trickle down his thin brown throat. 'Any ammunition is dangerous underwater. If it goes up, the Hoummet will go up with it. They'll have to redraw the charts.' He started packing the metal-stemmed pipe he smoked, lit it carefully. 'Times are hard, Sam, if you're wasting your time with a man like Baxter. If you're going diving on a time-bomb like this.'

'Times are hard.'

'Why are you doing it?'

'Money,' I said.

He blinked at me in disbelief. 'Sam, when did you last do anything for money? They're playing you for a fool. Either you're risking your neck for something they want, and what they're paying you isn't anything like what they're going to get out of it, or they're using you as a front for something. Baxter, and probably this bloody lawyer too, eh? They think you were born yesterday. But it's Baxter I'd watch out for.'

There wasn't much I could say to that. I sat and stared into the glass of rum.

'And another thing, make sure you're not drunk when you get down there,' he said. 'I like a drink myself, but drink won't help you. Drink never does.'

'All right.'

'Be careful, Sam. That wreck is a bomb waiting to go off.'

I said, 'I can handle it, Tom.'

20

'You'll get six months for this,' someone said to me on my way into the courthouse on the following Monday. I turned to look at whoever had spoken, but I didn't recognise anyone.

There was a dreamlike quality about the court-room. Even though it was me they were trying, or perhaps because of that, I felt detached, like watching a play. I'd put on a black linen Liberty jacket I'd saved from the shipwreck of my busi-ness, and a pink cotton Oxford shirt with button-down collar and bone buttons. And I spoke with a plum in my mouth. I wasn't just an ex-stuntman, I was also an ex-actor: I'd once had eight lines of dialogue as a British officer in one of those war epics which helped to sink the British film indus-try. I'd been parachuted out of an aeroplane and sodomised by barbed wire near the Remagen bridge. The voice coach had had the hell of a job with my cosmopolitan vowels – ex-Guernsey, ex-English, ex-Australian, ex-American, actor, stuntman and bum. But we'd come up with some-thing between us in the end, and I used it in court. I sounded like a cross between Margaret Thatcher and James Hunt.

But it was Evelyn who got me off. If she'd never made her mark as an actress on film she made it in court that day. She wore a dress of pale blue watered silk that made her hair glow like gold and her skin radiate something that had people hanging out of their seats.

Richard Guilbert shuffled his papers, gazed around the court myopically, and tried his best to look solid and British. He didn't quite make it; what I had been reading as a gestural clumsiness I was now beginning to see as an attempt on his part to disguise his Frenchness. Holding gestures back, not being as expressive as he'd have liked to be. But somehow, he'd made this clumsiness part of his act.

Guilbert led Evelyn through the events of Saturday night like a conductor leading an orchestra through one of those symphonies that has everyone crying halfway through the slow movement. While he ducked and weaved in the foreground, ostrich to her bird of paradise, she held the court spellbound.

She'd put a touch of pale lipstick on her mouth, dark make-up around her eyes. She looked vulnerable, wanting protection, pale, as if she was having her period; and she looked spiritual, if you didn't look too closely at the cleavage she was offering to the court.

It had been a terrible night, Evelyn said, with a catch in her voice. The men had thrust themselves upon her, had started to threaten her. But, thank God, I was there to help her. She told the court that I'd had a few drinks, but that was all. That I'd been provoked by the two men. That I'd fought to protect her, that I'd taken on these two thugs like a white knight on a charger. The police had got it all wrong. It wasn't me they should have been prosecuting, it was the two men I'd beaten up.

I was given a suspended sentence of three months,

and the usual heavy warning about my drinking and my behaviour, and next time I'd be put on the Black List, and who the hell did I think I was. Without Evelyn's testimony, and with the list of previous convictions I had tied to my tail, I'd have gone inside for certain.

De Jersey couldn't even bring himself to look at Evelyn, who stood beside me on the steps holding her hat on the crown of her head and smiling brightly at the TV camera like the bride at a smart wedding. Richard Guilbert came out and blinked at the cameras, shook hands with a few people, then shambled off down the street, brushing something from the lapels of his suit. Cobwebs. He was going home to climb back into his vault.

I stood on the steps feeling great – I was free. But then I saw a couple of policemen standing by my car, and coming up the street was the tow-truck they used to tow away mobile litter like my Traveller. Spooner, the bastard. I hadn't even enough money in my pocket to get me home.

Evelyn finished with the reporters and walked towards me. She'd stopped looking soulful and now looked businesslike.

'Come with me, Sam,' she said. 'It's time we talked.'

George Baxter Enterprises was in a modern block of offices fifty yards up St Julian's Avenue. It didn't overlook the harbour, but you could see the sea if you stood on a chair and craned your neck. Compared to the firm Richard Guilbert worked for, this one had just got a toe-hold on the ladder.

Baxter's offices were on the top floor. Evelyn and

I got into the lift, the doors shut and it trembled as it began to climb. She leaned forward and kissed me on the lips. Then she pulled away. I leered at her, surprised.

'What was that for?'

'For old time's sake,' she said.

There was no sign of a secretary in the reception room. Evelyn opened the door into the main office, where George Baxter was sitting in an easy chair watching a portable television.

It was the kind of office a film producer who hadn't quite made it would have, right down to an ivory leather casting couch. There were video screens, televisions, computers. Noticeboards on the walls covered with flow charts and year planners. Filing cabinets. Printers. A crowded, buzzing room vibrant with electronic interference. And about as healthy as the inside of a microwave oven.

'How did it go?' Baxter asked.

'Three months suspended,' Evelyn said, as if she were talking about the starting price of a horse. 'Christ, I'd like a drink.' She opened a door and went into an adjoining room, fiddled around while I made myself comfortable on the sofa, then came back with a bottle of champagne and three glasses. I opened the champagne, and we made the usual noises about getting a result, and what idiots the police were, and Baxter lit a Havana cigar, going through the usual process of skinning it of cellophane and circumcising it with a gold cutter.

'Policemen are like tax inspectors. Society may need them but I don't,' he said, something that sounded as if he'd learned it from one of the Harrods crackers he pulled at Christmas.

I undid a couple of buttons of my shirt and lounged back on the sofa. Evelyn put the champagne on the low coffee table and sat down next to Baxter. Her thigh came close to his, rubbing against it with a sound like something rustling banknotes.

'Did you ask the police to drop the charges against me?' I asked. 'It would have been easier than going through all that today.'

'I tried, but they wouldn't do it,' Evelyn said. 'Inspector De Jersey insisted on bringing the case to court.'

'So you went to De Jersey, did you? When?'

'When you were in the cells. Why? You haven't talked to him, have you?'

'No,' I said. I thought about that, about the conversation I'd had with De Jersey, remembering he hadn't mentioned such a visit. I said, 'Look, you don't really expect me to think you helped me out of the goodness of your heart.'

'I needed your boat,' Baxter said. 'And I needed you to work it. That's simple enough. Even a part-time Guernseyman like you can understand that, can't you? I wouldn't look a gift horse in the mouth, if I were you. Evelyn went a long way out on a limb for you today.'

On a glass coffee table on the silver Chinese rug was a carved ivory box. Evelyn took a cigarette from it and waited for me to pick up the lighter from the table and light it for her. So I did. Then I went and opened a second bottle of Krug. I was on my best behaviour.

'Do you know anything about hydrogen peroxide?' I asked when I'd done my duty and refilled the

glasses: easy to start acting as a servant to people who have a lot of money.

'What are you talking about, hydrogen peroxide?'

'You know, the stuff Evelyn puts on her hair.'

'But I don't need to put anything on my hair; this is natural,' Evelyn drawled, fingering a handful of her hair, which framed her face like an erotic halo.

'I took a look at that wreck you want me to turn over,' I said. 'I went out to the Hoummet in my boat and took a good look at it, close up.'

Baxter didn't like that. Then I told him about my session in the library and about my conversation with the Admiral. He didn't like that either.

I said, 'Sooner or later, sea water's going to work its way into the fuel cells of that torpedo. When it does, the hydrogen peroxide is going to explode. Any jarring caused by me banging around down there is likely to help it. The reason you've hired me, the reason Evelyn won't do the diving for you even though she's a better swimmer and diver than I am, came to me in a blinding flash yesterday. Guess what it was.'

He didn't answer me. He looked dumbfounded.

I said, 'I don't know what you've got in store for me, but I have the feeling you've worked out that if you're going to lose anyone in an underwater explosion, it may as well be me.'

Baxter looked first at Evelyn, then at me. He almost looked guilty.

'I'd have told you everything in due course,' he said. 'I just didn't want you knowing too much, not before I knew the result of the trial. If you'd gone to jail, I'd have needed to find someone else. I'm sorry you thought you had to start poking around on your own account.'

I said, 'If you don't tell me what's going on, I walk out right now.'

He didn't like that much either, but Evelyn ran a hand through his hair and smiled at me again, and rubbed her thigh against his. For a moment, I thought she even winked at me.

'You'd better tell him, George,' she said. 'He has a right to know.'

21

One of the machines made a meaningless noise. Baxter leaned over the back of the sofa and hit a button on a console near him. 'You've heard of Klaus Barbie, haven't you?'

'He was a war criminal, wasn't he?' I said, surprised.

'The wartime head of the Gestapo in Lyons,' Baxter said. 'He died in prison, not long ago, serving a life sentence for war crimes. He was the first man to use electricity as a form of torture. Civilisation has a lot to thank him for.' He grinned sourly at me, picked cautiously at his cigar with blunt fingers. 'Richard Guilbert worked for the French intelligence services for a number of years when they were investigating Barbie at the time of his trial, so he was looking into what went on in France during the Occupation. He came across some information which he didn't tell his bosses.

'The SS and the Gestapo kept so many files that a lot of researchers, Germans and Jews and French, are still sorting through them. It's the methodical German mind,' Baxter said, as if he was stating an eternal truth. 'Richard found some information about the SS who ran one of the concentration camps on Alderney. The Russians and Jews and the rest of them there were slave labourers, but they came from all over Europe, France, Poland, Holland. Quite a lot of them died. They were worked to death or they died of disease or they were shot, and the SS took their possessions, such as they were. Gold and silver from jewellery and from religious furniture some of the Jews had brought from their synagogues.'

'And gold from teeth,' Evelyn said, tapping ash from her cigarette. She seemed drily amused.

'But it's gold all the same, low-grade gold, but it would have been a pity to waste it,' Baxter said. 'Richard had found a lead to a German who'd been an SS guard in one of the camps. His name was Clausen. Richard was able to track him down through the old SS network. He moved to Holland after the war. He spent most of his life working for Philips and going to watch PSV Eindhoven at the weekends. He told Richard that when France was going to fall in 1944, some of the guards from the camp had tried to get what they'd stolen from the prisoners off the island to hide it so they could come back to it after the war, and by the time Liberation came in May 1945 they'd made all the arrangements and had already hidden it. A lot of what went on in Alderney never came out, you know, not even now there's been all this stuff in the press. They were very keen on showing film of atrocities in Buchenwald and Dachau after the war, but they kept pretty quiet about what happened on British soil.'

'Always the way,' I said.

'The guards took one of the experimental boats which were being tested around Alderney at the time, and they took it to the Hommet. They opened the cocks and sank her, but she turned on her back as she went down. The gold is aboard her, in a steel safe. There was a lot of other stuff on the boat – carpets and clocks, and small items of furniture they'd taken from Alderney, and Christ knows what – but it's the gold that really matters.'

'There won't be anything else left, not after that long in the sea,' I said. 'What about the other men? What happened to them?'

'Clausen said only a few of the guards were involved, and some of them left Alderney in 1944 and were caught in the Falaise Gap, and killed. Others were interned at the Liberation in 1945. Two died, one committed suicide. That left him.'

'And the gold is still there?' I said.

'It's still there.'

'Have you paid Guilbert for any of this information?'

'Six or seven thousand pounds, I suppose,' Baxter said.

'Anything else?'

'I pay him what I'm paying you. A thousand a week. It sounds a lot, but he's very useful to me, and he's spent a lot of time and money tracking down this story. And he says he's being squeezed out of the law firm he works for. Why?'

'Because it's a con,' I said. 'This story is crap from beginning to end.'

Evelyn looked angry; spots of scarlet burned on her cheeks. I hadn't seen her so disturbed for years. She smashed her cigarette into the ashtray and picked another out of the box.

Baxter simply looked surprised.

'I gave him the money in American dollars,' he said, as if that proved something. 'Ten thousand of them.'

I said, 'If there is a German, which I doubt, he's working with them. I made some enquiries about Richard Guilbert and his career. He worked in the French intelligence forces all right, he even had some tie-up with the CIA. After that, he came back to the Channel Islands, met up with you and did some work for you. You met Evelyn, who already knew Guilbert, remember, because she'd met him when I came over here to sort out my will. Evelyn may have made contact again when she called in at Guernsey on her way to Monaco after leaving me in the States. If they were both on the rocks financially, you must have looked like a goldmine to them. Somewhere along the line, Evelyn and Guilbert had an idea. There's been a lot in the media lately about Nazi material being found, in Russia and France. Why not in the Channel Islands, especially now some of the newspapers are getting hold of the story about the Alderney camps? So Guilbert traced an unmarked wreck near the Hoummet and he used that to spin this line. He's making whatever you're paying him a week, Baxter. But watch yourself. You're so soft a mark he thinks it's Christmas. I know about being conned. I've been conned. I know what I'm talking about. With her looks and his brains, they're skinning you alive.'

'I'll just assume this is another of your bloody awful jokes,' Evelyn said with a voice so level she must have been fighting down the trembling which showed in the way the smoke zig-zagged upwards from the tip of her cigarette.

I stood up and stretched, went out to the kitchen, found a bottle of whisky and poured some into a tumbler. Springbank again. Evelyn had probably

194

watched me drink cases of it, in the days when I didn't want to watch my marriage and my business collapse except through the bottom of a glass.

When I went back into the room they were staring at me as if I'd come through the wall.

'Tell me again, what are you paying me so much money to look for?' I asked.

'There's a fortune down there,' Baxter said. He turned suddenly to look at Evelyn as if she'd slapped his face.

She'd smoked no more than half an inch of her cigarette, and now she got rid of that and started fighting the cigarettes in the box. I went over and picked one out, helped her quivering hand to her lips, and lit the cigarette for her with the lighter from the table. I could smell her perfume. It was one I'd always liked, White Linen. That peacock-blue dress did a lot for her, bringing out the shape of her shoulders, the colour of her skin. The shape of her breasts was perfectly outlined by the clinging cloth and by the silk bra I could just see a wisp of in her cleavage. She'd never needed to wear a bra before; she must have been wearing it out of deference to the court.

'He's lying,' Evelyn said with cold savagery to Baxter, who shrugged helplessly. He had been staring at me for so long his eyes were watering.

'What do you mean, Richard is conning me? He told me all about his past. I know he worked for the SDECE. So what? No one's ever conned me. I'm not the sort to be conned. There're no flies on me, Breaker. Nobody cons George Baxter.'

'That makes you the easiest mark of all,' I snapped at him.

★ ★ ★

Evelyn was more controlled now, as if she'd forced herself back into character. 'He's lying, George, he's just trying to make trouble between us. I didn't think he'd be jealous of you, but he is. Don't listen to him.'

But Baxter was listening. He was going to tell me everything just to convince me that my version was wrong.

'I have transcripts of the conversations Richard had with the German, Clausen,' he said. 'And photographs. There's even an audio tape.'

'I made the tape myself,' Evelyn said. 'I was suspicious of what Richard told me, of course I was, at first, so I insisted on going back to Holland with Richard.'

'Was this before or after Richard told Baxter about the gold?' I asked.

'Before. George was away at the time. I didn't see any point in telling him a story I didn't believe myself, so Richard and I drove up through France and went to see Clausen. I took a tape recorder in my handbag and taped what he said. You can hear it if you like. I didn't want to at first, but I believed him when I talked to him.'

'Where's Clausen now?'

Baxter said, 'In a nursing home in Holland. He's dying. He has cancer.' He said the word as if it was something exotic to eat.

'When I saw him, he had a lump growing out of the top of his head,' Evelyn said, her face showing disgust. 'He was in pain, and he was taking a lot of drugs. His full name is Karl-Heinz Clausen. He'd been an *Oberleutnant* in the SS. He'd been married, but his wife was dead. He has a daughter living in Leipzig – she was a communist, and she disowned him years ago. Now that he's so ill, he's owning up to his past. He even gave me some of his insignia, which he'd kept hidden since the war. His serial number and the death's head he wore on his uniform. I've got them at the house.'

'The insignia is probably worth more than the gold you think you're going to find.'

But I had to look at some Polaroid photographs she showed me, photographs of an old man lying in bed; they meant nothing. Then Evelyn put an audio tape in a tape-player. A voice mumbling in German sounded as if it had been recorded in a broom cupboard. I leaned over and turned it off.

Baxter said, 'I've heard the tape. It's not all very clear, but I believe it's genuine. Later on, you can hear Evelyn and Clausen talking, as well as Richard.'

'Evelyn's an actress – and she wouldn't have to be to fake a tape,' I said. 'You put a tape recorder in a handbag and hand someone five-pound notes to talk in the background with a German accent. Even I could do that.'

'You mean, you don't believe her?'

I didn't know whether I did or not. I said, 'Why didn't Clausen come back and reclaim the gold himself?'

'The Hoummet's been off limits for years, and no one dives there because of the ammunition dumped on the sea bottom,' Baxter said.

'He did come back once,' Evelyn said. 'He came back in 1960. He even hired a fishing boat from the Breton coast. But he didn't have any diving

197

equipment and the currents were too strong. And what could he do? He knew the vessel had turned over, and that it would be a hell of a long job to get the gold out of there.'

'He hired the boat from Brittany because he didn't want to go back to the Channel Islands, least of all Alderney,' Baxter said. 'He told us he'd stamped a woman to death within ten yards of where the post office is now.' He was regaining his composure, relighting his cigar and puffing at it. 'You know as well as I do that French fishing boats aren't always welcome in Channel Island waters. But I believe Richard and I believe Clausen. It's you I don't believe, Breaker. You've been drinking too much. Your judgement's gone. What's Richard after, if he is conning me? He's taken a few thousand pounds, that's all. He hasn't asked for any more money. No one would set up anything as elaborate as this for the sake of a few thousand pounds. He could have walked off with a couple of my watches and cameras and done better than that.'

'He has a point, Sam,' Evelyn said.

'Do you want your money or not?' Baxter said. 'I've got a thousand pounds in cash waiting for you on the *Venus*, two thousand more if you turn the wreck over tomorrow, another three thousand if we find the gold. If you don't need it, that man of yours, Brouard or whatever he's called, does. He'll get free hospitalisation, but if he lives, he's going to need a lot of expensive treatment. How's he going to pay for that?'

Evelyn saw my face, and smiled triumphantly.

'Sam is just playing games,' she said. 'He likes to

needle people, George. He's been needling you, that's all.'

I probably looked as if that's exactly what I had been doing. I'd kept the trump card back, that Evelyn probably knew that Baxter was living financially on borrowed time and was just squeezing all the cash she could out of him. But I'd expected something to give, and nothing had. Perhaps there really was gold there; perhaps Evelyn was playing it straight. In that room, faced by Baxter's belief, it was suddenly easier to believe.

'You can't blame me for wondering,' I said. It sounded feeble, even to me. 'But I'm holding out for more money. Now that I know what's down there, I want five thousand pounds instead of three. And another five for turning it over.'

A look passed between them: two calculating people. Three, including me.

'All right,' Baxter said, a little too quickly for my peace of mind. 'But I'll only give you the other five if I find what I'm looking for. Ten thousand if we find the gold. All right?' I nodded – I had to: it was the best offer I'd had for several years. He said, 'I want you to take your boat out to the Hoummet today and set things up. Richard is already out there in the *Venus*, and Evelyn and I are going to fly in by helicopter. And you're going to earn your money, Breaker, believe you me. We'll see then whether you're full of shit or not.'

22

I'd almost reached the Hoummet before I saw the *Venus* in the bay. At first I couldn't see who was aboard, until a tall man appeared in the cockpit silhouetted against the rocks.

I brought the *Lady Day* up between the *Venus* and the pier, and Richard Guilbert brought the big cruiser in towards me, reversing and forwarding the engines with a delicacy of touch I hadn't suspected him of having. I juggled the *Lady Day* until the removable railings matched those on the *Venus*, tied up alongside the pier, then moored fender to fender, and opened the gates. Guilbert was wearing a pair of new 501s and a fade-wash shirt years too young for him. But he looked harder suddenly. Whatever made him convincing as a lawyer had dropped away.

'I've come to help you with the donkey engine.'

'I didn't know you could handle a boat.'

'Someone had to teach Evelyn how to handle the *Venus*.'

'So it was you.'

'I've done some sailing round here, I know the waters pretty well.' He rubbed his big hands. 'I thought I'd take a couple of days off from the office. Give you a hand.'

'I thought you liked being a lawyer?'

He looked mildly surprised, as if I'd turned out to be less perceptive than he'd thought.

'What do you think I like about it? Sitting in an

office all day listening to fluorescent lights and breathing recycled air, while you sail around the islands, and breathe in fresh salt ozone?'

'Debt-laden ozone. If you're going to help me, make sure you keep up with me.' I went to open the hold.

We spent most of what was left of the daylight shifting the donkey engine I'd brought from the scrapyard across to the pier with the *Lady Day*'s derrick. It was an awkward job – we had to improvise a bridge of planks to drag the donkey engine up over the rocks by a system of pulleys. He must have been ten years my senior, and I'd set out with the intention of tiring him out, but then I found I couldn't do it. Those gangling limbs of his were wiry. He wasn't at all what he looked.

When we'd got the donkey engine over to the edge of the pier where the Brew had set the shackles into the concrete, we covered it with nylon sheeting. By then, it was getting dark. We ate sandwiches in the galley, and Guilbert hauled a case of beer over from the *Venus* and we opened bottles. We stepped outside to watch the sunset, stood by the old bowsprit drinking the beer.

The evening star was shining like a distant searchlight between strips of cloud, and there was a watery yellow light in the west which meant bad weather, and rain. I hoped I'd be finished diving before any of the bad weather arrived. Even in the bay, big waves could move the *Lady Day* about. And if I lifted the hull of the wrecked boat close to the surface, the movement of the waves would shake it around enough to make things unstable. There might even be the possibility of the hull of my boat striking the hull of the wreck. That wreck was looming more and more. Whenever I thought about it, I shuddered.

Guilbert noticed. 'It is getting a bit chilly, isn't it?'

'Just a bit,' I said sourly. 'How long were you in the swimming-pool, Richard?'

'What?'

'La Piscine,' I said.

He kept on drinking the beer from the bottle, angling it against his lips, and then I realised that he'd stopped swallowing and was considering what to say next, whether to tell the truth or to lie. He sucked the bottle neck gently, tapped the bottle against his teeth.

'How did you find out?'

'I read the newspapers.'

'Why? I'm a respectable lawyer, in a respectable firm,' he said with amused disbelief. But I didn't comment on that, so he said, 'If you've been reading newspapers, how did you know which newspaper to read?'

I said into the silence that followed, in my best Californian drawl, 'Just lucky, I guess.' I drank some more of the beer and chewed on another piece of tired chicken breast. I didn't like the taste and threw the remains of the sandwich into the sea. A gull swooped and snatched it before it hit the water. Bird eats bird. It went flapping off seawards, pursued by other squawking gulls.

'I underestimated you. There's more to you than meets the eye,' Guilbert said amiably. 'Perhaps George was right to hire you after all. You must have contacts. Friends in the right places.'

'I found out you'd been in the SDECE, the French

intelligence services, now the DGSE, and I do have friends. But they're not friends you need to worry about. They deal in information, that's all.'

'That's all I've ever dealt in myself,' Guilbert said thoughtfully. 'Information is power. The trouble about being a lawyer, a middle-aged junior lawyer, in someone else's firm, is that one doesn't get enough information to have any power.' He brooded on that for a while. 'I did work for the French intelligence services, I even worked at their head-quarters, "La Piscine". So what?' I didn't say anything to that, so he tried another tack. 'You know, Breaker, a career in intelligence is just like any other career. With its optimism, its surprises, its ironies, and its disappointments. Especially its disappointments. I'd approached it with so much hope.

'When I left school I didn't like what was happening to the country. The election of a Labour government led to many of the best brains leaving the country. So instead of going to Oxford I went to the Sorbonne. My mother was French, my father was a Guernseyman. I was bi-lingual, legally trained. I have strong political views, and moving into intelligence seemed a logical thing to do.'

'You were an agent?'

'No.' He moved awkwardly against the railing. 'People have a lot of misconceptions about intelligence work, particularly, I'd say, about the SDECE, which has admittedly not always had the best of reputations. I was a lawyer, no more, no less, just as I am now. Intelligence services need legal advice, just like anybody else, and they need some lawyers to be cleared in security terms. If you take the *Rainbow Warrior* incident, for example, we had to do a lot of work on that. Or the Klaus Barbie investigations, in which we were involved.'

'Then how did you get that hole in your head?' I asked, but if he noticed my sarcastic tone, he didn't respond to it.

'That was the result of a misunderstanding.'

'My contact told me you had CIA connections and that the misunderstanding happened while you were in El Salvador.'

'I was visiting a friend at the time. His gas stove exploded.'

'I heard it was a grenade. You don't expect me to believe the story about the stove?'

He shrugged. 'It doesn't really matter, does it? But if I'd told the partners of my present firm the real story, I probably wouldn't have the job I have now.'

'If I told them what really happened, would you still keep the job?'

'Probably not,' he said, unconcerned; he didn't care whether I told them or not. He was dangerous. I wondered what he intended to do, about the job or about me. I could feel the cold air creeping up my back, where sweat was drying under my shirt; it was getting cooler all the time.

'I don't know whether I believe this story about Clausen or not,' I said. 'But it looks as if I'm going to risk my neck to find out.'

'I thought you once made a career out of risking your neck?'

'I was a stuntman, I made a career out of not risking my neck. You handled that boat pretty well. You ever flown a helicopter?'

'Yes.'

205

'While you were a lawyer for the SDECE?' I said sarcastically.

'Even lawyers have to move around.'

Some lawyer. He'd dealt in dirty money and in the lives of hostages, in confessions muttered into tape recorders. I could feel it.

It was getting cold. I shivered properly this time. The sun had dipped out of sight. Seagulls were black against the sky. The water in the bay was also black. Black for death.

'What will I find when I dive down there tomorrow?' I asked.

'What do you expect to find?'

'How the hell do I know? I don't know who to believe. Are you telling the truth?'

He grinned. His glasses glinted with the dying light, the depression in his forehead a deep hole filled with shadow.

'You're looking for a steel safe. That's not difficult. Either it's there or it's not. If it's got something in it, Baxter is right. If it's not there, or if there's nothing in it, he's wrong.'

'Ah yes, the steel safe,' I said. I heard the distant boom of an aeroplane going through the sound barrier somewhere up above. It was ominous, like a distant gunshot. A moment later, I saw it, a silver speck in the sky's eye.

I said, 'I had a look at the wreck yesterday, and for what it's worth I couldn't see a steel safe. The boat was upside down, the deck had rotted, it might have fallen through. I didn't see it, but I won't know until we lift the wreck.'

'Until *you* lift the wreck,' Guilbert said. He pointed to the hole in his forehead. 'I won't be there to help you. More's the pity.'

'Where will you be?'

'About a mile away, in case it does blow up.'

'Bastard,' I said.

'Why? You don't think you'll be risking your life going down there? You're going to be careful?'

'Of course I'm going to be careful.'

I drank some more beer. Becks. It wasn't my favourite. Too sour. Or maybe it was the thought of that underwater bomb we were floating above that left a taste in my mouth.

I had to get something off my chest, and it can be easier to talk to a stranger than to an intimate: coming clean was in the air. I said, 'I was a damned good stuntman once, one of the best. I've done a lot of things in my life badly, but that I did well. And I was careful, always careful. Except once.'

He didn't say anything. He just listened, like a confessor.

'Stuntmen like to break records – it's good for publicity, and it's good for their egos. My speciality was high diving, jumping off towers and buildings and out of aeroplanes. I used to break the world record for high dives off a tower on land, adding a couple of metres every year. The idea is, you tie ropes to your ankles and jump a couple of hundred feet and stop a foot or two before you hit the ground. It looks spectacular, but it's as safe as houses if you know what you're doing, like everything else in stunting. The ropes have enough give in them to stop you breaking your legs, and if you've done your calculations properly the ropes stop you just in time to stop you breaking your neck. I used to boast I could put a comb upright on the landing mattresses and stop my fall so close to it it would part my hair.

'One year, when I was rich and famous, and when I'd just won another contract from a film company, and when I didn't need to do it any more, for money or publicity or anything else, I did it anyway. Pride. I was standing at the top of the tower with the ropes round my ankles ready to make the jump, with no more than a dozen people watching, when Evelyn arrived with a television crew and made me wait while they lined up the shots. There was a thunderstorm coming. I could see it. Lightning struck and rain fell at the far end of the field. I stood at the top of the tower and watched it. And I felt the humidity change. I ought to have known the moisture would affect the ropes. When I jumped, the ropes had lengthened a couple of inches, and that was enough. I hit the ground and broke my neck.'

He chuckled gently. I joined in. We stood there and laughed.

'I didn't feel a thing,' I said. 'I just heard the bones crack. I could still hear it a fortnight later when I woke up from the coma.'

'No wonder you stopped living with her,' he said.

'I was a bloody fool for not trusting my own judgement. When I got out of hospital, after three months, I fiddled around a while in the business, but I was unfit by then, my wife had left me, and my partner had buggered off with my money. I knew I was gone. That was it.' I drank some more beer. 'I'd always thought I was immortal, till that day I woke up. April Fool's Day three years ago. It finished my career.'

'I thought you were too young to be retired,'

Guilbert said, showing his teeth in a stiff smile. 'She was trying to get rid of you, haven't you realised that?'

'What kind of a joke is that?' I said, and remembered Evelyn saying to me earlier in the day, 'I expect this is just another of your bloody awful jokes.' He was grinning, as if it really was a joke. I wanted to get rid of him, to get him off my boat. But I couldn't leave it alone.

'How could she have done it on purpose? She couldn't have known that thunderstorm was coming.'

He shrugged. Finished his beer and threw the bottle into the bay. 'Are you telling me she didn't read the weather reports?'

I said, 'Be careful where you throw things, there's a torpedo down there. With a trigger.'

'If your luck is that bad, you may as well forget the whole thing now,' he said, amused. He was relaxing. My confessions of weakness entertained him.

I felt uncomfortable, as if I'd peeled off some of the layers, that I'd shown him what was inside, under the usual mucky, crumpled pyjamas people use to cover up what they really are.

'I need a nightcap,' I mumbled. 'Something stronger than this German piss.'

I had two stone bottles of Bols Genever lying side by side in the Calor gas-operated fridge in the galley, with the dew on them solidifying into ice. I took one of them out, along with two chilled glasses and a couple more beers, and I sliced up a lemon into a saucer. I don't like salt with gin, but chewing lemon clears the palate.

We faced each other across the deckhouse table like distrustful card players. There was something about him that made me recoil. It was my reaction, intuitive or paranoid, to the talk that surrounded him, to the names that kept cropping up: 'La Piscine', Klaus Barbie, El Salvador. He wasn't the club bore at all, or the family lawyer; he was something more modern, more ruthless. He was the kind of man who'd ask questions in a little room where no one else would be able to hear the screams.

'I'm sorry you don't believe us about the gold. You're a cynical beggar,' he said, as if he were commenting on a clinical condition into which he was doing research. 'There really is a German, you know. Karl-Heinz Clausen. Ex-SS. I met him. I got to know him, even to like him.'

'A war criminal?'

'We can't always choose what we have to do, sometimes decisions are made for us,' he said, as if he was repeating a formula he'd lived by himself. He might even have been off guard for a moment, and took a mouthful of gin to cover it.

'He really did tell me about the gold down there. Of course, I don't know whether or not the story he told me is literally true. He's an old man with an obsession. He may not even know himself any more. But I do know that he was in the camp, and that what he told me about what happened did happen.

'He didn't approve of what was going on in the camp, of course – who would? – but it wasn't a death camp. I don't think the guards were motivated by altruism, but they weren't monsters. They probably realised fairly early on in the war that they would eventually be called to account. Of course, there

210

were acts of brutality. There always are in war.

'Clausen realised there was money to be made fairly early on, but he wasn't the only one. People died, or they were killed; their bodies were sometimes carried to a pit where they were burnt. Most of them had nothing, of course, but Clausen told me he went to look at the pit one day before the bulldozer filled it in, and among the ash and half-burned bones he saw the sun gleaming on a little river of gold running out of one of the skulls. Can you imagine that? He said, of course he'd heard of the SS taking the gold from the victims of the death camps, but it had never occurred to him to do it on Alderney before. He told me his father had lost everything before the Nazis came to power, and then he saw his way of getting it all back. Then he realised the senior officers had already confiscated wedding rings, bracelets, sentimental keepsakes those people had smuggled in in their baggage, and kept them – he got his hands on that little hoard when the camp was evacuated. Then he thought, why wait till the people are dead? They used a Ukrainian chap to pull out the fillings, then they melted them, burned away most of the impurities.'

'I wonder what happened to the Ukrainian,' I said.

'He was a Ukrainian, not an Aryan; what do you think happened to him?'

I took the stone bottle of Bols from the ice bucket and poured two more large gins. I drank mine gratefully. But he only seemed amused – a man, I realised, with immense reserves of self-control.

'Have you known Evelyn long?' I asked.

'I met her first when you came to me about your

will. We became . . . friendly. Two years ago, we renewed our acquaintance.'

'And you're her lover?'

He drank a large glass of the Dutch gin. He didn't bat an eyelid – a man who'd done a lot of heavy drinking in his time and who could hold his drink. 'I'm not saying I wouldn't like to be. I could do more for her than Baxter.' He poured some more gin, for both of us. Then he moved his hands in a way that he must have learned in France, or from his French mother. 'But I don't have what she wants.'

'What's that?'

'Money. That's all she's ever wanted. That's all she ever wanted from you, and she left you when you didn't have any more. There's something wonderfully simple about Evelyn.' He leaned forward suddenly. 'You interest me, Breaker. Why risk your neck? Why not turn around and sail away?'

'Because there's money in it for me, and there's money in it for the Brew. I need to turn the wreck over. I need the money.'

'I'm beginning to see what you and Evelyn have in common.'

'And I've got a point to prove. I'd like to prove Baxter wrong.'

'And me, I suppose. Winner take all?' he said mildly.

We went on drinking.

I felt like shit when I woke up. Served me right. I'm puritan enough to take the hangover on the chin. No paracetamol, no hair of the dog. Suffer.

I rolled over where I was sleeping – in the bows, with a covering of heavy sea dew. Christ knows what had made me decide to sleep outside; I couldn't remember. The sky was the green colour of a lacewing fly. Dawn. Hardly enough light to see anything but broad shapes. And my hands, like trembling spiders at the ends of my guernsey-sleeved arms. Bloody freezing, too.

I sat and shivered. I've slept outside so many times I've forgotten how many, sometimes from choice, more often not, and I've never enjoyed it. Not even sleeping on the top of Hedge Hope hill in the Cheviots with the daughter of a publican from Wooler had been worth it. She'd forgotten she was having her period and the horseflies had made a walking boil out of me. Now the deck, flat and cold and hard and old, seemed to have turned me into part of itself. I suppose I'm going to feel like that all the time one day. This seemed premature.

I stood up and stretched and yapped a bit, and peed over the side. Then I went through into the deckhouse. It reeked of drink. In the half-light it was difficult to see what was what. Guilbert was slumped back in his chair, snoring, his mouth a hole torn in his face. He could drink, but I could outdrink him. I'd beaten him. Not much of an achievement but just about the limit of what I could do these days.

Then I heard something. At first it was just growing out of the background, then it was a noise I could feel, a beating sound. I put my hands up to stop it, thinking it had something to do with my hangover, then I realised what it was.

I turned. The small angry bee of the helicopter was coming in low over the sea towards me.

23

Green water again, with blackness in the background. The water was colder than I'd remembered even from the previous day. I crawled over the wreck like a lobster picking over a corpse.

Baxter and Evelyn had flown in in the helicopter, which sat in the middle of the pier, and while Guilbert stayed with me they'd taken the *Venus* out of the bay. Now she circled a quarter of a mile away, engines burbling.

The *Lady Day* was moored fore and aft in the middle of the bay with her engine turning over slowly. I had half a dozen torches working from her generator lying on the sea bottom, the light making green globes between which I moved slowly, a moon-man on the set of *Alien*. Then I crawled under the upturned hull and was able to attach the hawser to the remains of the gunwale of the sunken boat. I found a place where it looked fairly sound and used shackles to make fast a loop of wire which I hooked the hawser to. It took me a full cylinder of oxygen to make sure they were fast: I was a model of paranoid caution.

Then I came to the surface and climbed up between the *Lady Day* and the pier on to the island. My hands were shaking. Getting drunk hadn't been the best preparation for what I was doing. And I was frightened.

I pulled off most of the aqualung equipment I had

on, and stretched, my arms and shoulders aching, my throat feeling raw from the oxygen. I felt light-headed: I'd been breathing too quickly, hyperventilating. Scared.

I went over to the donkey engine. This was the job the Brew should have been doing, and, my God, I thought, I need him here now. The metal was hot to the touch, the sun lancing down. The clearness of dawn had begun to haze over in the heat, and the Hoummet now lay in the bull's-eye of a ring of hazy sea. The horizon was grey with mist, while the sky overhead was deep Alpine blue. What I was doing was hidden from prying eyes as well as if I'd shrouded it in camouflage. The only visible boat apart from the *Lady Day* was the *Venus*.

From the shadow of the helicopter, I kick-started the donkey engine. I hit the gear lever which stood up from the squat bulk of the engine like the gear lever of an old tractor. I'd left a lot of slack in the wire hawser, and it began to uncoil slowly behind me, winding up over the pulley of the engine and depositing itself underneath the helicopter like a coil of excrement.

The hawser tightened slowly. The gear lever moved in my hand as I felt the engine take the strain of the underwater hull. I began to wonder whether the Brew had wedged the steel eyes the engine was chained to firmly enough into the rocks before he cemented them in. then the hawser began to screech over the pulley, and I snapped the lever into neutral and grabbed the brake to hold the hawser. It was taut.

I went to the water's edge. The hawser went into the water at an angle of forty-five degrees. It was thrumming like a guitar string. Sparks of water flicked off it into the vibrating air.

I put on a face mask and clambered down over the rocks into the water, swam down into the glowing lights. Mud smoking up from beneath the hull showed that it had already moved and the water was milky green from silt. I was down there long enough to check whether the shackles were holding before my lungs began to burst and I had to come up.

I crawled up over the rocks, and then had to rest, flippered feet in the water, the sun hot on my shoulders, getting my breath back. The *Venus* circled closer and someone shouted and waved from the deck, and I heard the radio on the *Lady Day* hissing and burping above the noise of the idling donkey engine. Fuck them, I thought, it's my neck, not theirs. It wasn't lack of air I was suffering from, it was fear. I'd seen the torpedo in the torchlight. It might have moved, it might not have done. I couldn't tell whether it had or not.

I got up and stood there looking down into the water where the dark hawser turned pale green. Fish had appeared, nosing around it as if expecting something to happen. The torpedo won't blow up, I told myself. It hasn't done for fifty years; why should it blow up now? It won't blow, it won't blow. Superstitiously, I kept repeating this mantra.

I went up to the donkey engine and gripped the hard plastic knob of the gear lever and jerked it. The note of the engine dropped, and a piercing shriek came from the pulleys as the wire hawser zizzed savagely. Jesus Christ, I thought, remembering a story the Brew had told me of a teenager working on a trawler who'd been trapped by a moving hawser against the side of a cabin and sawn in half like a piece of cheese, what if it snaps? I could imagine a flailing wire taking my head off. The hawser went on creaking away.

But then there was a convulsion in the water, and a huge sucking sound somewhere underneath. Something huge and dark rose up out of the depths like a surfacing submarine. Mud. It popped at the surface, scum boiling across half the area of the bay. The water clouded and darkened against the underwater lights as the hull backed up towards me and broke the surface, and I heard something breaking and tearing, and then the hull rolled over towards me, and there was a foul smell, and a broken sound. A jagged jaw of metal rose out of the water like the gape of a shark. I kicked the brake with my foot, then switched off, so that the hawser held the hull half-rolled towards me, part of the bow clear of the water.

Nothing happened. There was no explosion. The torpedo hadn't gone off, the peroxide hadn't exploded in the water. I'd just earned five thousand pounds in about a minute and a half.

With the prow of the wreck jammed up against the rock, I drank tea made grey with condensed milk, and stared over the side of the *Lady Day* into the bay, where the movement of the ebbing tide was slowly sucking away the clouds of dark mud from the blacker forms beneath. A bloated green eye slowly appeared and began to stare back up at me. Then another. The torches were burning where the water was cloudiest. Slowly, they were beginning to burn a paler green.

I heard an outboard motor, looked up to see the inflatable from the *Venus* bouncing over the waves towards me. Guilbert.

He swung in alongside and threw me a rope, which I looped over the rail. He cut the outboard and climbed aboard.

I said, 'I thought you were going to stay out of range.'

'The danger's over,' he said, drily amused.

'Are they going to be all right out there?'

'Evelyn can handle a boat all right.' He peered over the side. 'How much longer? The water's clearing.'

'So it's clearing. I'm not going back into the water until it's clear enough to read a book down there.'

'You're in charge,' he said, unimpressed.

'Damned right I am.' I strengthened the tea with a shot of Calvados.

'You want to be careful how much of that you drink,' he said. 'It'll be dangerous enough down there without that.'

Christ, I thought. I drank some of the tea. My fingers were trembling.

Above the sounds of wind and sea and the noise of the *Lady Day*'s engine ticking over, I heard music playing on the *Venus*, floating over the water. I looked up from staring into the water to see Evelyn at the wheel a quarter of a mile away, with Baxter leaning on the rail and staring at me. A moment later, I heard the engines race and the *Venus* slid away into the haze. They were looking for calmer waters, so they could drink their cocktails without spilling them.

★ ★ ★

I went in an hour later, and spent a lot of time tying ropes to places on the hull and taking them up to Guilbert so he could attach them to the steel eyes the Brew had set into the concrete. These would hold the wreck firm so that when the tide began to fall it wouldn't move around too much. I used a length of heavy-duty chain and a lot of rope. When I'd finished, the part of the wreck that was clear of the water was festooned with blue and orange polypropylene, wrapped like a fly in a spider's larder.

I waded in from the side of the bay until the mud-clogged water came up to my face mask, then swam down slowly. I turned on my hand torch. The lights made cones of green glass; in the dirty water, the torch beam was a club solid enough to break them with.

A shoal of shrimps fled from me, and small rockfish darted on the bottom. There was a black crater where the wreck had been, and a lot of stuff lying there: crushed boxes, half a small boat, twisted metal shapes.

I swam around in glowing greenness between walls of darkness, digging around in the mess. Mud bled up between my legs. But wherever I turned, whatever I looked at, the torch returned, over and over again, to the blunt phallic tip of the torpedo.

It was more precariously balanced than before; it even seemed to have moved – whether it had or not, I thought it had. I'd once used hydrogen peroxide as a disinfectant on a suppurating burn on my arm, and I could remember the blood bubbling like raspberry fizz at the edges of the wound. Now I could imagine the peroxide beginning to bubble as sea water seeped into it. The mercury fulminate fuses must

have been corroding for half a century. I pictured
the explosion. Boom. They'd see it in France.

I couldn't see a safe. I went back up to the surface,
clambered aboard the *Lady Day*, changed oxygen
cylinders with wrinkled hands, then went back into
the water. The tide was beginning to run rapidly
now. I could hear it rustling past the Hoummet, the
waters around the island beginning to boil and swirl
as the currents began to move. I'd give it another
half an hour, no more. I didn't want to be underwater when the tide started moving the wreck around.
Half an hour. I looked at my watch. Half an hour
and I'd be finished with this. Half an hour to survive.

I'd almost given up, when instead of looking
down, I looked up, and I saw something in the huge
bulk of the hull looming over my head. It was
wedged in a couple of the steel cross-members where
the planking had rotted away. Something poised
above my head like a booby trap, dark against the
black background of the cavernous inside of the hull.

It was a steel cube a metre across, webbed with
seaweed. I used a crowbar to lever it out of the hull
like ripping a giant tooth out of a rotten skull. It
freed itself suddenly and came ballooning down
towards me while I struggled to get out of its way. It
hit the sludge. I stood frozen and waited for something to blow up. But nothing did.

I put the crowbar into the mud beneath it and
began to move the safe across the bottom of the bay.
I think I might have cracked a few vertebrae rolling
it over the mud to where I'd laid a sling of netting on
the sea bottom. I rolled it on to that, then I swam to
the surface.

Aboard the *Lady Day*, I stripped off the wetsuit

and towelled myself down, doing my best to pretend I'd been shaking because of the cold. I tried hard, but I didn't convince myself, let alone Guilbert. My stomach was heaving and my knees were as weak as if I hadn't eaten for a fortnight. I felt light-headed, weird, a half-starved mystic coming down from the mountain. I was breathing like an emphysemic old man.

'I found something,' I told him. 'It's in the net.'

'Good for you, Breaker,' he muttered.

He engaged the gear on the derrick to lift what I'd found out of the water, and the old boat tilted as if she was going to turn over as it took the weight. Together we swung it aboard and let it fall to the deck hard enough to crack some of the planking. Sea water, seaweed, fish spilled out of the net.

'Jesus Christ Almighty,' Guilbert said disbelievingly. 'This is it, this is exactly what Clausen said we'd find.'

I felt no joy, no satisfaction, just relief, the mixture of physical and emotional exhaustion that follows fear. But I could hear the hawser and the ropes holding the wreck to the rock creaking as the running tide shifted it. There were bigger and bigger waves outside the bay, more and more movement inside it. So while Guilbert hacked at the safe with a crowbar I hauled the anchor up and slipped the *Lady Day* into gear, and slowly, very slowly, I steered her out of the bay. She began to pitch and heave in the running tide. Seagulls came clamouring around her.

I could hear Baxter barking at me from the flying bridge of the approaching *Venus*. She stood up in the water as she came powering in towards us.

★ ★ ★

Evelyn clambered on to the *Lady Day*, while I put fenders over the side and made the vessels fast, lashing the *Venus* alongside the *Lady Day*, fifty yards or so below the Hoummet, at anchor. If there was going to be an explosion, I was going to make sure there was enough rock between us and the bay to protect my boat.

Baxter followed, grinning.

'So Clausen wasn't lying, and you were wrong,' he said to me. 'See? See that?' He seemed to have grown an inch or two, in height and in girth. Confidence. Victory. I was wrong. I didn't answer him. I did my best to look as if I knew how to lose.

They crowded round the safe. Guilbert had stripped most of the seaweed away but fifty years in the sea had made it as coarse and layered as an oyster shell. Guilbert had made a gap around the door of the safe; now he was using the crowbar to lever the hinges. They snapped and the door tumbled to the deck.

'There's something in there,' I heard Baxter say, his voice thick with excitement, and he reached into the rusty water with which the safe was filled.

'For God's sake, drain it out first,' I said.

'What do you expect, a booby trap? There's something in there all right. Something I came here for.' He plunged his arm in and started scrabbling around in the safe. But I thought I saw something else move, something that wasn't his arm. Then his body jerked, and he screamed at me.

'Aaahh!'

He ripped his arm out of the water but it kept coming, a length of threshing black rubber, and as Baxter stepped back and stumbled, it followed him and writhed across the deck. Evelyn screamed as blood spurted. I grabbed the crowbar. I knew what it was.

Baxter had fallen against the deckhouse, the conger eel clamped on to his arm. I hauled him down to the deck, then dropped the crowbar across the eel's neck – it had been curled round inside the safe and now it was fastened on Baxter's arm like a leech. A coil of shiny black muscle. I trod on the crowbar, then took the knife from my belt and began to cut through the eel's neck. There's an air sac behind the head, and it barked at me as I cut, a man coughing for life in a hospital ward. I put my foot on Baxter's wrist and used the knife to cut the jaw of the eel away, ripped the teeth out of his flesh while the goggling eye of the eel glared at me, then threw the remains of the head into the sea.

It was one of the biggest I'd seen, and if it had got a better grip on him he might have lost his arm. There must have been four or five feet of the body, as thick in the middle as my thigh, with enough strength to have bitten through a car tyre, let alone Baxter's arm. He'd been lucky it had got mainly flesh, not bone. The headless body was threshing and lashing wildly in the scuppers. But I've seen a severed head bite the nose of an inquisitive dog, and conger eel steaks leap out of the frying pan. I kicked it over the side.

Baxter was lying with his shoulders in the scuppers, face drained of colour.

'Bastard,' he said. He rocked with pain, his bleeding arm locked between his knees.

I squatted down and looked at his arm.

Evelyn brought the first-aid box from the wheel-house, and I used a bandage and a length of wood to make a tourniquet, then tipped TCP over the wound while Baxter stared dully at me. His arm had both swelled and shrunk so that it looked deformed, a flap of flesh the size of a wallet lying back to show a piece of whitish bone rinsed with sea water and blood.

He tried to sit up. I wound gauze and lint around his arm and held it in place with surgical tape, taping down the ripped-open flesh. He looked confused, his face swollen around the eyes. He was hard to recognise as the man who'd hired me. He grunted as if he had something wrong with his stomach.

'I need something for the pain,' he said.

'Whisky, paracetamol. But we'd better get you back to a hospital,' I said. 'This needs stitches.'

'I can do the stitching,' Evelyn said. I looked up at her. 'I've stitched you up often enough, Sam. There's a full first-aid kit on the *Venus*. Some butterfly stitches will probably do it, and we have antibiotics if we need them.'

'What about the gold?' Baxter asked.

'There isn't any gold,' I said. 'There's nothing in there but eel shit and mud.'

'He's right, there's nothing in there,' Guilbert said. He put a foot against the safe and tipped it over. Water vomited out of it, staining the planking the colour of blood. He crouched down and ran his fingers through the muck.

'There's nothing there,' he said. 'There's really nothing there.'

'And there's nothing else in the water either. Even if there is, you can get someone else to look for it,' I said. I rubbed my neck. Immersion in the cold sea water was making it ache. I was relieved but I wasn't happy. I'd made some money, but not finding the gold had cost me – and the Brew – the bonus.

24

Later, I left the *Lady Day* and crossed over to the *Venus*. I couldn't see Guilbert, or Evelyn, but Baxter was in the cockpit. I felt irritable; tension and fear had worn away most of the self-control I had.

Baxter didn't look any better than he had the last time I'd seen him. He looked feverish and crumpled, an old man suddenly; the cigar butt plugged into his mouth looked like a handle to lift him with. The creases in his jowls were deep trenches full of shadow. His bandaged arm lay in front of him on the table like a club. He'd been drinking, a lot, and alcohol didn't go too well with whatever else he'd had – something for the pain, and something to make him buzz too, I guessed; his red-rimmed eyes glimmered feverishly. He looked up at me as if he'd never seen me before.

'What do you want?' Baxter asked.

'I want my money.'

'You think you've earned it?'

'Yes, I've earned it.'

'It was pretty easy when it came to it,' he sneered. 'All that worrying for nothing, hey? No gold, but no big bangs either.'

'That wreck's an armed bomb; I must have been out of my skull to go anywhere near it. I'm going back to Guernsey, and I'm going to tell Trinity House what state it's in. I wouldn't go any nearer the Hoummet than you are now, if I were you.'

'Chicken, hey?'

I grinned at him. I'd have liked him to start something; I'd spent the last hour lying in my bunk thinking how close I'd come to blowing myself to pieces because of his fantasies about underwater treasure. I batted his cigar smoke away from my face. I was ready for a fight.

'Baxter, I want my money,' I said. 'If you don't make a move to get it for me in the next thirty seconds, I'll break up your state room, then I'll break up your boat. Then I'll start on you.'

Baxter's forehead wrinkled. He looked surprised, as if he'd misunderstood me before now.

'Give him the money,' Evelyn said from the door behind me; I hadn't heard her arrive.

I thought for a moment even then he wasn't going to, but he struggled to his feet and went through into the state room. I heard him moving around, hampered by his wounded arm. He unlocked and opened a drawer and came back with a bundle of notes the size of a Swiss roll. He trapped the roll on the table with his elbow and peeled off notes with the other hand.

'Five thousand pounds, as we agreed. One thousand for hiring your boat, four thousand pounds for turning the wreck.' I took the money. He said, 'Now I'm going north, going to visit Herr Clausen in his nursing-home. Check his information.'

'And pay out more money?' I said.

He didn't like that. He didn't like anything I said; he never had. His lips curled back from his teeth.

'Then I'm going to get someone else to do the diving, someone who doesn't chicken out when it gets tough.'

'Good luck,' I said. 'Try my wife.'

I didn't count the money. I just nodded to him and left.

Evelyn grabbed me as I walked past her.

'I want you to come back with me, Sam,' she whispered fiercely into my ear.

'With Baxter? You're joking.'

'No, without him.'

'Forget it,' I said, and went on past her without looking at her, and crossed over to the *Lady Day*. That was it. I was finished with them.

I put my money into the rucksack under my bunk, then put the gun in on top of it. Then I used the radio to put a call through to the Princess Elizabeth Hospital. It wasn't good news. The Brew's condition was worse, not better; they were flying a brain surgeon over to the Island, but it sounded as if the Brew was likely to die anyway. I sat there in the wheelhouse staring at the radio and trying not to think. Trying to fight off the feeling that the Brew was one of the human beings I really cared about, and that there wasn't a damned thing I could do to help him.

I thought about having another drink, then thought I wouldn't. My arms ached, my head ached, and I'd forgotten how exhausting it was working underwater. I sat in the wheelhouse and waited for the weather forecast, listening to the gulls clamouring on the Hoummet. The forecast said the storm in the Atlantic was blowing itself out, but the remains of it would arrive the next day, bringing heavy seas. I'd turned the wreck over just in time.

I cast off and got under way, and by the time I

remembered I still had the safe aboard I was well clear of the *Venus*. But all I'd done was leave without telling them, taking an empty safe with me. And as I cleared the Hoummet, and the *Venus* sank out of sight behind the shoulder of rock, I caught sight of Evelyn standing on the flying bridge. She was staring after me, and I think she waved at me as if trying to get me to turn round. I didn't wave back.

As the *Lady Day* lumbered through the haze and the swell, I looked again at the safe where it lay on the deck. It wasn't much of a safe. It was heavy enough, but it seemed to be made out of tin. Wartime rubbish. I poked around it for a while, even thought of throwing it over the side, but then I gave up and made some coffee. I sat in the wheelhouse and drank it.

Then I went below, and took out the rucksack. I took four thousand pounds of the money Baxter had given me, put it in an envelope, wrote the Brew's name on the front, and locked it in the small lockable drawer in the deckhouse. Then I put a Betty Roche tape on the tape-player. I think it was a Jerome Kern song. The music filled the air, above the sound of the engines and the sea. Her voice was filled with pain.

When I got back to St Sampson's I was tired, but I made myself tidy up the mess on the decks – I'd left it, of course, while the Brew would have done it straight away. The safe lay tipped over in the slurry that had come out of it, among the shells and the dead fish and the net and the seaweed. Where the sea water hadn't dried, it was like a bloodstain on the planks. I made it all shipshape, shovelled the mess on the deck into the scuppers, watched it stream away into the harbour.

I felt listless, worn out by too much tension, too much drinking over the last week, but I was hungry, and I walked along to the Southside Café for eggs, bacon, beans and chips. Then, almost as an after-thought, I used the pay phone and dialled Jenny Mahy's number. Unfinished business – not that it mattered much now.

She was a long time coming to the phone. She sounded out of breath.

'I'm sorry. I was bathing Ray.'

'Did Lizzie find out anything?'

'I said I wasn't going to tell you.'

'You said you weren't even going to ask her.'

'Yes, I did say that. And I shouldn't have asked her really.' She was silent for a moment. I heard her saying something, to Ray, I supposed.

'What's the answer?' I asked.

Her voice dropped, as if someone were listening in.

'The Land Use Committee, the one chaired by Milliner, has been looking into land use in the St Sampson's area. It probably involves your land. That's all she knows.'

'And they've just recommended that some land here is designated as building land?'

'It seems as if they have,' she said cautiously. 'I'm in a hurry, Sam. Do you mind?'

'My land, right?' She didn't answer. 'And you don't know who's trying to buy it from me? Is it Milliner?' Still no answer. 'Did you find out who Milliner's having an affair with?'

'Some Jersey woman, no one I've heard of. But haven't you heard?' she said, her voice metallic with surprise.

'Heard what?'

'Milliner's dead.'

'What?'

'He killed himself yesterday. Just before the receivers were called in.'

'Are you sure?'

'Of course I'm sure. They tried to find his wife, but she didn't leave a forwarding address when she went to Spain. Financially, he'd been living on borrowed time for the last year. She must have got sick of it.'

'Where did she get the money to go to Spain?' I wondered out loud.

'She must have had some money put away.'

'There isn't a chance anyone killed him, is there?'

'Not a chance. He took an overdose and left a note. One of his children found him.'

'I'll buy you lunch next time,' I said, and rang off. Alarm bells should have been ringing by then – but I was too tired. I just couldn't make out the significance of it. I couldn't fit any of them into the puzzle any more.

I went back to the *Lady Day*, where someone had put an envelope in the wheelhouse. I opened it. It contained faxed photocopies from Nathe Bernstein of newspaper articles from an English-language paper published on the Riviera two years ago. They were about Theo Bradley.

I read them, had a drink, then went to lie down.

I woke instantly. Something had disturbed me. Early

morning. Sunlight burned almost horizontally through the open port.

Someone was moving on the deck. Quietly, as quietly as a cat, but I could still hear them. I lay there, coming round slowly, feeling exhaustion drain gradually out of my limbs. It had been a hard day the day before: nothing tires the body like fear.

I pulled on some shorts, eased myself through the cabin door. My fists were bunched as I stepped around the corner. Someone was in the deckhouse.

Evelyn.

'What the hell are you doing here?'

'I've got to see you.'

'What about?'

'I want to hire your boat.'

'Oh Jesus, don't give me that!' I said. I yawned and stretched, unclenched a fist. 'I've just got rid of that bastard Baxter. Now I've got you. Come off it. Leave me in peace. Go back to the *Venus*.'

'I can't. I brought the *Venus* back from the Hoummet, but that's the last time. I intercepted a call from the company he's hiring it from the other day. They want it back.'

'He told me he owned it,' I said, to fill up a space in the air.

'He doesn't own a damned thing,' she said, with the contempt of someone who'd once owned a lot of things. 'He's in hock up to the eyeballs. That's why he put everything into Clausen's story – he needed it to be true. And I've had enough. I'm getting out while I can.'

'Where is he?'

'Richard flew him in the helicopter to Cherbourg to get his arm stitched up properly. After that, they're going to Holland to look for Clausen. And I'm going to leave the Island.'

I'd never seen her look so tense. With the white-framed sunglasses, scarlet lipstick, a white blouse and tight pants, she looked magnificent, the sort of woman I think I'd just been dreaming about. What I hadn't been expecting was the state she was in.

'You're going to leave?'

'For good. It's over with me and George. I want to get away from him. I'm going back to his house, I'm going to get my things, get a few things I've got coming to me, then I'm getting out.'

'Where to?'

'France. I want you to take me to France.'

'Balls,' I said.

'I'll pay you two hundred.'

'You could fly there for a fraction of that.'

'Not with the luggage I want to take with me. And I'm paying you to keep your mouth shut. I want you to forget you've ever taken me anywhere, that you've ever seen me since the Hoummet. I don't want George coming after me.'

'Two hundred,' I said; if I gave most of my share to the Brew, I would need the money. 'Plus diesel?'

'It's a lot of money,' she said. 'I'm offering you two hundred pounds for an old boat, and someone who probably isn't the world's greatest navigator. How much will the diesel come to?'

I picked a figure out of the air. 'Thirty quid?'

'All right. Come back to the house with me, and you can help me pack.'

'I'd rather have breakfast and go for a swim,' I said. 'On my own.'

She smiled thinly, her fingers pulling at the halter

neck of the shirt she was wearing. I caught a glimpse of her nipple through the thin cloth. 'Bloody typical, isn't it? When I've got rid of George, I've only got you to fall back on.'

But I went with her, as I later realised she knew I would.

I washed and dressed, checked over the *Lady Day*, closed the doors, and, at the last moment, picked up the rucksack from under the bunk. Banknotes, and that reassuring weight in the bottom.

Up on the harbourside, I climbed again into the passenger seat of the Jaguar. She eased into the usual traffic jam and let the speed drop. The air-conditioning whispered. She lit a cigarette. She swerved out past a bus, accelerated smoothly up the wrong side of the road, forced her way back into the traffic queue again.

'Milliner's dead,' I said.

'Dead?'

'Took an overdose. Suicide. You knew him, didn't you?'

'I told you, he was a friend of George's.' She shook her head. 'I didn't like him, but I'm sorry he's dead.'

'There was a time when I thought you were having an affair with him.'

'With who? Milliner?' She snorted with laughter.

'I thought you were using him to get at information held by the Land Use Committee.'

'I can't imagine why.'

'Perhaps he was going to be your way out of Guernsey, the way you used Baxter to get out of Monaco.'

'That was different. Baxter turned out to be a bastard who likes degrading women, but I had to get out of Monaco, and I didn't know then what he was like. I was in trouble and I was in debt. And I was ill. Really quite ill. George was my way out. I've slept with him, and now it's come down to it, he's done his best to leave me with nothing. You know George is only a millionaire on paper?' I did my best to look surprised. 'You only got your money because he was afraid of you. And I think if that conger eel hadn't bitten him, he'd have seen you off the boat with his shotgun. The jewellery he gave me is false, the pictures on the walls of his house are fakes, the furniture is repro. He doesn't own the house any more, the bank does. He doesn't even own the Jaguar.'

I was beginning to think I'd been misreading her. Perhaps she really had stayed with him because she liked him; perhaps she'd always known he wasn't worth staying with for his money. But how much lying had she done?

She wasn't looking at me when she said, 'Why are you angry with me, Sam?'

I said, 'You knew about the warheads on the torpedoes, and the peroxide, and you wanted me to dive on the wreck. You didn't tell me about the danger.'

'I would have done before you made the dive. But I knew you'd be all right, Sam. You're the best.' I didn't say anything. And she said. 'He won't be back for at least two days.'

She seemed to be waiting for me to say something, but I didn't; it was as if she was dangling something in front of me, waiting for me to react. I waited, I didn't react.

The Jaguar had stopped at some traffic lights. It was ridiculous, but for a moment I thought of getting out. I even put my hand on the door handle. I could have opened the door and stepped out, walked up the hill to a café I knew, and had breakfast. Eaten well, then found a few friends and gone fishing. Or gone to see the Brew. Or gone to see if I could apologise to Anton. Or gone to do any damned thing.

But I didn't. I stayed in the car.

25

She slid the Jaguar into the garage alongside the off-road vehicle and the red Mercedes with the broken sidelight, while I stood in the starfish shadows of the palm trees, clutching my rucksack.

'Who's is the Merc?' I asked as she closed the garage doors. 'I thought it belonged to Henry Milliner.'

'He ran out of money. George called the car in to settle a debt – Milliner owed him some money. George has his finger in all kinds of deals. I don't understand what he's up to half the time. I don't suppose he does either.'

'There isn't anyone else in the house, is there?'

'No, there isn't. I told you, George and Richard won't be back for days. By then, you and I will be sailing down the French coast in the *Lady Day*.'

She'd never spent a night on the *Lady Day*; I didn't mind shifting her and her luggage over to France, but sharing my boat with her would be too intimate. The *Lady Day* was mine. My home.

'I didn't know you wanted to move in with me. I thought you said you wanted me to take you to France.'

The Dobermanns grumbled at me through the wire. We walked up the drive, past the swimming-pool into the house through the french windows. The large living-room, furnished in off-white and ivory, smelt of stale cigar smoke.

I threw the rucksack down behind the sofa. I saw her looking at it and said, 'That's my bank account. I feel safer if I have it with me. I don't trust banks.'

'Are you crazy, Sam? Nobody robs banks any more.'

'Not from the outside,' I said. 'I can't leave money on the *Lady Day* because there's no way of locking it up.'

She went through to the kitchen, came out with a bottle of vintage champagne. She held it up for me to see.

'This stuff costs a couple of hundred pounds a bottle. George has been saving it for something. I'm going to drink it. I'm going to drink all his bloody champagne before I leave. And if I can't I'll put it in the bath and wash my hair in it.'

I opened the bottle and poured two glasses. She sipped hers while I drank one glass as if it were medicine, then took my time over a second. Champagne isn't bad at that time of the morning, I decided, not bad at all.

'Do you want breakfast?'

'Not particularly.'

'What do you want to do?'

'I want to load your stuff into the car, take it to the *Lady Day*, and take you to France. Then I want you to pay me.'

'You're still angry, then?'

'I'm not angry.'

'You've been angry all your life.'

There wasn't any mileage in this: I wasn't there to be psychoanalysed.

'Have you got much stuff?' I asked.

'Several suitcases, but I have to pack.'

'Then you'd better get on with it.'

She didn't like that; I think she wanted me to be pliable, to fall for her, to admit how charming and attractive she was. I didn't feel like doing any of those things. I walked round the big living-room instead, went into the other downstairs rooms. There was a lot of the furniture covered in ivory leather that Baxter seemed to go for – he probably got it in some insurance scam – and big ivory curtains, and bone-coloured fitted carpets, and some rosewood furniture inlaid with mother of pearl that comes from Thailand or somewhere. The wallpaper seemed to be raw grey silk. The metal banister that followed the curving, open-plan staircase was gold-plated. I followed it upstairs, the metal slimy under my fingers. She watched me.

'Where are you going?'

'I'm just looking round.' She didn't stop me.

The first time I'd been to that house I'd felt as if I was being watched. I was still uncomfortable, as if the winking magic eye of the burglar alarm up in the corner of the room had a human eye behind it. But I didn't find anybody. What I did find were four upstairs bedrooms furnished in tones of off-white and grey, cream, silver and mushroom soup, with en suite bathrooms for each and a solarium on the roof with electronically operated windows and shutters. In the master bedroom there was a circular bed large enough to have taken the chorus line from 'Fame', if you'd wanted them all there at once. I could feel horny just looking at it.

I went back downstairs. She was still watching me.

'There really isn't anybody else here, you know. Don't you trust me?'

241

'I was just looking round.'

'I'd better go and pack,' she said. But she didn't.
She poured another glass of the arm-and-a-leg champagne and drank that.

'We'd better get on with it,' I said. 'From now on
our relationship had better be professional, Evelyn.
Go and pack your things.'

'I lied about what happened when I left you in the
States,' she said suddenly. 'When you hurt your
neck, when you were unconscious. I sat by your bed
for a whole day.'

'Oh good,' I said. 'I was out for a fortnight and
you waited for a whole day.'

She got up, walked towards the french windows
and stood against the light. A beautiful clean-limbed
shape. The reflected light from the pool played
around her like lightning on a hilltop.

When she spoke, I didn't hear her the first time –
or perhaps I did and didn't believe it – so she
repeated it.

'I was pregnant.'

'Pregnant?'

I felt like a sap. Mouth open. I was gawping just as
much as when she'd walked into me nude. 'You
can't have been pregnant. I was using condoms –
people with our kind of lifestyles always did. Of
course, they don't always work, but . . .'

'It wasn't your child,' she said. 'It was Theo's.'

I looked at her standing at the window with her
back to me. I looked down at the glass I was
holding. I looked at my hands, which seemed to
belong to somebody else. The water of the
swimming-pool made liquid shadows on the ceiling

of the sun-flooded room. It was like being in a fish tank. I tipped some orange juice into my glass of champagne and swigged that.

Theo.

Theo Bradley was a short, weedy guy who must have been thirty-five or so but who still looked like a college kid. He wore college-kid clothes, he wore John Lennon glasses, he had a Stephen Spielberg haircut, and he had the spotty complexion of a chocolate-eating teenager. But he had brains. A financial whizz-kid. Evelyn had brought him in, and he'd transformed the finances of my stunting firm. Until he'd run off with my goddamned money. I could have broken him over my knee; but perhaps that was his appeal, that I could have done.

'That bastard ruined me,' I said.

'He ruined me too,' she said.

There wasn't anything I could say to that. I grabbed some more of the champagne. Straight this time, without the orange juice.

'Well,' I said. 'What am I supposed to say?'

'You don't have to say anything.' Still with her back to me.

'So you had sex with Theo. Okay. Big news. You got me here to tell me that. I fooled around too, Evelyn. I had a few women here and there.'

'You had hundreds.'

'Dozens,' I said. It seemed like a joke to me.

'What's so funny?'

'I was thinking about our marriage. What fun it was. The year before I broke my neck, a friend of mine and I went to bed with four girls. He got herpes and I didn't. Then he crashed a plane into a field in

Normandy and killed himself. I think about the virus sometimes. Spreading across France like a slime mould.'

'You've always been the same, Sam. Every time I try to say something serious, you tell me a silly bloody story.'

'So do you,' I said. 'Theo Bradley, hey? Good old Theo.'

'You suspected it. You said so.'

'Well, all right, I suspected it. I even suspected, when I was feeling particularly unpleasant, you might have been behind his move on my money. We hadn't been getting on for a while. I thought you might have been sick of me, might have wanted to get your share. After all, you weren't really getting on in Hollywood, were you? Only as part of me and my business. I thought you might have got Theo to embezzle the money and then gone to join him in Monaco.'

'That's not what happened,' she said. She turned and came to sit opposite me again. She put her hands on her knees and showed me a heart-shaped face of childlike innocence. 'I'm so ashamed,' she said. 'This isn't easy for me, Sam. This is my life I'm talking about, my whole life. You see, you didn't want a child . . .'

I hadn't. With my lifestyle it would have been ridiculous. I didn't want to be tied. I didn't think she had either.

'Theo and I made love only a few times, and I was fond of him. But I didn't expect it to happen. The day after you hurt yourself, the pregnancy was confirmed. The day after that, I found out where Theo had gone and I went after him.' Her face crumpled with pain. 'They'd just said you weren't going to come round, Sam. I had no choice. Stay with you, and watch you die. Or go with Theo, the father of my child.'

'No contest,' I said.

'Don't make fun of me.'

'I'm not.'

'I didn't know then that he'd taken the money. He was just away in Europe on vacation. I found out later it wasn't until you'd been in hospital for two or three weeks and the bills started piling up that anyone realised what had happened. I had a key to his flat, and when I went there I found enough in his papers to tell me he'd gone to Monaco. I went after him, impulsively, just like that. I found him, but not for several weeks – he'd been on a cruise in the Mediterranean, with a card school. He'd lost more money in three weeks than we'd made in three years. And when he got back from losing his money at poker, he went straight into the casinos to lose the rest. But it was my child, and he was the father,' she added simply. 'I'd had an abortion when I was fifteen, and my insides were all messed up. I didn't think I stood a hope in hell of conceiving, and when it happened I thought it was the best thing ever to happen to me. The only problem was that the baby wasn't yours.'

She was looking at me in surprise, and I realised I'd made a sound, something like a snort of laughter. Me, a father. I shook my head dismissively; it was a bloody silly idea.

'Then Theo disappeared,' she said. 'And I was alone. I had the film script, which I'd taken with me, but I hadn't got any money. And I'd started to bleed. I was terrified I was going to lose the baby. Then I met George.'

'I get it,' I said. 'The sugar daddy.'

Her face was crumpled with real pain. 'Don't make fun of me, Sam. I couldn't bear it.'

'I'm not making fun of you. I don't know what the hell I'm doing, but I'm not making fun of you.'

'I had to go into hospital. While I was there, George looked after me. The bills were mounting up and up – hotel bills, medical bills. Theo had disappeared. George even offered me a job. And the night he did, I lost the baby. And then I realised I'd never have children.'

'This isn't the script you were trying to sell in Monaco, is it?'

'It's true, Sam, all of it!'

'But it's very, very neat.' I drank some champagne, then regretted that; I needed to think clearly. 'Did you know that six months after you say Theo disappeared they dragged his body out of the sea? They identified him by his dental work.'

She nodded her head vigorously. 'That's right. It was only later I found out that he hadn't just disappeared, that he'd actually killed himself.'

'Open verdict,' I said. 'Probable cause of death, something that disagreed with him. But hard to tell. He'd been in the water too long for them to be sure. Why not suicide? Wouldn't you? He'd gone to Monaco and played the tables. The report that turned up in the newspapers said he must have lost a million or so inside two months.'

'How did you find out about Theo?' she asked.

'Someone sent me some cuttings.'

'Who?'

'Someone I know. Bernstein.'

I couldn't remember whether she'd met Nathe Bernstein or not. Had she ever used Links herself? I should have asked Nathe if she'd contacted him. But I hadn't.

'Poor Theo.'

'Yeah. Poor Theo,' I said.

She was shivering. 'The last time I saw him he was standing at a roulette table throwing chips on to the baize. He was a lousy gambler.'

'Did you ever take an English-language newspaper when you were in Monaco?'

'I can't remember. Why?'

'I'm just wondering when you'd have known that Theo was dead.'

'I never read the newspapers anyway.' She sighed. 'Poor Theo. I thought he'd abandoned me. Instead of that . . .'

Her face was a ruin of emotions. I reached out to touch her but she pulled away from me.

'He abandoned you the way I abandoned you,' I said sarcastically.

'No. The way I abandoned you.'

So that was it. Confession time. She'd left me because she was carrying someone else's baby.

She was sitting on the sofa crying into a handkerchief. I stood and watched her. It was like watching a bad drama on television, but I thought I'd better do something. I went over to her, sat down next to her and put my arm round her. She slumped over on me. More tears.

'It's nothing to cry about,' I said. She straightened up, wiped her eyes, blew her nose.

'You're right,' she said. She stood up. 'I'm going to go and pack. All right?'

'It's all right with me.'

I watched her go up the staircase, with the lightness of step of someone who'd just got something off their chest. She danced up the steps. I could watch her for hours. I could watch her do anything – walking, dancing, swimming . . . The thoughts began to come. I still fancied her. I always would. I stood up too. I thought of going up after her, then thought I wouldn't. Life was too bloody complicated already. I'd take the two hundred quid. I'd take her to France. That really would be much simpler. But I still felt pretty sick. I'd been cuckolded by a corpse, among other things. And college-kid Theo had impregnated my wife.

While she went upstairs I went out through the french windows to the pool. The sun beat down. Nathe Bernstein owned a David Hockney canvas of a naked man in a swimming-pool. No one had ever looked properly at a swimming-pool until Hockney started to paint them. The underwater lights were on even in the sunlight, and in my mind's eye I could see a naked body in the water, caught in the ripples like a fish in a net. Her? Or me?

Perhaps this really was all there was to it, with Guilbert and Baxter on their way to Holland, with Evelyn wanting to explain her past so that she – or we – could sort it out. But my judgement was clouded: too much feeling. Too much past.

I stood there. I could smell cut grass, and the chemical smell from the swimming-pool. I drank the champagne. I heard a window open above, and looked up. She was standing on the balcony of the master bedroom which overlooked the pool, wearing some kind of wrap.

'Will you come up here a minute?' she called down. 'I can't get the wardrobe drawer open. I think the bastard has locked up my best clothes so I can't get at them.'

'What do you want me to do?'

'Smash the lock.'

'All right.'

I went in through the french windows, through the living-room into the kitchen, picked a selection of utensils I could use as blunt instruments, and went up the stairs, thinking about locks, innocently. Into the bedroom. Saw what must have been a walk-in wardrobe with sliding doors. It wasn't locked.

I turned round.

Her wrap was open. She wasn't wearing anything underneath. My eyes drooled down her. Throat, cleavage, navel, vulva. Whether I thought getting involved with her was a good idea or not was already academic.

Her arms snaked up round my neck.

'There's another reason I wanted you here, rather than back on your boat,' she said.

'What's that?'

'Your bunk on the *Lady Day* is within a few yards of men walking their dogs and women walking their children. What I have in mind for you, they'll hear you in France.'

26

Hours later, I stood on the balcony looking down, this time at a real body in the pool. Evelyn. She swam unhurriedly, length after length. The underwater lights fought the glare from the sun. Her body was a pattern of light and shade, of shadow and gleaming highlights. Length after length after length. I stood and watched her.

We'd been making love for most of the day. On a towel by the side of the bed there were four used condoms, lying side by side like fish thrown up on a riverbank. 'Guernsey whiting', the locals called them, when they saw them floating in the harbour. I hadn't made love like that for a long, long time. I felt, as they say, like a million dollars.

She climbed out of the pool suddenly, in a single movement, bringing a great wave of water out with her, stood for a moment on the pool's edge, as sleek and naked as a seal, breasts and shoulders heaving with the effort, sweeping the water from her limbs with her hands, then looked up at me. The dark blue swimming-goggles she wore made her look like something inhuman. Her blond hair was black with water, slicked back tightly over her skull. A blond, beautiful death's head.

She smiled at me. Walked away and disappeared from sight, the water dripping from her body leaving scribbles on the paving-stones. I tried to make sense of them, but couldn't. I was holding a glass of whisky she'd brought me. Lagavulin in a big crystal glass which must have held a pint. She'd served it with the smoked salmon and scrambled eggs we'd eaten a couple of hours earlier, the right drink for that menu.

It was a single Islay malt, but not one I was familiar with. I nosed it cautiously, sipped it. Standing there with the sun on me, and the breeze cooling my skin, I felt tired suddenly. The champagne catching up with me perhaps. Or the whisky. Instead of drinking it, I went through into the bathroom and poured it into the hand basin: I didn't want to get drunk. If she'd had too much champagne to drive the Jaguar back to St Sampson's, I'd have to. And then I'd have to be sober enough to steer the *Lady Day*. Otherwise we'd be spending another night here.

I went back into the bedroom and lay down on the big double bed. Light flooded in from the wide windows, against which ivory curtains moved gently in the draught.

The door was open. I heard her padding up the stairs. She came into the room. She was towelling herself down, and shivered in the breeze from the window, goose pimples prickling on her arm. She snuggled next to me, her skin cool and prickly, then warm, and as smooth as the gold I'd been diving for. She poured some more whisky from the bottle into my glass.

'Lagavulin,' she said. I tasted it again. Certainly a stronger flavour than Springbank. 'Nice?' she asked. I didn't know. It contained all kinds of tastes, some of them delicate, some of them overpoweringly strong, and not always pleasant. Caramel, peat, spring water, TCP. And something else I couldn't place. An encyclopaedia of tastes. Some I hadn't expected, but that could have been the hungover taste in my mouth. I was beginning to wonder whether I liked it at all.

'Too strong a taste. Anyway, I've been drinking too much lately. I'm going to lay off it for a while.'

She took the glass from me, put it down on the bedside table, and said, 'You didn't believe us, did you? We didn't find any gold, but we found the safe. And you thought we'd made the whole thing up.'

'Not the whole thing. What I couldn't understand was, what was the point of such a complex con? I still don't understand it.'

'That's because it isn't a con, it never was. I know Richard's taken more money from George than he should have done, but the story's true. You weren't wasting your time risking your neck, you know. We believed there was gold there.' She rubbed her body gently against me. 'We've got days together, Sam. And we've always been good together. The older you get the more you realise that's important. I've never had another man like you.'

She rolled over on to her back alongside me, and I leaned over her and put my head on her breasts; I could smell a faint tang of the chlorine from the swimming-pool. I looked down at her body, looked at the glimmer of pubic hair, and at the horizontal scar along the edge of the hair, above her mound of Venus. A thin and beautiful scar, a very expensive scar. No more than a slit in an envelope. A hysterectomy scar.

'Have you ever lied to me, Evelyn?'

'Not recently,' she said, amused and not even

surprised by what I'd said. Her stomach moved gently under me.

I knew she had. But how much? Was it true that if she'd lied about one thing she might have lied about others? I kissed the thin, puckered lips of the scar, and her fingers moved down to touch it.

'I had it done after I lost the child,' she murmured. 'No more children for us.'

I was beginning to feel rough, as if the diving, the love-making, had tired me more than I'd thought. I lay back. Her hand strayed down my body, her fingernails picked at loose skin between my legs. I thought about her. I'd married her for her looks, and for her love-making, and for her ambition: a tough-minded English girl making her way in the ruthless world of the West Coast of California in that miraculous year, when I'd been making money, when I was being paid a fortune for doing something I liked. When everything seemed easy.

My penis stiffened. I breathed in deeply. Oh Jesus.

'And you're still going to tell me that you and Guilbert really spoke to a man called Clausen, who was an SS guard in the camp on Alderney?'

'Yes,' she said. 'It's true. All of it.' She kissed me. 'I want you to keep it up inside me for hours. Whisky keeps you hard, doesn't it?'

'Sometimes.'

'Then you'd better have some more,' she said. I let her tip some of the Lagavulin into my mouth. Not much, but enough. I felt strange. Light-headed. Drunk, perhaps. Worn out too.

She put a hand down and felt my cock. It was hard by now. And sore.

But I didn't feel like doing it any more. Too tired. I have the constitution of a horse but I was feeling rough. The aches in my muscles caused by physical labour, by healing bruises, were beginning to reawaken. Too much tension, and anger. Too much fear.

Evelyn played around with me for a few minutes but even she didn't seem that interested. And I wasn't. I'd been thinking about the wreck for so long, other thoughts hadn't had much of a chance to develop. But now they were coming back. That conger eel in the safe. Theo after all that time in the sea. The wreck roped against the rock, waiting for someone to come and make it safe.

'I ought to contact Trinity House, or the States,' I said. 'There's a storm coming. If that wreck moves around too much . . .'

'It won't move around in the bay,' she said. 'Relax.'

I lay back on the pillow and stared at the white-painted ceiling. Too much drink. Far too much drink. My head felt heavy. The ceiling was beginning to crawl around in front of my eyes, like milk curdling in a glass.

'I think I'm going to have to go to sleep,' I said. 'I'll be all right after a few minutes.'

'I'll wake you,' she promised.

'Ten minutes, no more.'

'I promise I'll wake you, darling,' she said. 'Trust me.'

Those were the last words I heard for a while: comforting, motherly words. They eased me into the dark.

I struggled up out of some nightmare. Some darkness. I lay there, watching the ceiling revolve slowly
around my head.

Something had woken me; I'd no idea what. I
thought back, reached back into my memory. There
were dreams there. Nightmares. I'd dreamed I was
back on the Hoummet. Underwater. Drowning.

There was something wrong.

I went to get up but, as I moved, nausea went
through me. I came upright, eyes shut, and tried to
get out of bed. My hangovers must have been getting
worse. So much worse that my legs went from under
me. I fell to my knees. Fell forward. I must have
blacked out. Not for long, just for long enough for
the floor to spiral round a couple of times and come
up and slam me in the face.

When I got myself upright again, I'd split something in my mouth and I could taste blood. I had to
make the bathroom. I half crawled across to it,
butted the door open with my head, dragged myself
upright, vomited into the wash basin and then peed
into the lavatory bowl. I made a mess of things. I
found I was wearing my trousers. I couldn't button
them up properly and I couldn't remember putting
them on.

I struggled upright and reached for the bathroom
cabinet. I saw my face in the mirror on the cabinet
door. I stood in the half-gloom and peered at my
face in the mirror. There was something wrong with
it. I couldn't work out what. I looked bruised. Or
smeared with lipstick. Or something.

I groped for a light and couldn't find one, then
started running the tap. Water gushed in the basin
and swirled up over my wrists. Something dark

stained the water. Coming out of whatever was soaking the woollen sleeves of the shirt I was wearing. My shirt, but unbuttoned, and clinging to me like wet seaweed to an exposed rock. As dark as black coffee running out of a coffee pot. I felt the hairs standing up on my spine.

I found the light switch. What was running into the water was the same as what was on my face. Blood.

I grabbed a hand towel and wiped the blood from my face – or tried to; I was covered with the stuff. The sleeves of the shirt were as heavy with liquid as if I'd been trailing them in the sea. Drooping with it. But then I realised it wasn't my blood.

I grabbed a bottle of aspirin from the cabinet and took four of them. Swallowed a mouthful of tap water, threw it up, with the pills foaming in the juice, swallowed again. I drank more water, grabbed the shower nozzle from the bath taps, turned it on and hung my head over the basin. The water helped but my head throbbed as if it was fractured, and my tongue felt like a piece of raw liver. I've had hangovers before, but not like that.

I drank more water, pulled myself upright. I steadied myself against the basin and pushed the bathroom door open and looked back into the bedroom. In my crazed state, I still expected to see Evelyn there waiting for me.

But the bed was empty. The duvet thrown back, pillows on the floor. A bottle of yellow pills had been thrown across the bed and the bedside table. The bottom sheet was mashed down and stained; blood trailed out of the bed. I'd left a trail of it across the ivory carpet like a badly shot grizzly bear across snow.

Evelyn's blood? Had I killed her? I couldn't remember. I couldn't remember going to bed and I couldn't remember going to sleep. I couldn't remember putting on the clothes I was wearing. I couldn't remember a damned thing. I could hardly remember who I was.

The light was grey gel, Vaseline, solid enough to hold me upright, to wedge me there against the cupboard door. I was helpless. I stood there in the bathroom, looking at the bath and the mirror and the cabinet and the ivory silk wrap hanging on the back of the door, watching them reel and lurch around me, and feeling the fog thickening and clearing again in my brain.

Time passed – it must have done. In a series of leaps, the light thinned. And as it thinned it stopped holding me upright. I began to shake. The weakness came from my knees and made my thighs tremble. If I stayed there any longer I knew I'd fall through the greyness to the floor.

I moved. Another mistake. Pain banged in my head. Then I began to realise. Not long ago, it must have been dark. It wasn't night-time at all. It was dawn. I'd lost the whole night.

A lot of time. Too much alcohol over the past few days might have explained it, and Spooner smashing me over the head with his truncheon. But I didn't believe that. Not this long. The gap in my memory yawned at my feet, big enough to drop a wardrobe into. Or a life. Evelyn's. Or mine.

The light was growing. What had happened the

night before? I couldn't think. I could hardly even stand.

I tugged the shirt over my head and dropped it into the bath, and stood there for a moment, shivering, watching blood leak out of it on to the porcelain. Then I made my way slowly back into the bedroom. I grabbed hold of the back of the chair in front of the dressing-table, and used it like a walking-frame to get me across the room to the head of the stairs. The french windows were open. Cold dawn air was rolling up the stairs, as cold as sea water. There was blood on the stairs too.

I went down the stairs slowly, a step at a time, moving air in and out of my lungs as if it was water. As the thick grey waxy stuff that I'd brought with me from the bathroom began to clear from my eyes, I knew I was going to find it. I'd felt it coming from the moment Evelyn's hirelings had tried to beat me up in the restaurant. But I'd tried to be too clever. And now I was going to pay.

I was halfway down the stairs when I saw where the blood must have come from. The open-plan stairs came down in a sweep to the sitting-room. From my position I could see something crumpled up behind the sofa. I went down into the living-room.

When I took a good look at what was lying there, I almost felt relief because I'd thought it might have been Evelyn. But it wasn't. It was Baxter. He was dead.

There was blood sprayed over the walls and soaking the carpet. He'd been beaten to death, and beaten a lot after death, with a club or something like it.

259

However much blood there is in a human body, most of it had been beaten out of him, and his flesh was the colour of candle wax. The right side of his face and neck was pulped, bones protruding through what was left of his cheek. He stared up at me with one eye. The other eye was half out, a snail sprung from its shell.

I stood there trying to think, trying to gather myself, trying to become somebody again instead of just a space filled with currents with no more meaning in them than the currents in the sea. The house moved around me like the *Lady Day* moving in the water.

This wasn't fraud or blackmail or theft, it never had been. This was murder. Baxter's murder. And I was set up for it. Why hadn't I seen that before?

I turned round. Where was she? Where had she gone? For an insane moment I could imagine her running along the road to call the police, her silk wrap trailing behind her, her heels kicking up like a child's. But I knew that wasn't the truth. I'd fallen into the trap. I'd trusted her.

Then I thought I heard something. A voice. Probably from the back of my mind somewhere. I listened. Some seagulls making a hell of a fuss about something. Then a car. Then the first of the early-morning planes; I glimpsed it through the open french windows, glinting like a chip of glass in the sky. I stood for a moment longer, listening to it droning away towards the airport; nothing else, except for the gulls and the sea, but my stomach had tightened up into something metallic and cold. I could feel it there, a painful shape inside me. Guilt and fear. Guilt because I should have pulled out of all this days ago, I should have gone to De Jersey and told him everything I suspected, not just everything I knew. Fear because I knew now they were after me.

There wouldn't be anyone else in the house, except me. This was it. This was what they'd been building up to, not just ripping Baxter off but murdering him. And I was set up as the murderer. I was more scared than I'd ever been before in my life.

Then I heard something. A squeak that might have come from a mouse in a trap. The gates at the end of the drive opening.

I went to the front door. It was open, like the french windows. I don't know why the hell it was open, but it was. It allowed me to see down the curving drive past the cage where the Dobermanns were to the wrought-iron gates glinting in the early light of dawn.

And Spooner, walking slowly towards me.

27

Spooner was walking slowly. Looking round him. A tourist straight off the boat. He had his two-way radio in his hand but he wasn't using it. He was dressed in off-duty policeman's blue – shirt, anorak and trousers – and he was wearing dark glasses, to keep the early-morning light of truth out of his eyes. He looked happy.

I went back into the living-room and found my old rucksack by the side of the sofa and thrust my hand into it, rustling among the notes, and found the plastic bag. I lay down on the far side of the sofa out of sight of the door. I took my shoes off and removed the plastic bag from the gun I kept in there. My insurance policy. The only one I had left.

It was a long time before he came into the room. And when he did come, he came quietly, much more quietly than I'd thought a clumsy bastard like him could have moved. It wasn't until he reached the further end of the sofa and saw the corpse that I heard him. A short, sharp intake of breath.

I sat up, slowly and carefully. Spooner was standing with his back to me, one hand gripping the back of the sofa. He was looking down at what was left of Baxter and holding his two-way radio as if he was just about to use it.

I stood up. He didn't hear me. He stood there looking down, and then, instead of looking towards me and the french windows and the swimming-pool, he looked round to the right. Up the stairs. He took a single step towards the stairs, then stopped as if he was thinking about something.

I set off. I walked around the sofa. It was hard work, like walking up the deck of a capsizing ship. But I was going to make it. I was the inevitable, the necessary, the force of history. I was fate.

I walked across the room and came up behind him. I was breathing like a bulldog on a choke-collar but he still didn't hear me.

I put the barrel of the little .32 automatic inside his ear.

He jumped, then froze.

'This is Breaker,' I said. 'Move again and I'll fucking shoot you.'

'Turn around,' I said.

He turned around slowly. His face was a picture. Moon-shaped. Slack-mouthed. He took a long time to react, but then he started to try to hide his two-way radio behind his back. I put the snub barrel of the gun further into his ear.

'I mean it,' I said. I was shaking. I was shaking so much I could feel saliva dribbling down my chin. 'Don't do it,' I said.

'Don't do what?' he asked.

'Don't use the radio,' I said. 'Drop it.' He did. I kicked it away. I grinned at him.

'I feel like death. The only question is, yours or mine.' I felt a giggle bubbling up inside me. He shook his head in fear. 'Damnation, Spooner, you bastard. You're going to do something for me. If you do it, you'll be all right. If you don't do it, I'll kill you. That's my word on that. Okay?'

He nodded. I wiped what I thought was sweat from my face and saw that I hadn't wiped off all the blood. Blood and water dripped from my face. I must have looked as if I meant what I said.

I grabbed a raincoat from a hook in the hall and pulled it over my shoulders. 'We're going to my boat,' I said. 'We're going to your car, and you're going to drive me there. I've got nothing to lose, Spooner. You put a foot wrong, I'll kill you.'

He shuddered and almost looked relieved. 'All right,' he said.

The sun must have just been appearing above the horizon to the east, and there was a thin greenish light in the sky. The trunks of the palm trees made strange shadows across the lawn. We walked past the swimming-pool down the drive. Spooner walked like an old man. He jumped when the Dobermanns started yammering as we went down the drive.

'Not used to it?' I said to him. 'I thought bloody coppers like you liked guard dogs. Hold it.' I looked in through the side window of the garage. The Mercedes was still there but not the Jaguar. 'Keep walking,' I said, my voice as high and strained as a keening dog.

We went through the gates. It was still early enough for there to be no visible neighbours, no milkman, no postman. We climbed into Spooner's Granada, him in the driving seat, me in the back.

'Start the car,' I said. He did. 'Drive,' I said.

'Where to?'

'St Sampson's. Go down St Julian's Avenue and along the Esplanade.'

He let out the clutch, and the car jumped and

stalled. I saw his face looking like a frightened dog's in the rear-view mirror as the barrel of my gun touched his ear.

'Drive,' I whispered.

The Granada stopped and started along the road, bumped over the sleeping policemen. My breathing and his fear fogged up the inside. He turned on the heater. A blast of cold, then suddenly hot, air filled the car. I reached forward and flipped off the fan. I didn't want the noise to stop me hearing anything else.

At that time of a summer morning, Guernsey is as quiet as the grave. Seagulls fought over something left in a garden. A cat wandered past, sat down in the middle of the road to wash itself. A car went past, the driver's head turning slowly towards us as if worked by wires. Spooner slowed down and his head began to turn.

'You'd better hope the car doesn't stop because if it does I'll shoot you right now,' I said. He kept driving.

'Relax, Spooner,' I said.

I was finding it difficult to concentrate. My head swirled with every movement the car made. If he'd swung it round in a couple of circles I'd have lain down and wept like a child. But he kept looking back at me in the rear-view mirror and I held him with my eye. The Ancient Mariner. I knew what I looked like. White, and mad-eyed. 'I'm still drunk, Spooner,' I said. 'And dangerous. I think I'm out of my mind.'

'Oh Jesus,' he said. 'Just take it easy with that gun.'

He drove down into Town, down St Julian's

Avenue and on to the Esplanade. I made him draw
up at the kerb. The *Venus* wasn't in her usual berth.
There was only one other place she could be: the
Hoummet. If she wasn't there, I'd never find her.
Making a run for it wouldn't take me far, not now I
had Spooner in tow. If I didn't find the *Venus*, I'd
had it.

'Do we have to go through with this, whatever it
is?' Spooner asked.

'Spooner, if it's the last thing we do, we're going
to go through with it.'

'What are you going to do?'

'We're going on a trip,' I said.

'Jesus,' he said. He gripped his chest. 'My heart,'
he said. He was getting his courage back, trying
anything; I heard him gulping. 'I bet that gun isn't
loaded,' he said.

I just laughed at him. A rich, demented laugh. I
clicked the safety catch on and off. It made a
satisfying sound.

'Drive to the Bridge,' I said.

There wasn't any traffic at that time of the day and
soon we were in St Sampson's. We came in under
the shadow of the cranes. I got out of the car,
opened the driver's door and pushed him towards
the *Lady Day*.

'We're going to get on that boat now,' I said.

'Leave me here.'

I said, 'You're coming with me. You do what I
say, you're all right. If you don't, click click.'

'You're mad,' he muttered. But we clambered on
to the boat. I leaned the gun against the back of his
neck and pushed him towards the wheelhouse. I felt
him shudder. But I didn't want to scare him shitless,

267

I just wanted cooperation. I pulled the gun back.

'I've got a wife and child,' he said, as if he'd just learned to speak, but I didn't answer him. 'I can't steer a boat,' he whined. 'I've never steered a boat.'

'You'll learn,' I said.

He went into the wheelhouse, gripped the wheel while I opened the hatch in the floor and started the engine.

'You'll never get away with it,' he blurted suddenly.

'Do you think I don't know that?' I said.

With Spooner standing at the wheel, I sat on the stool at the back of the wheelhouse, holding the gun in my lap. I'd thrown away the coat and put on some of my own clothes, a tee-shirt and a guernsey. The *Lady Day* went out of the harbour. An early fisherman waved at us from the end of the quay. I waved back.

Even through the thumping and walloping of the old diesel, I could feel the change when she left the harbour and reached the sea. Just like sliding a hand off the polished woodwork of a snooker table on to the green baize. A shiver in my buttocks through the seat of the stool and through the soles of my feet. Waves began to slap against the bows.

'I didn't kill him, Spooner,' I said when we'd cleared the harbour.

'If you say so,' he muttered. I could see him eyeing the radio. So I leaned forward past him and yanked the wires out from underneath it, throwing the handful of bits over the side. Then I leaned past him to open the throttle. I opened it as far as it would go. A cloud of black smoke burst from the

268

stern and hung there. As we flogged through the water, it followed us. I could see the unevenness on the horizon which meant big waves ahead. On top of everything else, we were sailing into a storm.

My head was clearing, but whatever I'd drunk the previous night, whatever had been in what I'd drunk, had left everything seeming filtered, bright but remote. Like looking through a prism, as if rainbows had just vanished from the edges of everything. The fresh air and the fear had blown a lot of the cobwebs away, but those that were left didn't allow me to think very clearly.

I sat there, hunched up. Three hours out to the Hoummet, perhaps four. Hours to think and brood and remember. Spooner didn't say anything. Neither did I.

Spooner made a pretty good job of bringing the *Lady Day* in through the undulates. Better than I would have done. Some sailor I was. I owned the bloody boat and even with a gun pointing at the back of his neck this tyro could handle her better than I could.

I didn't see the *Venus* at first, and I thought I'd had it then. But then I began to make out the shape of the Decca navigator and the radio mast sticking up above the rocks. She was there, moored in the bay against the pier, as she'd had to be. And the helicopter, sitting on the circular concrete pad of the pier. Lashed down in the rising wind. The wreck of the German boat was visible, the bow rising out of the water on the falling tide, held there by the hawser from the donkey engine on the pier and by the chain and by the ropes.

269

'Kneel down,' I said to Spooner. He let go of the wheel and turned round to look at me. I showed him the gun. 'Kneel on the floor. Put your arms over your head.' I could see the fear on his face, and something else there too; I couldn't decide what. 'I won't hurt you,' I said. 'I'm not going to kill a copper, am I? Not even you.'

He squatted down clumsily. I reached forward and gripped the wheel as the *Lady Day* nosed into the bay of the Hoummet. She kicked through the undulates and came into the smoother water of the bay. I jammed the gear lever into reverse. She swung in heavily across the bay. I cut the engine. She kept going, her momentum propelling her, like a wardrobe sliding downstairs. I let go of the wheel, put my feet on Spooner's back to keep him there, and braced myself for the collision. She was slowing when she hit the *Venus*, but her bulk turned what might have seemed a slight blow into a major impact, like clubbing a china vase with a sock full of wet sand. I saw the *Venus* rise in the water like a whale, tilt, and grind against the pier. I heard half a million pounds' worth of overpriced hull crack like a coconut. Water geysered up on the other side. A frightened face appeared in the state-room window. Seagulls rose like flies from the rocks.

'Okay, Spooner, get up,' I said. He did. I ushered him out of the wheelhouse, grabbed the painter from the stern of the boat, and hopped across the yard of sea water between the two boats.

'Come on, Spooner,' I said to him. He looked down at the space between the boats as if it were a gap between skyscrapers. 'Jump!' I said. He did, suddenly, climbing up on to the gunwale of the *Lady*

Day and landing on the slippery deck with a thump. I looped the painter over the rail and tied it, one-handed. The deck was splintered upwards where the impact had occurred.

Then I pushed him into the cockpit of the *Venus* and went in after him, grabbing hold of his anorak at the back of the neck. I held him away from me and stood there listening. I heard frightened voices below-decks. Heard someone moving.

Evelyn came up out of the companionway. Evelyn was wearing a lime-coloured leisure suit which, as she came up into daylight, made her resemble something alien rising from the bottom of a pond. She looked stunned.

I pushed Spooner on to the bench in the cockpit, grabbed Evelyn's hair and forced her down on to the bench, jamming the gun into the back of her neck.

'What are you doing, Sam? What's going on?'

Guilbert came next. He was naked apart from boxer shorts decorated with orange fruit. He was trying to pull a white trainer on to one foot, and he stopped when he saw me, holding the other shoe.

'What have you done?' he said. 'You've sunk the boat!' He turned to me, his face flat and dead and vicious. 'Are you crazy? There's water coming in the front of the boat. If I don't pump it out, we'll sink.'

I said, 'Then do it.'

'I have to start the engines. The pump runs off them.'

'Then start them,' I said. I waved the gun. 'You know I'll kill you if there's any trouble.'

Guilbert passed the starter buttons and the engines began to rumble beneath us. He engaged the pump, and foam, then water, began to spray out of

271

the sides of the boat. He leaned over the side, then turned back to face me.

'What the hell's going on?' he asked. He stood with the shoe in one hand, looking at Spooner. 'What are you doing here?'

'He's here because of Baxter,' I said. 'Baxter's dead.'

'Dead?' Evelyn said. 'What are you talking about, Sam?'

'He's dead,' I repeated. 'He's been murdered.' I gestured at Spooner. 'Tell them, Spooner.'

He licked his lips. 'Someone telephoned the station and they put the call through to me,' he said. 'I was driving in to work in my car. When I got the call, I drove to your house, Mrs Breaker.'

'George is dead?' Evelyn said. Her face began to change. I had the impression of someone assembling an expression, like shaking jigsaw pieces on a tray hoping they'd make a picture. 'You're not making this up, are you?' she asked. 'I don't believe this.' She looked around. 'What are you doing with that gun, Sam? Is this a joke or something? Where's George?'

'He's back at the house with his brains beaten out. And you killed him, Guilbert. And Evelyn.'

'I don't believe you,' Guilbert said.

'It's true,' Spooner said.

'He's dead,' I said. I could feel the hammer pulling back on the gun, as if I wanted to shoot somebody. 'For Christ's sake, Guilbert killed him and beat him with a club. Beat him so it'd look like a crazed attack from the Island drunk. I've got a grudge against Baxter, for all sorts of reasons. After the kind of newspaper coverage I've had lately I'll go

down for good for this. And that's without any of
you getting in court to give your version.'

'He doesn't know what he's talking about,' Guilbert said.

'Sam, stop doing this,' Evelyn said, pleading with
me. 'You've been drinking again. You're paranoid,
you're making this up. You've imagined the whole
thing. We spent yesterday together . . .'

'Then what are you doing here?'

'I wanted to see Richard.'

'How did you know he was here?'

She shook her head, put her hands in her hair.
'Sam, put the gun down. This isn't the way to do
this. The boat's sinking.'

I said, 'I found Baxter dead, this morning. Then
Spooner found me. And assumed I killed him. Isn't
that right?' I growled at him.

Spooner licked his lips again. 'Of course I did,' he
said. He was staring as if in supplication at Evelyn.
The sun had gone, and a great skein of grey cloud
had been drawn across most of the sky. The weather
was getting fouler. In the bad light, Evelyn's green
clothes glowed. There was a scattering of rain.

The *Venus* moved under us suddenly.

Guilbert said suddenly, 'We're sinking, for
Christ's sake!'

'Then we'll sink,' I said. 'You must have gone
back to Guernsey in the *Venus*, come into the house
and killed him last night.'

'He's been with me here all night,' Evelyn said.

'But you were with me.'

'No. I've been here. Ever since you left yesterday.'

'You're lying,' I said.

273

Evelyn put a hand to her forehead. She looked as if she'd just woken up, as if she'd just got out of bed, still with that unformed, provisional expression on her face. I felt a pang of something – jealousy, anger, I don't know what it was.

I said, 'Tell Spooner the truth and we can radio the police and we can get the hell out of here.'

Spooner made a move towards me. I looked at him, and he stopped, the expression of fear frozen on his face.

'What the hell is going on?' Evelyn asked.

28

I didn't answer. Guilbert looked at me as if he expected me to explain. Evelyn shook her head. She looked angry and frightened. The *Venus* lurched. The wind whistled through the handrails.

Evelyn slowly and carefully removed a pack of cigarettes from the breast pocket of her top, lit a cigarette with her Zip lighter, which she dropped on to the top of the table in front of her. I stared at it. It was an effort to move my eyes away.

'You look pretty awful, Sam,' she said.

I said, 'Guilbert, what were you going to tell the police? That I got drunk and got in a fight with Baxter, and that last night I beat him to death because I was jealous of him screwing Evelyn?'

Guilbert grinned at me. 'That popgun of yours has bullets in it, does it?'

'It does,' I said. He shrugged. I said, 'I had a lot to drink yesterday. Lagavulin. Malt whiskies are my favourite drinks, but Lagavulin is so strong-tasting that even if there was any taste to the stuff Evelyn spiked my drink with, I wouldn't have noticed. What did you use, Evelyn?'

'You're mad, Sam, you're insane,' she said.

I said, 'Listen to this, Spooner. Before she got her break as a model, Evelyn worked for a pharmaceutical company. It must have been child's play for her to add something I wouldn't be able to taste to that Lagavulin, something that would combine with the

275

alcohol enough to make me sleep all night. They'd have found me drunk. And if I hadn't tipped most of the glass of whisky she'd doctored down the sink they'd have found me dead. If they found anything in the blood test they'd have found something like a barbiturate, which I might have taken to get me to sleep, or to get rid of a headache. There were pills all over the bedroom when I woke up.'

Slowly and carefully, Guilbert rubbed his Adam's apple between forefinger and thumb. 'Quite an elaborate story. How long have you had to work this out?'

'The time it took to sail out here. I thought about a lot of things. Like the Brew. Spooner, the Brew didn't get run over by accident. He heard something on the *Venus*, heard Evelyn say something so vital she had to try to kill him. So Guilbert lured him out of his house with a phone call, clubbed him from behind, and was going to fix him for good, by running him over or beating him to death, when things started to go wrong. Spooner turned up. If it hadn't been for Spooner he would have died.'

They were staring at me, as if in disbelief. I thought Evelyn's face cracked into a smile for a moment, as if she hadn't understood what I'd said.

I said, 'I was stupid enough to think I could go on playing everything along from the inside. The trouble was, I didn't think it through. I thought you were just interested in stripping Baxter and I wanted to be able to prove it and then go to the police with what I knew. I didn't realise it was me you wanted. And that you wanted me wrapped up nice and tight. For ever.'

'Why would I do that to you?' she asked breath-lessly.

'I can tell you why,' I said. 'Because of the scrapyard.'

'It's an interesting, theory,' Guilbert said. He seemed ironically amused, a circus master audition-ing an inferior act. But his eyes kept staring at the gun; he couldn't help it.

The *Venus* lurched again, the lighter sliding sud-denly across the table. I could see the calm of their expressions changing. The engines growled. The pumps were losing their battle against the water seeping into the hull. The *Venus* was sinking. That suited me.

I went on. 'There isn't any gold here, there never was. The Clausen story was a way of tangling Baxter up, getting me involved so you could trap me into looking as if I'd killed him. The real gold is back on Guernsey. And I own it.

'My guess is, there's a multi-million-pound build-ing project waiting to go through on my land. I didn't want to sell up so I ignored the offers. In the end, when GHH made their big offer, I went to Richard Guilbert and told him I wasn't going to sell. Not very bright of me, but I didn't know he was at the heart of it. I should have begun working things out then. But I didn't.

'Let's say you'd already decided to kill Baxter, partly because you hated him. Your idea was to get rid of me at the same time as you were getting rid of Baxter. It was a good idea, with a beautifully simple formula at the heart of it. Kill Baxter and make it look as if I did it. That would get rid of both of us, two birds with one stone. Me, who was stopping you developing the land. Baxter, who might have caused all kinds of trouble when you had. You were finished with Baxter when you realised he hadn't any money. With him out of the way, your syndicate would develop the land, and you'd get rich. And my will gave Evelyn any rights I might have had to what was coming.

'I was just right for the murderer. You hired a couple of thugs to start a fight with me in my favourite restaurant, the one place you knew I'd be, the only place I ever visit regularly, every Saturday night. That helped to set me up. You made sure I got off, but the point was made, especially to the police. I was dangerous, unstable. I might just kill someone rich and successful, like Baxter, if I was working for him, and if I knew he was also screwing my wife.

'The rest was easy enough. Probably the hardest part was talking Baxter into hiring me for this scheme about finding gold on the Hoummet.

'Evelyn played me along. She knows me better than anyone. She knows what kind of cunt-crazy animal I am. I'd have had her that first day I got out of the cells, given half a chance. But Spooner turned up, and stopped me dead. Otherwise, I reckon she'd have had me.'

'Don't flatter yourself, Sam,' Evelyn said, with something of the detached amusement I'd once liked her so much for. She had nerves of steel: I'd never seen her frightened, I'd never been able to tell whether she was bluffing or not.

Spooner was goggle-eyed, moon-faced. I almost felt sorry for him. The *Venus* was tilting more and more. Bottles must have fallen off the shelves in the bar because I could hear them smashing in the state room. Evelyn jumped, a wire twitching around her mouth.

I kept going. 'The plan was to get me back to Baxter's, but I'd had enough of all of you after the dive, and the conger eel did the rest – Baxter wasn't going anywhere for a while after that. Evelyn had to wait until the next day. And when she asked me to go to Baxter's house, I went, because I was frustrated, and curious. Then what really got me was her story about the pregnancy. What pregnancy? On the way out here, I realised the timing was wrong. I'd found out she had a hysterectomy after she left California and before she went to Monaco. She wasn't pregnant in Monaco, even if she was pregnant before. What she told me about Theo's baby was balls.'

Evelyn moved her head, almost smiled. Touché.

'How did you find that out?' she asked.

'Just lucky, I guess,' I said to her. 'So I went back with Evelyn to the house where she'd always known Baxter was going to be killed. There was sex, to keep me occupied. Alcohol and the drugs to keep me in the house. But I was cautious enough, worried enough, to get rid of most of what I'd drunk. Otherwise, I'd be dead, or in the cells by now, and De Jersey would already have thrown away the key.'

The pack of cigarettes started to slide, and Evelyn plucked it from the table-top, flicked one from the pack and stuck it in her mouth. Guilbert grabbed the lighter and lit it for her.

Spooner licked his lips. 'Any witnesses to any of this?'

'Only witnesses against me.'

'And no one saw Guilbert or Baxter come or go?'

'In that road? People don't come and go in that road. Most of the houses are empty. Those rich neighbours of hers spend the summer in Brazil. They got Baxter back to Guernsey last night – either by helicopter to the airport, where they made a big show of getting him a taxi to take him to the house, so everyone would remember where he was going, or they brought him in on the *Venus*.

'That put Baxter in the house, with Evelyn. And me, upstairs, stoned out of my mind. Guilbert killed him. Then he and Evelyn left Guernsey for the Hoummet on the *Venus* last night when it was dark. The Hoummet was the safest place – who could prove they hadn't been here at the time of the murder? They'll say they left Baxter at his house, and I broke in, drunk, and killed him.'

'And no one saw us?' Evelyn asked ironically. She looked more and more relaxed, as if what I was saying was reassuring her.

'After they'd killed Baxter, they came out here, probably arriving here an hour, perhaps an hour and a half, after they left the house. Guilbert can handle the boat all right, even in the dark. No one will be able to prove the time of death accurately enough to pin the murder on them. They must have called the police and since then they've been sitting here waiting to hear about my arrest. While I lay in Evelyn's bed and stiffened up in Baxter's blood.'

'If there are no witnesses to any of this,' Spooner said, 'it's all supposition. It's never going to stand up. What if someone saw your wife on Guernsey? If she's saying they've been on the Hoummet all day yesterday and someone saw her, her story's gone.'

'No one saw her, and even if someone did, she'd talk her way out of it,' I said, even more wearily. Rain started to fall. I wanted it to end. I felt awful, physically and mentally. My hand was tired from holding the gun – I'd been holding it for about four hours. I felt as if my fingers would never work properly again.

Spooner ran his hands over his face. He had to steady himself, as the *Venus* tipped more and more.

'This boat is going down,' Evelyn blurted out suddenly.

'If I'm facing fifteen years in gaol for killing a man, I'd just as soon I went down with it,' I said.

'Sam!' Evelyn said in alarm.

The *Venus* lurched again, nose down. I could see spray rising up on the other side of the rocks. Sea water must have been pouring into the state room in spite of the pumps; a tongue of water moistened the bottom of the door that separated the cockpit from the state room, then more slopped through.

'Guilbert, tell Spooner the truth,' I said. 'Give yourself a chance. If you tell the truth, Spooner will call up his friends on the radio upstairs, and we can all go and argue about this in a nice safe dry cell.'

'The truth?'

'Tell him you killed Baxter.'

'All right,' he said. 'Sergeant Spooner, I killed Baxter.'

Evelyn reached out for his hand. I lifted the gun.

'Say it again, you bastard.'

'I killed him.'

'Did you get that, Spooner? Now tell him why, Guilbert.'

He spoke without emotion. 'What does it matter why? I killed him for money, what other reason is there? I've no pension from the SDECE, nothing. This way, Evie and I will get the profits from the scrapyard. We are Grande Havre Holdings, of course. We used the name Harkin when we registered the company. When you came to my office, I told you Carl Martin had made the offer to put you off the scent. It wasn't going to matter: you were supposed to be dead before you found anything out. Yes, dead. You weren't supposed to wake up this morning at all.' He shrugged. His big hands moved together, dancers on the Formica. 'I killed him last night. Killing him was easy. Then I beat him to look as if you'd done it. Then we came back here on the *Venus* during the night, and called the police this morning.' He raised his eyebrows and his hands stopped moving. 'Do you really want me to go on?'

'Yes,' I said.

Guilbert said, 'There is a man called Clausen, but I didn't give him the ten thousand dollars, I kept that – he was more interested in clearing his conscience, once I'd tracked him down. And it was easy for me to lean on him. He didn't want his picture in the papers,' he said sardonically. 'Clausen had some yarn about gold from the camp that should be lying around on the sea bottom around here somewhere. He said there was a safe on the boat, and that the boat was scuttled, but he didn't know what was in it. The gold might have been there, but he didn't know, he wasn't one of the big fellows. You are right. That land of yours is a lot more valuable than any gold there might be underwater. We got Baxter interested in the search for the gold because it gave us the chance to kill him.'

I should have felt elation, or relief, but I didn't; I just felt tired. 'You'd better call your friends, Spooner,' I said. 'Tell them we're in a sinking boat and we're going to go ashore on to the pier to wait for them. Tell them I'm holding the murderers of George Baxter here. Tell them about the gun, and that I might use it.'

He moved slowly behind me.

'All right,' he said. 'But if what you say is true, and you didn't kill Baxter, give me the gun. You're in trouble, Breaker. It's time for the law to take charge. If you go along with me, I'll do my best for you.'

'You just can't stand me telling you what to do, can you? Make the bloody call,' I said. The *Venus* shifted again. Water appeared under the door of the state room in a flood.

'Sam!' Evelyn said in alarm.

I said, 'Make the call, Spooner. Go on, call them.'

Spooner got up slowly and went past me and began to clamber up the steps to the flying bridge. I'd never noticed before that he walked as though the sinews round his ankles had been cut through; he went up to the flying bridge, his feet flopping on the deck over my head. I heard him using the radio without hearing what he was saying.

'I even know who your inside man was,' I said, then produced my rabbit from the hat. 'Milliner. He was the chairman of the Land Use Committee. He was upstairs the first day I called on you, Evelyn; his car was there. He was at the restaurant on the

Saturday night the fight started, so he could appear
as a witness in court if you needed any help. He was
up at the restaurant the night I went there to ask
Anton who'd called the police on that Saturday night
– I'd already begun to think there was something too
glib about what happened. Milliner's been having an
affair for the last couple of years: his secretary knew
about it, I found out through her. I'd thought he
might have been having the affair with you, Evelyn;
now I'm not so sure. He must be involved, somehow. And now he's dead. Evelyn, I wouldn't put it
past you to have found something in your pharmaceutical kitbag to help him to die.'

She didn't react, except to smile gently.

'Milliner?' Guilbert said.

'The one with the red Mercedes sports car,' I said.

I wasn't ready for what Evelyn did then: she
laughed.

'You're telling me you think Henry Milliner was
involved in George's murder?' Evelyn said.
'Because you've seen a red car around?' She
couldn't keep the smile off her face. 'That Mercedes
used to belong to him, but it wasn't Milliner who was
driving it when you saw it round at my place.
Richard was. He took it in kind for some legal work
he did for him – didn't you, Richard?' She smiled at
me. 'Richard had come round after the initial hearing, Sam. I would have told you, but when I went
into the house to get the beers, Richard told me not
to.'

Guilbert said, 'I was called in to give Milliner
some advice about some of the things going on in his
business life. I was his last resort, he said. I couldn't
do anything for him.'

'When Milliner was up at Anton's, so was the car,' I said. 'And it was at Carl's garage too.'

'Carl was servicing it for me,' Guilbert said. 'He spent a couple of days driving it around over-revving the engine to clean the plugs. It was me, not Milliner, who'd driven it to Anton's the night you turned up there.

'That's all,' I repeated, like an idiot. My face felt as stiff as the fingers of the hand holding the gun.

Spooner began to come down the steps behind me.

'Did you call them?' I asked over my shoulder.

'They'll be here in an hour. They're sending a car up to the house too,' he said. 'You'd better put that gun down now. You hand's shaking. It's likely to go off.'

'Fuck the gun,' I said. 'I thought Milliner was the key to this. You must have had someone on the Land Use Committee . . .'

Guilbert said, 'We didn't need anyone on the Committee. We only needed someone who had access to the relevant papers. They've been discussing using your yard on and off for years, but secretly, as usual, so speculation doesn't start. And some months ago, they took the decision to do something about it. All we needed was that information. Everything else was in place. You wouldn't sell, we had to do something.'

'Spooner, are you listening to this?' I asked over my shoulder. 'This is it. He's giving us everything on a plate. Evelyn, who gave you the information?'

'Milliner used to take his work home all the time,' she said. She smiled at me.

I thought back. To something Jenny Mahy had

said. The *Venus* lurched a little. Guilbert stood up.

'We'd better get off this boat, Breaker, or we're going down with it.'

'Stay there,' I said. 'Milliner took his work home. So his secretary wouldn't see it. But his wife could have done.' I remembered Carl Martin speaking to me on the night of the fight. 'His wife might have wanted to get her own back, because of Milliner's affairs, and his business failures. She might have turned to someone else for help. She's a Guernsey woman, so she might well have turned to her family. She's linked to one of you. What was Margaret Milliner's maiden name?'

'Spooner,' Spooner said.

Then he hit me.

29

It was the second time the bastard had hit me in a week. Light exploded in my head and down I went. Right off the stool head first and across the slippery sloping floor up against the door into the state room where the sea water was seeping in. I lay there with my face in the water. It tasted of oil. I lay there wondering what he'd hit me with.

'Pick up his gun,' Spooner said to someone, his voice sounding flat and remote.

What gun? I felt around. I'd let go of it. A great man in a crisis. I'd held a gun for four hours and dropped it the only time I really needed it.

I rolled over. Spooner was standing where I'd been moments before, towards the stern, holding a shotgun on me, the over-and-under weapon Baxter had used to shoot at seagulls. It must have been that he'd hit me with. He'd got it from the bridge. And he'd known where to get it.

Voices came from a long way off. Somebody moved out of my sight. Spooner seemed to have shrunk into the distance. When I looked at him, it was like staring into a tunnel.

Then Evelyn walked into my vision. She bent down and picked up my gun from where it had skidded across the floor under the table. She broke out the magazine, looked inside, then closed it and tossed it to the floor.

'You fooled us, Sam,' she said. 'It's empty.

You've got a lot of nerve, I'll give you that. Or perhaps I should have remembered you have.'

I spat blood out of my mouth. 'You don't think I'd keep a loaded gun lying around, do you? I don't like explosives.' I tried to fight the wooziness. 'Spooner, I didn't kill Baxter. What do you think you're doing?'

'I know who killed Baxter,' Spooner said. 'Richard Guilbert killed Baxter. And if he hadn't, I would have.'

He settled his haunches comfortably against the table, cradling the shotgun, its barrels pointing at me.

'Richard and I are like that.' He crossed his fingers. 'We used to work together. He came to me because my sister was married to Milliner, and he wanted information about the Land Use Committee. He knew about your will; he'd worked out this scheme to get hold of the scrapyard.'

'And your sister's in on this too?'

'She was. We tried to buy your land through Grande Havre Holdings, but when you wouldn't sell we found another way of getting the land. We'd kill Baxter, then let you die, so the land would come direct to Evelyn and there wouldn't be any Baxter to mess up what we were doing. With you around, we might have been tangled up in the courts for years.'

'You were going to let me die,' I repeated. The gawping victim, the sucker.

'You should have died last night. The courts would have swallowed it, all right. First you killed Baxter, then yourself. Murder, then suicide.'

'And you'd visited the house. The Dobermanns didn't bark at you when you found me with Evelyn by the swimming-pool. Or today. They only barked at me.'

He nodded, grinned. Moved the shotgun comfortably.

'I often visited the house,' he said. 'I'd overrated you, Breaker; you didn't notice.

'When my sister came to me to complain about Milliner's affairs, we persuaded her to get us the photocopies of the papers we needed. We've paid my sister off, and she's already left for Spain. It's a nice little scheme, Breaker. Luxury homes for the overseas market. They're talking about a profit of around eight or nine million pounds.'

'Spooner, you're crazy. They'll rob you.'

'They've already put a hundred thousand pounds in a bank account for me, the same amount they gave my sister. A hundred thousand pounds of what used to be Baxter's money. A good investment. It was having Richard Guilbert as a solicitor and adviser that cost him so much.' He grinned broadly at that; he liked the joke. 'I've already spent some of it, got some stuff for my daughter. Two million follows towards the end of next year. That's a lot of money, Breaker. I'll leave the Island and they'll never find me. Early retirement.'

'You're crazy, you're crazy,' I mumbled.

'Listen, I've been in debt for a long time,' he said – there was a smouldering anger behind the smile. 'It's been hard watching people like Milliner make fortunes and then waste them. Throwing money away on other women, humiliating my sister. And men like your father, Breaker, coming in and buying up what they liked. You're an outsider, Breaker, a fucking outsider.'

289

'You mean Evelyn isn't? And Guilbert? What have you fallen for?'

He snarled at me, 'We've already got your bloody scrapyard. You've written a will, remember. You're going to leave everything to your wife. And you're going to die. It's all legal. Apart from this.'

'Apart from this?' All I need to do is stand up in court . . .'

'You won't be standing up anywhere, darling,' Evelyn said. 'You're going to be dead.'

Richard Guilbert appeared in my vision, stepping down into the cockpit. He was wiping his hands, and smiling at me. 'You never did get the hang of it, did you?' he said, quietly amused.

I was suddenly afraid. An eruption of feeling rose up through me, but I could do little more than stir my limbs clumsily; I couldn't do what I wanted to do. I wanted to kill him. And Evelyn. Loyal, loving Evelyn, who'd stood by me through it all. Evelyn, who must have married me for money, left me for money, come back to me for money.

I moved my head, slowly because of the shooting pain in my neck, and I looked up at her through the haze. She'd walked through the whole thing – deception, sex, murder – without a flicker of feeling, for me, or for anyone. Jenny had been right about Evelyn, and she'd tried to tell me I'd been wrong. But I hadn't believed her. Now Evelyn was looking at me as if she'd never seen me before.

I tried to control my trembling limbs. I was going to have to do something. Soon. But as my shoulders rolled against the doors, I felt that the water I was sitting in was ice cold. Fresh sea water. The *Venus* was sinking fast. Just as I'd almost given up hope, I suddenly found myself thinking, I've got some kind of a chance.

'You bastards,' I said weakly. 'You're all bastards.'

I looked into the muzzles of the shotgun. Blue-black. The boat lurched. Spooner staggered.

Guilbert said, 'This boat's going down, I don't want to go down with it. Let's get it over with, get rid of him, then get on to the island.'

The *Venus* lurched heavily again. I could hear more bottles falling out of the bar. The door swung open suddenly as if pushed by the flooding water, and there was a sudden overpowering smell of alcohol. Guilbert hopped up on to the steps behind me and looked around over the sea.

'There're a lot of waves coming into the bay, the *Venus* is sinking. If she bumps against the wreck, it'll blow the whole island sky high.'

I started to stand up, but Spooner stepped towards me. Bang. Light exploded in my head, and I was woozy again.

'That's for what you've put me through, you bastard,' Spooner grunted at me. I looked up past the gun barrels into his face. It was congested with blood, like a man straining for an orgasm.

'Get up when I tell you to, not before,' he said. I nodded at him. 'Okay. Do it now.' I got up slowly. The water lapped at my feet, snuffling for a scent. I looked around, for anything, any sign, any way out. Watercolour sheets of rain wafted in towards the Hoummet. I could see sea water exploding on the far side of the island. Big waves, without much wind. I was registering what I could see, but I couldn't

291

think. My mind was empty. I was helpless.

'We've got to get out of here. We'll have to take the helicopter,' Guilbert shouted. 'Let's get it over with, then make the call to the police.'

Spooner's moon face was red and shining and content. Something hit me in the back. I staggered forward. I licked my lips, tried to get my mouth working properly.

I thought, I've had it – I'd never thought that before. Ever. But the auxiliary control panel was there behind Evelyn, with the throttle controls for the engines and the gear lever, and I could hear the engines running, the pumps working.

'I want to do this,' Spooner said. 'Get out of the way,' he said to Evelyn.

'Give me a break,' I said.

Another laugh. The men were behind me now, and Evelyn, suddenly alarmed by a sickening movement of the *Venus*, began trying to push past me, moving towards the stern. I leaned forward, as if weakening. I put my hand to my face. Blood was coming out of my nose. As I straightened up again, I reached past Evelyn and made a lunge for the throttles. And jammed them forward.

It must have been a second before anyone reacted to what I'd done, the engine note of the big diesels hesitating. Then the scream of the engines came out of the air.

I kept pushing Evelyn behind me and I grabbed the gear lever and dragged it towards me. The propellers churned in the sea, the *Venus* lurched and began to power backwards across the bay, tilting like an accelerating dragster. A wave formed in a huge fold beyond the stern. The deck tilted and angled

away from under our feet. I grabbed the wheel.
Spooner and Guilbert stepped backwards and
started to tumble, Evelyn clawed her way towards
them up the tilt of the deck.

The wreck of the German boat, lashed in its blue
and orange spider's web, moved in slow motion
towards me. I heard Evelyn cry out. The wreck hung
there; Evelyn twisted against me and I was fighting
free of her. Then the wreck rushed at me. The stern
of the *Venus* smashed into the visible part of it hard
enough to dump Spooner and Guilbert on the deck.
The *Venus*, on the rebound, spun in the bay, one
propeller smashed so that the engine raced uselessly,
the other pulling her round, opening up sea between
her and the wreck.

It gave me half a second of time. I threw myself at
Evelyn and my weight took her over backwards on
to Spooner, who was trying to get to his feet. I saw
the muzzles of the shotgun begin to rear upwards. I
pushed at them and hurled my weight on hers. The
gun went off somewhere near my ear, but he went
over backwards and Evelyn went over on top of him,
screaming. The back of Spooner's head hit the deck.
I reached over Evelyn's shoulder and hit him, right
in the middle of his face.

'God!' Evelyn screamed, under me.

I put my elbow on her throat and put my weight
on it, and hauled myself up her body a little further,
using my left forearm as a club to knock the gun
barrels upwards again so I could hit Spooner with my
right. This was a better blow. I felt his nose snap. I
liked that. I lifted my fist and hit him again. He was
trying to raise his head and this blow smashed the
back of his head against the deck. I could see into his

eyes. Hatred. I've never seen so much hatred. But it wasn't anything like the hatred I felt for him.

I was reaching out for the shotgun, which had flopped up above Spooner's head on to the deck, when hands grabbed me from behind. Guilbert. I could see Spooner stretching up for the butt of the gun, knew what he was going to do with it. Guilbert reached round my shoulders and pulled me back as I crouched there.

I stood up, taking Guilbert with me. Backed away from Spooner. He looked as if someone had smashed a watermelon in his face; blood was leaking on to his shirt. He was turning the gun towards me. He was going to use it. My hands went up in front of my face as if they were being worked by wires.

'Shoot!' Guilbert screamed in my ear.

I saw it before I heard anything. Something grew suddenly on the turbulent open water between the smashed stern of the *Venus* and the wreck. The surface of the bay curved upwards, an upturned bowl of glass, and I could see fish in it, and seaweed as green as fresh lettuce, and something yellow. Then the globe exploded. A white torrent. Then an impact.

The shock-wave picked up the *Venus* and pushed it across the bay as if it was caught on the front of a runaway train. She slammed into the side of the *Lady Day*. I caught a glimpse of Evelyn's face, frozen in fear, then felt myself falling.

I went into the sea over the stern.

30

It must have been ten yards to the *Lady Day*. I couldn't see a thing in the soup around me, but then I felt clothing and skin being scraped off my back. I'd come up under the belly of my boat, under the barnacles the Brew was always telling me to remove.

I surfaced and hung for a moment, gulping air. Then I reached up and grabbed the handrail, hung there, pulled myself up on to the deck where the deckhouse hid me from the *Venus*. Sea water and muck were still falling out of the sky.

I scrambled into the wheelhouse and hit the starter button. The engine coughed and churned, and didn't catch, and then did, and clouds of black smoke burst from the stern. Above the thudding of the engine, I heard shouting. I looked up to see a figure on the deck of what was left of the *Venus*, which was skewing round in the pieces of wreckage and weed all round her, a spar rising from the yellow water like a swimmer's arm. Guilbert, pointing something. A puff of smoke was snatched away like a handkerchief in the wind. Something hit the side of the wheelhouse like a slap from a hand. Glass splattered me. The bastard wasn't going to give up.

I jammed the gear lever into reverse and wound the wheel and felt the *Lady Day* move ponderously under me. Something was holding her back. It was the painter tying the two boats together. It was as tight as a bowstring. The *Lady Day* pulled against it, and I thought for a moment it was going to hold. Guilbert was loading the shotgun. With the heavy shot Baxter had told me about he could have blown the wheelhouse apart, piece by piece. But then the handrail of the *Venus* came out of the deck like a rotten tooth.

I backed the *Lady Day* out of the Hoummet, crouching down in the wheelhouse. Waves started splashing over the stern, and then I turned her into the waves.

Fifty yards or so away from the Hoummet, I risked standing up and taking a look out of the window. I kept low, but there were no more shots. I was out of range, and free. If I survived the storm.

The waves were coming in from the long reach of the Atlantic, big oceanic rollers, remnants of a big storm, running into a big tide which piled them up. Big, barrelling waves, shouldering the horizon out of true. Instead of rolling the *Lady Day* with a long, predictable motion, they pounded her.

As she cleared the lee of the Hoummet, a wave caught her almost sideways on, and for a few seconds I thought she'd go on rolling right over – that bloody mast! But she righted herself heavily. I opened up the throttle as far as it would go and turned her bows towards what I hoped was the shore. Another wave hit her, hard enough to jolt every timber in her hull. And my teeth.

I looked back at the Hoummet. It stuck up there, an ugly white-tipped thumb against a lowering sky, foam smashing around it. I could see the helicopter, dark-bodied, lashed down against the wind. Something moved on the wet rocks, green, like a maggot wriggling. Evelyn. Then someone else. Guilbert? Spooner?

Then I was too far away to see. The *Lady Day* went on hammering into the waves.

I didn't fancy trying to make Alderney in those conditions. It wasn't far to the French coast, but there was a squall of rain ahead, and I couldn't see it. Visibility was poor. There were no landmarks at all apart from the Hoummet, and that was barely visible now, just the huge waves rolling in from the west, spume lifting off their caps. I needed the Brew, I needed him now. Even being able to see the Hoummet didn't help because I wasn't sure of my position in relation to it, and out of sight of the Hoummet, I was wandering around in a shifting desert of currents and waves, and rocks which didn't shift but which lurched suddenly out of the water.

The *Lady Day* went into another wave, and the shock rocked through me. I had to ease back on the throttle to stop her turning over.

I checked the compass. It was spinning wildly, and I could hardly make sense of it. But if I kept heading roughly east, I'd hit something. Europe. France. Rocks.

I looked astern. No sign of pursuit. The *Venus* was finished. But I was still scared. I tried to control my breathing, braced myself in the wheelhouse as well as I could, trying to let my heartbeat get down to something like normal because it was shaking me like a rat.

I didn't feel good. Where Spooner had hit me on the back of my head, there was a swollen mass of flesh and a ridge which was the open mouth of the wound. The back of my shirt was soaked with blood;

I could taste blood in my mouth.

I took a mouthful of Calvados. It didn't help. I needed food of some sort. There was some Kendal mint cake in the wheelhouse drawer and I swallowed some of that, washed it down with more of the Calvados, and with the mineral water I always kept there, next to the nailed-down ashtray the Brew used . . . What would he have done?

I did my best to steer by keeping a lighter area of sky away on my right. Time passed – twenty minutes, half an hour. I had the engine at full throttle, the pistons hammering underneath me. Diesel fumes soaked up through the decking. Astern, the wake of the *Lady Day* vanished into a maze of currents and waves. She was being pushed around like a paper boat in a Jacuzzi. There was nothing I could do but keep going.

I took me a long time to realise it, but the boat was moving strangely, more and more strangely, as if something was trailing underneath her. There was something wrong, there had to be.

I lashed the wheel to the binnacle with a piece of rope, hoping she'd still keep end-on to the waves, and, taking a Maglite torch with me, I left the wheelhouse and got down into the hold. There was already water in there, slopping and fizzing about my ankles, cold sea water leaking in somewhere between planks which the shock of the explosion must have sprung apart. I should have expected it.

At the far end of the hold was a small door leading to the storage lockers and the bows. I shone the torch on it. Water spurted through a crack like a squirt from a soda syphon. I went to it, tried to open it. It was jammed shut. I jerked it open. Water that

298

must have been piled up behind there spilled over my knees. Another wave came up astern and pushed the bows of the *Lady Day* down, and another wave tumbled over my legs, less than before but still enough to show me that the boat was sinking. And that there were live sand eels in the hold.

I slammed the door and turned back into the hold, just in time to see something dark flash across the sky through the hatch. I could hear it then. The grumbling, slapping roar of the helicopter.

The Brew's fireworks were piled under plastic sheeting in one corner. As the *Lady Day* rolled, water washed up to my ankles. I slipped on the grating, pulled back the tarpaulin. Boxes packed in plastic, the contents dry in spite of the sea water. I grabbed as much as I could manage and clambered up the ladder to dump the fireworks on the deck. Rockets, bangers, a couple of the aerial bombs and one of the sawn-off cylinders he'd used as launchers. Anything to attract attention, I thought – I'd no clear idea then of what I was going to do. The *Lady Day* was sinking, that's all I knew.

Another wave. A gush of water came through the door I'd just shut, pushing it open.

I went into the wheelhouse through the rain and spray. I couldn't see the helicopter any more, or hear it. The radio was dead, there was no lifeboat aboard the *Lady Day*, and I was heading for a coast I didn't know in waves that were likely to sink the boat before we reached it. I was a good swimmer, but I couldn't expect to survive in that sea, with or without a lifejacket. After getting away from the

Hoummet, it looked as if I was going to drown after all.

In the wheelhouse, I suddenly found I couldn't breathe. My face was wet with rain, my hands shook in front of me. I didn't want to go through with this . . .

I struggled into a lifejacket, then cut the rope holding the wheel. I opened the throttle again, and the diesel started thumping under my feet. But then I thought I heard something above that, the racket of the helicopter again. The machine passed overhead, blurred through the window of the wheelhouse by the rain on the glass. Guilbert. Spooner. I started to shift the fireworks into the wheelhouse.

The *Lady Day* went into another wave. The force of the blow almost pitched me backwards out of the wheelhouse. She'd hit bottom.

It's a different feeling to anything else. The pounding of the *Lady Day* into the waves was bad enough, but it was nothing like this. After the slugging of the waves, hitting the rocks was a hard and metallic shock, like being hit by a hammer. The noise came up through the planking. I pitched forward into the binnacle. I spat out blood.

She'd stopped in her tracks, like a train hitting the buffers. A wave broke over her stern and water rushed past me and went tumbling into the hold.

Now I could see the helicopter, hovering half a mile away, as if she'd overshot me. The Atlantic storm went rolling towards it. It was eerie because there wasn't much wind, but the waves were big enough. During the Fastnet Race years before, the sea had bulged over the sea bottom and had swallowed up dozens of ocean-going yachts, plucking the masts out of them and breaking a couple of them in half. The *Lady Day* wasn't half the sea-boat that they were. She was on the bottom and she was already down by the bows.

I felt her shift, break free of whatever was holding her. She moved forward a dozen yards in a sweep, then a wave picked her up and dumped her on something else. A crack went through her – I felt it come up through my legs. The main mast moved. It snapped out of the tabernacle and went over the side – derrick, gaff rigging, furled sail, the lot. Only a tangle of ropes attached it to the deck. Over the crest of one of the breakers I glimpsed something. Low clouds, I thought, then saw it was land.

I left the wheelhouse and went forward with the binoculars, and stared, through spume and foam, towards part of the shore I'd never seen before, with a wilderness of breakers between me and a coast that would have been as black as coal if it hadn't been for the foam and spume combing off the top of the waves.

I struggled back to the wheelhouse – uphill. The door was banging in the gale, the glass smashed. Rain was pouring through the windscreen. Even with a lifejacket on I didn't fancy my chances of surviving in that sea. For the second time I thought, I'm going to die, I'm going to die on board the *Lady Day*. She was my home. I'd got free of those murderous bastards only for her to let me down. The bows were already almost under water. The big yellow-topped waves came at me slowly astern, then speeded up until they seemed as fast as cars speeding down a motorway, coming straight in over the stern and exploding and breaking into the hold.

I jammed myself on to the stool in a corner of the wheelhouse. I found a flare, opened the window and stuck it outside. The bright crimson flare rose like something from a Roman candle, hung for a moment, and was swallowed up. I tried again. It cast about as much illumination as a spark from a bonfire. So I tried a couple of the Brew's rockets, holding the sticks in one hand while I lit the touch-paper with a lighter. They went whizzing into the air.

Then I heard it again, above the pounding of the surf and the banging of the door, clattering overhead. The helicopter came swinging back, perhaps a thousand feet up. It began to descend. It couldn't have been easy flying in that wind. I could see a face through the windscreen as it came down towards me. Through the bulging screen of tinted glass, it was as white as a speck of fat. Richard Guilbert.

The noise of the helicopter increased to a clattering roar. I could see the waves and the spray round about being flattened. It was coming closer. Closer and closer. With no mast to get in its way, it could have landed on the deck. I stuck my head out of the door. Mistake. I'd just identified the shape of someone hanging out of one side of the cockpit when he flashed a signal light at me.

Bang.

The roof smashed inwards as if someone had put their fist through it, and I was sitting staring at my hand by the wheel. It didn't look like my hand any more, it looked like a jam sandwich. I couldn't feel a thing. I pulled it towards me. It left a lump of blood the size of a strawberry on the splintered wood. Jesus, I thought.

Bang. The compass exploded like a grenade. Glass and fluid and bits of metal spurted around the room.

Bang bang bang bang. The shots came in through the roof – I was sheltering under an eggshell. I screwed my head round and looked up. Through the colander of the roof, I could see the swollen belly of the helicopter, so close I could have jumped up on the roof and reached up and touched it.

My left hand felt as if I'd had it in a freezer for long enough to turn it into a piece of dead meat, useless, so I jammed the sawn-off cylinder between my legs and used my right. The Brew fired bags of gun-cotton propellant electrically with a mercury fulminate fuse, so I ripped the terminals from the battery of the starter under the cowling, stopping the engine. I pulled the plastic covering from the wires on the fuse with my teeth and dropped one of the cylindrical bombs into the barrel. I manoeuvred the cylinder between my legs so that it pointed up through the roof like a mortar.

I remembered hearing about the fatality at the fireworks display, the shell taking the man's head off, and how he had stumbled wildly across the lawn until he had suddenly flopped down, the blood fizzing through the grass. The memory of it made my face tighten up like leather drying in the sun. I looked up. Then I put on the goggles I'd been using for swimming. The world turned blue.

The helicopter was settling down on the roof, a dinosaur squatting on its egg.

Count three. Don't act too soon. Don't be satisfied with getting away with your life. Stop these bastards; it's the only way you're going to get out of this.

One.

I saw something, a man scrambling out of the door of the helicopter on a line. Spooner. I could see the shotgun slung over his shoulder, some sort of handgun in a holster. He was abseiling down to the *Lady Day* to make sure of me, ready to jump down to the deck.

Two.

He must have been trying to land on the roof.

Three.

I scraped the bare wires of the fuse across the terminals of the battery. They sparked. I felt the cylinder kick like a horse between my legs, and there was a whooshing sound, then a louder, sharper boom. For a moment I was blinded, the sound of the helicopter roaring like a train in a tunnel. I blinked away the stars and saw that the roof above me was burning like ragged sacking. Through that I saw the helicopter. I could see the black smear which meant that the bomb had hit the helicopter, even what might have been a hole there where a panel had sprung loose. But Spooner was still swinging down towards me, the shotgun strapped over his shoulder, a handgun on his hip. I could see Guilbert in the cockpit. I could see the black hole of his mouth, the black hole in his forehead. He'd begun to shout something, over and over. Then something began to happen to his face. As if someone had shone a torch on it from underneath, it was starting to light up.

A huge moth appeared underneath the helicopter, between the skids, a spreadeagle of crinkling pattern, the wings starting to flap, red and white, red and white, flapping faster and faster. Then the redness whitened into the glare of a blowtorch.

The helicopter began to rise and veer to one side. It tilted, and Spooner swung underneath it like a pendulum. Then someone was alongside him in the sky, pinned there somehow like a shape on a wall. Someone wearing lime-coloured clothes. Evelyn. She hung in the air for a moment, and then went bicycling slowly and terribly down into the sea.

The helicopter rose, up and into the scudding cloud, a spinning shape falling into the sky. Then the rope carrying Spooner began to tangle as the helicopter came down into the surf.

I didn't move for a long time. The *Lady Day* was resting on rocks, but she'd stopped moving, she wasn't going to sink. Waves broke over her from time to time, coming over the stern and washing as far as the wheelhouse, but they were helping to put out the fire I'd managed to start.

I felt all right. I'd got through, I'd survived. I ate some more of the mint cake, drank some of the Calvados. Slowly, as if the sensation was coming from a long way off, my wounded hand began to hurt.

Half an hour later, the yellow rescue helicopter arrived.

31

Jerry Rossetti owned a Matisse nude which he'd had stylishly redrawn to look like the BT logo, and this was at the top of the letter he sent me after the trial. I got an advance against his promise that he'd ask me to do some stuntwork in his next film, and used that to buy the *Lady Day* back from the French salvage company who'd repaired her; I paid off the Australian plastic surgeon who'd sewn my hand back together by taking him fishing all summer for nothing, and then sailed the *Lady Day* over to Weymouth. I spent a couple of days listening to Jerry's high-pressure salesmanship – he'd got interested in me again all of a sudden, something to do with the publicity – then borrowed one of his cars and drove to Kent, to the women's prison where Evelyn was doing her time.

I didn't know what to expect, and when I saw her I didn't recognise her at first. She'd shaved her hair off, and it had grown back to a soft stubble, like a hayfield in autumn.

She propelled her wheelchair through the door and across the room until she faced me in the visiting-room, with its pale blue Formica-topped furniture, the grilled window looking out over the lawns, towards the wall and the trees that bordered the road. Two women talked in low voices at the other end of the room, their heads close together.

'Four years, two years suspended,' I said. 'That's

307

not bad. Not bad for murder.'

'That's not what they called it.'

I gave her a packet of cigarettes, and she lit one with a paper match, turning her head to one side as she did so. She winked at me.

'I'll be out next year. Just you watch me. I'll have the parole board eating out of my hand.'

'Did you get my letter?'

'Of course. We should have got divorced years ago. I should never have married you.' She smiled at me. 'You needn't worry about me, Sam, I'm all right in here.'

'It's not supposed to be a holiday camp. There must be some things you don't like doing without.'

'Oh, I don't know. You know me, Sam. Any port in a storm. I have friends.'

This made me look towards the two women, who'd started kissing each other. I looked back at Evelyn. Her eyes were twinkling. She squeezed my hand.

'It's a good thing you're not the jealous type, Sam.'

'I stayed with Jerry Rossetti last night,' I said. 'He's thinking of casting you in a film about your life. The only problem is your back. You've got to be able to walk if he's going to use you, so if you want a job when you get out start exercising. You know Jerry – you'll be spending most of the film without your clothes on.'

'Another of your jokes, Sam?' she said, but I could see she couldn't make up her mind whether I was telling the truth or not. 'I'll probably be out of the wheelchair next month. There won't be any scars.' She smiled at me. 'We'll let the divorce go through, Sam, but I'll be sorry to lose you. You and I are a matching pair.'

I said, 'No we're not. We're different. I've had a year to put things together, and I wanted to say this to you, just so you'd know someone else knows about it besides you.'

'What a dramatic remark,' she said, and widened her eyes mockingly. 'What are you leading up to, Sam?'

'The prosecution was able to establish that you drugged me the night Baxter was killed; what they couldn't establish was whether you knew anything about Guilbert's plan to kill Baxter. I know you did. It was your idea.'

'You haven't driven all the way out here to tell me that, have you?'

'A year before you got Guilbert to kill Baxter, you poisoned Fiona Maugham in Monaco. She was your rival for what you both thought was Baxter's money. She had an attack of what people called food poisoning just when she might have been threatening your position with Baxter, and it nearly killed her – but perhaps you intended to kill her, the way you killed Theo Bradley.'

'Poor Theo,' Evelyn said.

'Theo died of an overdose after he'd gambled away most of the money he'd taken from me. You went to Monte Carlo to meet Theo, whatever you told me later. You can forget the film script you said you were trying to sell – it doesn't matter whether you were or not. Theo had embezzled my money and he was going to share it with you. But he messed you around, he blew the money, he gambled it away. So you got your own back. You killed him, and he went over the side. You can tell me about it because you're safe now. No one could find out how the overdose was administered after he'd been in the water for as long as he had when he was found. No one will ever know. Just us.'

She smiled at me. 'You sound like a policeman. You haven't got a tape recorder hidden on your person, have you?'

I kept going. 'If you ran away to join Theo, that makes me think you must have tried to get rid of me while we were both living together in the States. If you had done, things would have worked out differently for you, things would have been a lot easier. You'd have inherited the company, you wouldn't have had to get Theo to rip me off. But it didn't quite work. Remember when I broke my neck, jumping off that high tower? Did you . . .?'

'No,' she said. She shook her head. 'No.' She looked frightened; for once, I'd got under her skin.

'You guessed about the humidity, about the ropes lengthening. You tried to kill me.'

'Don't be silly,' she said, and leaned forward to touch my hand. 'I wouldn't have done that to you, Sam. I loved you. I still do.'

We sat, holding hands, knees touching, like lovers. I looked at her pale face, examined it like a man turning a vase in his hands. Blue irises, ringed with a darker purple. A tan faded to the colour of silver leaf. Blonde, gypsy eyelashes, a mouth plump and crooked with voluptuousness. A truncated halo of cropped hair.

Where she'd been resting a hand, her cheek had a patch of blush; a delicate rosy capillary had wormed its way across part of her eye. The flaw delighted me. She was the most beautiful woman I'd ever seen.

'Why are you here, Sam? Have you come to gloat?'

'There's nothing to gloat about. The States cancelled the building scheme. I'm just as broke as I was this time last year. Well, almost.'

She caught the edge in my voice. 'What do you mean, almost?'

I said, 'You missed something. There *was* gold in the safe.'

Her eyes widened. She snatched her hands back from me. The claws turned into fists.

'You're lying! You bastard, you've just come here to make fun of me.'

'I found it a month ago, when I started cutting up the safe with a thermal lance. It has a sturdy steel frame, with metal panels fitted into it, but they're not the original panels; they were much thinner. The gold had been poured in between the new panels like the inner layer of a sandwich. When I started heating it up, the gold melted before the steel did and some of it just trickled out on to the floor.'

'How much?' she snarled.

'If I cashed it all in, I'd never have to work again.'

'If?' she said.

'Yes. If. I'm not going to. It's not mine. I've taken just enough to pay off the Brew's back rent and set up the scrapyard as a business which hc can run for me.'

'What are you going to do with the rest?'

'What you'd want me to do,' I said sarcastically.

'You cunt,' she said. Her mouth worked. I moved

311

back from her. If she'd been sitting any closer, she'd have gone for me.

I steered the *Lady Day* out of Weymouth Harbour, and then took all day to cross the Channel, dodging container ships until the traffic began to thin out and the sun began to sink. It was late summer, and the sun had been hot, but there'd always been that coolness that's never far away at sea.

Closer to the Hoummet, a man in a yellow rubber apron stopped pulling up crab pots long enough to wave at me from a fishing boat rocking in the swell. A French yacht moved slowly out of my way. A gannet went flapping slowly past.

There was a slight haze. I watched the horizon, and thought about the past, and the future. It would be a good year, I decided. Better than the last, anyway. I'd make sure of that.

A glimpse of the French coast, with the nuclear power station like a tooth on a green rug, Alderney sticking up out of the sea like a flattened cake on a tray. Then, suddenly, the Hoummet.

There was a red flag flying on the beacon now. Explosives experts had shifted some of the stuff but not all of it. Landing was prohibited. When the birds nested there, they'd be undisturbed.

I came in towards the undulates, slipped the engine into neutral, and let the *Lady Day* wallow in the waves. I've never been a good sailor, and standing there with the boat rocking in the swell, inhaling the exhaust fumes, the sunlight glittering on the waves, I felt queasy.

The safe I'd taken from the wreck stood on the deck, part of it ripped open like a half-opened

Christmas present. I opened the gunwale section like a gate so it was open to the sea and put my foot against the safe.

A small fortune in gold. Someone else's gold. Gold from a concentration camp.

The safe tilted.

In court, Baxter had been portrayed as a sexually exploitative monster, Guilbert as a sadist who'd beaten him to death in a fit of rage. Evelyn had been the helpless victim, and I'd been shown up as a fool. And perhaps they were right about all of us; I'd thought about it for so long I'd given up caring. I just knew I didn't love her; I didn't even feel sorry for her any more. I felt sorry for the Brew, who'd barely been out of hospital for three months and who was having to learn to read and write all over again.

Something for me, something for the Brew. That was all I'd taken. That was it.

But just as I was about to kick the safe off balance and into the sea, a heavy swell came and rolled the boat, and it toppled in anyway. The air inside it held it up for perhaps two or three seconds, and then it hissed loudly, and disappeared. After that, the sea was empty, and I turned the *Lady Day* for home.